Dirty Bad Savage

Jade West

Dirty Bad Savage

Dirty Bad Savage

Jade West

Dirty Bad Savage © 2015 Jade West

The moral rights of the author have been asserted.

All rights reserved. No part of this publication may be reproduced, distributed, or transmitted in any form or by any means, including photocopying, recording, or other electronic or mechanical methods, without the prior written permission of the publisher, except in the case of brief quotations embodied in critical reviews and certain other non-commercial uses permitted by copyright law. For permission requests, write to the publisher, addressed "Attention: Permissions Coordinator," at the email address below.

info@jadewestauthor.com

Editing by John Hudspith http://www.johnhudspith.co.uk
Cover design by Letitia Hasser of RBA Designs http://designs.romanticbookaffairs.com/

First published 2015

Jade West

For Nancy
Thank you for fourteen beautiful years of companionship.
I hope they have squeakies on the other side.
Miss you, Baby Boo.

Warning

As readers of Dirty Bad Wrong will already be aware, I don't use my warnings lightly. This book, like its predecessor, does exactly what it says on the tin. It's dirty, it's bad, and some parts of the book are pretty damn savage.

There will be sexual practices some readers may well find offensive. All of the acts within this book are performed by sane, fully consenting adults. Please don't try some of this at home, people!

Thank you so much!

P.S. If you're sick in your mouth all over again, please don't blame me. I did warn you. ☺

Prologue

Sophie

A deep breath, fists clenched tight against the leather padding of the flogging bench. I arch my back.

Cain's voice, practised and gravelly, "Get ready."

I've been ready all week, craving the bite of the cat o'nine against my skin, craving the hot sting of palm against my thighs. Craving a hard fucking pounding of cock with a side of tongue, and the intrusion of his thick meaty thumb in my asshole. Craving the release he used to give me. *Used* to.

"Count for me, Missy," he says.

I splay my hands flat on the bench. "Just hit me, will you? I don't want to count."

A swat at my ass. Hard enough to sting, but not hard enough. "You'll count for me, *Missy*, and you'll be grateful."

I choke back a sigh through gritted teeth, forcing myself into the zone. "Yes, *sir*."

"That's my girl."

I'm not his fucking girl.

He lands the tails hard between my shoulder blades. *Yes! Thank Christ.*

"You fucking love that, don't you, baby?"

"Yes, sir," I manage, but already my nerves are on fire, demanding more. I hear the flogger whirring in the air like a helicopter.

I stay silent until I realise he's still waiting. "One."

"Good girl."

He lands another, but this one is weak, nothing but a tickle. "One point five."

"Cheeky."

A heavier blow nips at the soft skin of my hip. "Fuck, yes, *two*."

This is it... why I'm here... what I crave... The beautiful rhythm of pain is the only beat that consumes me. My only release. I need this.

I urge Cain on without words, baring myself wide for everything he has to give. If he notices, he doesn't respond. His movements, as always, are steady and composed. His breathing even. He strikes, then waits, repeating on loop. Waiting too long, performing too hard. Like an actor. A professional. Like someone who's played the game too many times.

We've played this game too many times.

The inevitable line, "Fuck, yes, Missy. Are you ready for me?"

I know my part—what I'm supposed to say. I'm *supposed* to be in the zone, endorphin-high and floating on air. *Supposed* to need more, need cock, need *him*. But I don't.

"Answer me."

"I'm..."

"You need cock, don't you, baby? I know. I know just what you need."

I *need* to feel alive... out of control... possessed... consumed... out of my fucking mind.

I wrench my head around, knowing exactly how I'll find him. His dick is already in his hand, flogger discarded, his eyes on the spectators outside. They know the drill too. Club Explicit, BDSM haven for dirty freaks like us. We come to play and we come to watch, and that's all great fun, until you realise you're playing the same movie on repeat, all of us, over and over. And suddenly I'm angry, angry beyond all rationale. Angry with Cain for not being the dom I need him to be, angry that he's not the man I knew before him—the man who could turn my insides to jelly with one single command—angry with myself for needing everything I need from this place.

"No. I'm *not* ready."

Cain shuffles, surprised. He shoves his dick back in his jeans and goes for the flogger.

"Oh, ok, um, sure. You want more of this, then? Is that what you want?" he approaches my head, leaning in close enough to whisper. "You took fifty, I thought that would do you. How about another twenty?"

And that's it. Done. Over.

I'm so far out of the zone I may as well be at the office discussing housing benefit claims.

"Surely *you* should tell *me* how much more I should have? You're the dom, aren't you?"

His cheeks flush pink as he turns to the window, checking out the faces as he considers they may well have heard my criticism.

"I'm a dom, Missy, not a psycho. You normally take fifty."

"I *normally* take whatever you dish out. I've got a safeword, Cain, and a tongue. I'm capable of using them."

He retreats, and I hear the flogger whirring. I dare to hope, dare to believe he'll put me back in my place and give me what I need.

"Count for me," he says again, and this time I'm really done. I'm already up, slipping through shackles that are too loose on my wrists, another oversight on his part. "Hey!" he says. "Get back into position! I didn't give you permission to move!"

"It's over," I sigh. "I'm just not feeling it."

"I'll make you feel it," he barks. "Just get back in position." Again his eyes flit to the window and the shocked observers. It's then I know for certain. He's scared of losing face, more concerned with what they think than what I need.

"A couple of lashes would have done it, by the way. Maybe a couple of decent slaps. A *fuck you, Missy, I'll be the one to tell you what you need*, and then a proper pounding. Maybe in the ass, that would have been good..." I shrug.

"And I'm supposed to be a mind reader, am I?"

"A body reader, a *person* reader. We've been doing this how long? Six months?"

"Five," he snaps. "What's wrong with you these past few weeks? Nothing seems fucking right for you anymore."

He's right, nothing does seem fucking right anymore. Nothing at all. "I'm sorry, Cain."

"Yeah, well, let me know if you sort your fucking head out, will you?"

He doesn't hang around to hear my response, and it's probably just as well.

***

"Whoa, baby." Mistress Raven slid her glass along the bar in my direction. "You look like you need this a ton more than I do."

"That obvious?" I took a seat, wincing as I sniffed the purple concoction. It smelt like liquid gasoline and gummy bears.

"A *garnet crow*," she said, "vodka, rum and other unimportant shit. Get it down your neck."

I risked a sip, keeping my eyes on Raven as Cain stomped away across the main dance floor. She'd dressed to match the cocktail, seemingly. A purple leather mini-dress over fishnets, and the darkest violet sweep of shadow over her eyes. She made my black-PVC ensemble look positively vanilla, her black-and-red-curled mane putting my straight blonde bob to shame.

"Great outfit."

"Cara picked it out." She gestured to the pretty little minx at her side. They really were a beautiful couple, solid in their love of gothic clothes and hardcore sex. I'd have envied them their solace in each other, but they were just too bloody awesome for bitterness. Some other couples, however…

Raven raised an eyebrow, mind-reading as usual. "So, what's eating you, pussycat? Still pining for Masque? I know he's left some big fucking boots to fill."

And there it was, in a nutshell. The real reason for my frustration. Masque, the beautiful beast of BDSM club Explicit. The man I'd been relying on for my hardcore kicks for the past twelve months, and now he was off the market, shacked up in bliss with his green-eyed little submissive, Cat. Monogamous. Faithful. Taken.

I wasn't the only one pining for him; he'd left a hoard of frustrated women in his wake. I hadn't even subbed for him all that much, but he'd been *there*, available. His shadowy presence on the outskirts of our kinky little community offered absolute dominance, the shattering of boundaries you never knew you had. He was really fucking good. And really fucking gone.

"How *are* the perfect couple? Please tell me he's bored of her already."

Raven smiled, and it lit up her face. "They're doing good. First proper holiday. Mauritius. Sun, sand and a fortnight of filthy sex…"

"You aren't helping," I groaned. But I was smiling. Raven's smile does that to you.

"So, what's gone down between you and Cain? I thought you guys were finding your groove," she purred.

"Too much of a groove. I can't reach the zone anymore. It's all so... structured."

"And you can't switch it up a bit? Put the sizzle back in the spice, so to speak."

"We haven't talked about it," I admitted. "Hence he's pissed. Embarrassed probably. I was a bitch in there."

"He'll get over it. He's a big boy."

"Yes, he is," I smirked. "But that's not enough. Not anymore."

Her eyes glinted with wickedness. "Maybe you need to show the old dog a few new tricks?"

"I don't *want* to show him anything." I tried to put my frustration into words, staring out at the familiar crowd on the dance floor, wishing I still felt the magic of the place. "I want something *raw*... something *wild*... something... I dunno..."

"Something dangerous?" she finished. "Some*one* dangerous? That's dodgy ground you're drifting into."

"Maybe I need to expand my horizons."

Raven moved in closer, red lips tight in an uncharacteristically serious pout. "Masque is a savage, Sophie, but he's a *sane* savage. He wouldn't *actually* fuck you up, not really. The guys in here don't match his kind of brutal, sure, but some of the wackos out there, lurking around in the dregs of online chat, they really *will* fuck you up. Masque's so good because he keeps his shit together. He's in control of you, he's in control of the scene, and he's in control of *himself*. There aren't many like him out there, but there *are* a shitload of weirdos who'll get their kicks at your expense." She waved to the barman for another cocktail. "All I'm saying is keep yourself safe, will you? This place is safe, the people here are ok. They might not give you the adrenaline spike that Masque did, but they'll leave you in one piece."

"Yeah, yeah, I know. I'm not thinking straight."

She touched my hand. "Real life getting too much again?"

"Am I that transparent?"

"I just know you."

I sighed, loudly, letting go some of the tension I'd been carting around all week. "I need this, Raven. It's the only thing that lets me unravel."

"You're preaching to the converted, Missy. I get it. I'm just saying be *safe*."

"I'll be safe. Nothing crazy."

"You're lying," she said.

I rolled my eyes. "I'll be safe! Couldn't have Sophie Harding of the great Hardings veering off the rails now, could we?"

"Your family own a national property business, not a dynasty."

"Try telling my dad that."

"Maybe *you* should," she said. "Don't hide under a rock all your life complaining you can't see the sun. It's *your* life. Stand up to them."

"Ouch. That's harsh."

She held up her hands. "I'm a tough love kinda girl."

"Don't I know it," I smiled. "Thanks for the pep talk, *Dr* Raven. I'll bear it in mind when I'm next over at family dinner, jousting with Dad over the moral value of choosing social housing over the private sector."

"Anytime." She pulled me in for a kiss. Her lipstick tasted of strawberry, and most likely of Cara. It was at times like this I wished I were gay and Raven were single. "You take care of yourself, Missy, seriously. Promise me, at least, that you'll bring him here. Whoever your Mr Dangerous turns out to be, make sure you're here where we can at least keep an eye on you."

"When I find him, you'll be the first to scope him out," I said. "That's a promise."

I waved goodbye to Cara, and Tyson, and Trixie, and all the other people I'd come to know so well at Club Explicit, and then I turned my back on them.

Once out in the cold London air, I stared back at the doors that had welcomed me into a whole new world. A world of acceptance and release… of friendship and excitement. Doors to a world of pleasure I'd never known existed.

I'd never have believed the Explicit excitement would dull. Never have believed I'd need something else, something more than the beautiful games I'd learnt to play in that place.

Masque had a lot to bloody answer for.

***

Chapter One

Sophie

"Have you heard the news?" Christine leant over my desk, armed with tenant files for the anti-social behaviour briefing at midday. Her grey hair was up tight in its trademark bun, glasses perched on her nose in her usual display of tenant-liaison efficiency.

I hadn't heard any news, not that my ears were particularly open for it. I'd been glued to my phone the remainder of the weekend, checking out profiles on Edgeplay, the dating network for kinky freaks like me. The handset was now on my lap under the desk, while I compulsively checked for new messages.

"What news?"

"You really haven't heard? Crikey! It's about your patch as well."

"My patch?"

She tutted condescendingly. "Well, you *are* the estate manager of the East Veil block, aren't you?"

"Last time I checked."

"You'd think someone would have thought to tell you, then, wouldn't you? There's no communication round here these days, it's all about email, email, email, no damn given for *talking*."

"What's the news on East Veil? Someone thrown a fridge from their balcony again? A car-jacking? Piss in the communal hallway?

More graffiti?"

"You need to take this estate more seriously, Sophie, it's not like Haygrove. East Veil has a damned sight more problems than a bit of urine in the corridors."

"I know, I know," I said. "Sorry. Let's start again. What's happened in East Veil?"

Her face took on the utmost sincerity, like war itself had broken out amidst the tower blocks. "Callum Jackson – he was released this weekend."

Now she had my attention. "I thought he was inside another six months?"

"Good behaviour, apparently. If you can believe that."

If what rumour said about Callum Jackson was even half-true then no, I wouldn't have believed it. He was red-flagged on our system, a troublesome tenant of the most ferocious variety. Except he wasn't really a tenant, not officially. He'd been raised on East Veil by a mother well known to our housing association. She'd had two children taken into care since Callum, but social services had come too late on the scene for him. By all accounts he was unpredictable, violent and virtually feral. Hannah Jackson, mother of the year, had thrown her son onto the streets several years back—I'd read about it in the East Veil block file once I'd been assigned the estate—and since then he'd coasted around the place, bedding down in the garage block, or the maintenance huts, or even in vacant properties if you didn't get them boarded up in time.

Callum Jackson had been arrested for assault, theft and vandalism more times than the files could keep track of, and finally they'd sent him down last year. A twelve month stint the management had bemoaned wasn't in any way long enough, and yet seemingly he was out again, on the loose and on my newly-assigned patch. Great.

My email pinged, and Christine cranked her neck around without

any consideration for confidentiality.
From: Central Hub
Subject: Hannah Jackson, 57 East Veil.
Talk about timely.

"See," Christine said. "What did I tell you? It'll be kicking off already, you mark my words."

"Weren't you on your way somewhere?" I asked, trying my best to maintain a civil tone.

"Meeting preparation," she said. "Someone needs to make sure these things run smoothly."

"I'll see you midday, then, thanks for the heads-up."

She hovered. "You be careful with those Jacksons, Miss Harding. They're not to be trusted. None of them. They're trouble. No, they're more than trouble, they're downright dangerous."

"I'll be sure to keep that in mind."

I waited until she was long out of view before I opened the email.

Ms Jackson called today. She would like an urgent visit pertaining to additional security. She advised that if we don't respond and anything should happen to her property or possessions she will seek compensation via Lawyers-R-US - she's seen them on the TV. Please respond.

I'd only had the pleasure of meeting Hannah Jackson once since becoming estate manager, and that was for chasing down some rent arrears on behalf of the income recovery team. She'd seemed to know more about the system than I did, exceptionally clued up on exactly what benefits she was and wasn't entitled to. I doubted she would be bluffing about the compensation threat, she'd bleat about unfair treatment to anyone who would listen, and those idiot firms advertising on daytime TV would be more than happy to hear her out. They love a case against the establishment. They'd probably truss her up in a pastel suit and play a violin soundtrack as she recounted her tale of woe in a testimonial study. I'd have to go out there, the sooner the better.

I looked over to see Christine rounding up the team for her midday meeting, two full hours of her nit-picking and waffling on about how things were so much better in the days of old, before social housing had come under Housing Association control. I could do with getting out of that crap.

Hannah Jackson or Christine White? Who would I rather spend my afternoon with?

I grabbed my coat.

***

The East Veil estate has its own guidelines for tenant interaction. The handbook says no individual visits, strictly pairs only, and I normally stick to it. *Normally.* East Veil has its problems—as do all London social housing estates—but in the broad daylight of a Monday morning the rules seemed grossly overkill. Maybe the management feared it would be one of us on the Lawyers-R-US testimonials if things went awry. Anyway, if I'd have pulled someone else out of that meeting to go along with me I'd have been shut down faster than a raw-chicken takeaway shack.

I signed out of office with nothing more than *tenant visit*, perfectly vague. I'd be back in a lickety-split, before they'd even noticed, full of apologies at having to skip Christine's meeting. Such a tragedy.

I rode the tube down the southern line to East Veil, clipboard in hand and ID badge clearly visible for anyone who cared to look. The place was undeniably depressing: towering blocks of concrete splattered with graffiti, shuttered retail units with kicked-in windows. A couple of kids, who should have been at school, kicked a tatty football around the road and wolf whistled at my rear once I'd walked on by.

"Hey, blondie. Fancy some cock?"

"Posh totty!"

"We love a bit of MILF!"

Sure they do. Little shits.

57 East Veil was at the far end of the estate, a blotch of dilapidation on the fifth floor of tower one. I walked confidently, quickly, with an air of authority I relied on to keep people at arm's length. Estate manager equals demon to a lot of these people; it means rent arrears visits and spot checks, and the power to issue notices seeking possession.

I'd worked so hard on Haygrove, implementing a whole host of community initiatives and pushing through a load of improvement funding. I'd done well, really well, well enough that I'd been commended with an inter-agency award and given a pay grade promotion. Now they'd given me this place; a whole new community to understand and a whole load of new tenants to build a working relationship with. I was still the enemy here, an outsider from the *council*, not to be trusted. Curtains twitched and people hushed their conversations as I walked on by, staring with the same hostility I'd had to work so hard to overcome last time around. I'd like to say I wasn't nervous, but I'd be lying. Christine was right, East Veil wasn't Haygrove, and for all my bluster I knew it. My pulse raced like a train, a familiar rush of adrenaline fizzing through my veins. This was the adrenaline I craved so badly, but not here, not today.

I picked up pace, zooming through a connecting alleyway to avoid a small huddle of youths, right into the garage courtyard of block one. I was pacing too fast to change my route, already committed to my trajectory. My blood froze to ice as I realised I'd committed to walking headlong into a street fight.

I'd seen scuffles before, it's part of the job. I'd seen the tail end of plenty of punch-ups between locals at Haygrove, where the contenders would be jeered on by crowds of onlookers. They'd always seemed a bit of a spectacle, more like a stand-off than a genuine fight, but this one was nothing like that.

The two men brawling amongst the garages of tower block one were gunning for blood. There was no shouting, no hysterics, just the low growls of exertion as the fists flew. One of the men was bigger, considerably bigger. He moved on heavy feet, swinging meaty fists with purpose. I heard one connect, a terrible crack, right on the jawbone of the man facing up to him. I forced myself into action, flattening myself into the wall behind while my jittery fingers searched for my mobile.

The smaller man railed backwards from the assault, spitting out a gob-full of blood, but he still had his wits, ducking out of reach and coming back for a counter attack. His fists were a flurry, landing full and hard into the big man's nose. Fresh blood splattered the tarmac, the air heavy with grunts of pain and curses, until again they were squaring up. I caught sight of the smaller man's eyes—dark pools of rage and pain, like a wild animal. He was chiselled and wiry, with an unkempt mop of dark hair and the perfect ghosting of stubble. A beautiful thug. A beautiful, vicious, monster.

Again the thump of fists on bone gritted my teeth.

The bigger man found some distance and charged at his opponent, a raging bull of muscled flesh. He was an ugly brute, skin-headed and scarred, with a jagged tattoo across his scalp. I knew his tattoo, a tribal eagle above his right ear. This had to be Tyler Jones, another problem case, one known primarily for domestic abuse. He'd beaten his girlfriend black and blue a few summers before, landing himself a suspended sentence and a non-molestation order. I knew it well, another entry in the East Veil case file.

My fingers wouldn't work, landing on just about everything in my bag besides my mobile. *Pissing hell.*

Tyler missed his target, lurching forward in his own momentum and losing his balance just enough for the other man to strike. Strike he did, a kick to the back of the knee knocking out Tyler's legs from under him and landing him in a heavy heap on the tarmac. I flinched as a bellow of rage rang out, a feral war-cry and the beautiful thug continued the assault, kicking the man under him, over and over and over again.

Just as he stopped, spitting blood on the ground beside his defeated opponent, I found my mobile.

"Piece of shit!" he raged. "You fucking piece of shit!"

"Fuck you, Jackson!" Tyler crawled away, clutching his side, keeping a wary eye out as he stumbled to his feet. "I hope they've beat her to death already, you cunt."

"If they've touched her, you're fucking dead. I swear down on my fucking life."

"Not if you're dead first, you fucking asshole."

I held my breath as Tyler stumbled away, letting out a sigh as he moved out of eyesight. Thank fuck for that.

I entered the unlock code into my handset, keyed in the number for emergency services.

"Emergency Services, which service do you require?"

"Police!" I wheezed. "I need the police!"

A shadow across my vision, blocking out the light.

"No, you fucking don't."

And that's when I realised the beautiful thug was whole lot bigger than he looked.

***

Chapter Two

Sophie

The beautiful savage was quick as a flash, snatching the handset from my fingers before I could move a muscle. He dismantled it with a grunt, snapping off the back panel and wrenching out the battery.

"Jones had it coming, piece of shit." He thrust the pieces of phone at my chest and I grabbed them from his hand. But his stare was on me. He was close. Too close. Close enough to scare me. And close enough that I could smell him. He smelt wild: of sweat and damp and pure fucking rage.

Fuck. Adrenaline, fear, and hot, sweaty man flesh; a combination I crave, but shouldn't. I definitely shouldn't.

"You should let me call an ambulance. Your jaw..." I swallowed the croak in my voice.

He hacked up blood, spitting so close to my feet it splattered my shoes. "Taken worse."

I watched him watching me, hollow eyes unreadable. I flinched as he reached for my chest, but he was only going for my name badge.

"Sophie Harding. *Estate Manager.*"

"On my way to tower one." I gestured to the looming hulk of my destination. Shadow and grime had never looked so safe.

I should have been more careful with my paperwork. In the chaos my clipboard had lolled carelessly, and I was too slow to avert it from his eyes.

"You're going to me mam's."

"I'm, um, making some local visits."

"She says any shit about me, she's a fucking liar. I didn't touch her."

I struggled to hold my nerve. "Tyler Jones said he hoped someone had been hurt... was he talking about her?"

"Me mam?! Fuck no."

"Throw me a line here... I should be screaming blue murder and calling the police."

"Pretty sure of yourself, ain't you? What makes you think I'd let you call the pigs on me?"

I dared to stare right back at him. "What are you planning on doing? Keeping me here forever?"

"Dunno yet."

"You could just tell me what's going on. If someone's in danger..."

I flinched as he thumped the wall above my head, convinced I'd made a terrible mistake. Christine's words smashed around my brain. *Dangerous, dangerous, dangerous.*

"Like someone like *you's* gonna help someone like *me*."

I dropped my eyes to the floor, kept my voice neutral but firm. "I know Tyler Jones has history... with women..."

"You ain't gonna help. You won't give a shit."

"Try me."

"You're gonna call the pigs anyway, as soon as I let you go."

"Then what's to lose?" I chanced. "I won't say anything about the fight. Jones would never talk, I know that as well as you do."

He clenched his fists, pressed them hard against the wall on either side of my head, caging me. "I can't go back inside, not until she's safe."

"Who's in danger, Callum?"

His eyes flashed with surprise at the sound of his own name, and for one tiny moment he was human. The pain I saw in his face nearly took my breath.

"Casey," he said, simply.

"Casey?"

"My dog. They took her."

I felt the tension leave my body enough to breathe freely. "You were fighting over a *dog*?"

His face turned sour, as though I'd struck a blow.

"Yeah, *just* a fucking dog. I said you wouldn't give a shit. You can piss off now, *estate manager*."

He turned his back on me, gathering up a load of strewn clothes and shoving them into a tatty holdall.

I brushed myself down, ordering my thoughts. My suit felt crackly, crumpled and tight. "What are you going to do now?"

"Like you fucking care."

"Why did someone steal your dog?"

"They didn't. My stupid fucking mam gave her to Jones while I was locked up, then that sack of shit sold her."

"And you don't think the new owners are taking care of her?"

He shot me a look over his shoulder, one that made me feel about four years old. "The *Scotts* bought her. You know them? Dog-fighting cunts."

I knew them. And yes, they were. They were right at the top of my eviction hit list.

"Have you asked for her back?"

He didn't even grace me with an answer. "Piss off and see me mam. And get some of those pissing bars she wants on the windows. She'll need them if anything's happened to Casey. Tell the pigs all you want, I don't give a shit. She's the only reason I'm out."

"The early release for good behaviour... that's because of a dog?"

"Never had a dog, have you?"

He was right. I'd never had a dog in my life. Never had a pet, in fact. My parents weren't ones for mess. I watched with my heart still pounding as Callum Jackson dug around in his bag, returning to wave a picture in front of my eyes: a battered photo of a scruffy black mongrel.

"She's not *just* a dog to me." He took it away and shoved it deep in his bag. "I'm all she's got."

And she's all you've got. I daren't speak it aloud. "How long have you had her?"

"Few years. She was a stray, like me." He slung his bag over his shoulder.

"What are you going to do?"

"Whatever it fucking takes."

I reassembled my phone, weighing up my options. I *should* call the police, *should* call the office, *should* explain to anyone who'd bloody listen that Callum Jackson was embroiled in his usual round of shit and needed putting away again. Should, should, should, fucking should.

"If you go up there starting trouble they'll lock you up sooner than you can blink. Who's going to take care of your dog then?"

His shoulders stiffened. "Got no choice."

"You could let me call the police, they could get the rescue people out... take the dog away from them."

"Sure they will, yeah, and then they'll just hand her back to me, won't they? No fucking chance."

"At least she'd be ok," I tried. "She'd be safe."

"She wouldn't get a good family," he said, sadness etched across his brutal features. "She's no good inside, not trained."

I looked over to tower one. The Scotts were on the top floor, flat fourteen. "You're sure they've got her?"

His eyes were black as coal. "Course I'm fucking sure."

In spite of every shred of common sense in my body, I closed the distance between me and the man they call savage. "I could go up there, see if they'll give her up."

His eyes narrowed, searching me. "Why the fuck would you do that?"

Fuck knows. "It's my patch, I won't sit by while tenants abuse animals."

"No pigs?"

"Let me try speaking with the Scotts first."

"If it don't work..."

"If it doesn't work *you'll* do whatever you have to do, and *I'll* do whatever I have to do."

Dangerous. Every inch of him screamed danger. "If you're fucking with me..."

"I'm just doing my *job*." But I wasn't. This wasn't my job.

A grunt in the affirmative and he walked away, dropping his holdall to the floor and taking up position against a garage door. His eyes burnt my back as I set off for tower one. I walked slowly, shoulders high in an effort to convey a confidence I wasn't feeling. My mind whirred. I was off script, procedures cast aside without care, and for what? To help a convict? A thug? Callum fucking Jackson?

To help a dog. A dog in need.

I held the thought like a mantra. I'd fucking need it.

✶✶✶

The lift stank of piss and poverty: a dingy, rickety contraption that had seen better days, just like the rest of the estate. I kept my breathing shallow, fearful of inhaling any more of the stench than necessary. The communal hallway wasn't much better, littered with beer cans and a whole sea of cigarette butts. Number fourteen was right at the end. The door was fist-battered, tacky red paint flaking around the edges. Music blared from inside, so loud it took three attempts at knocking before it dulled down.

Janine Scott's beady eyes looked out through the crack. They narrowed as she registered it was me, a look of pure disdain.

"I've turned it down already!"

"I'm not here about the music," I said. "Can I come in?"

"What for?"

"I've had some complaints."

"What the fuck about this time? I paid a fiver off my rent last Monday, check my statement if you don't believe me."

"It's not about the rent, Mrs Scott. It's about a dog."

She unlatched the chain, swinging the door wide. "Who's been saying shit about my dogs?"

"I'm not at liberty to say. You have a black dog, yes? I've had reports it's been barking, causing a disturbance."

"They're full of shit. The black dog don't fucking bark, it don't do shit, see?" She stood to the side, shifting her flabby ass enough for me to peer into the gloom beyond. A toddler darted into the kitchen, nappy-less and pissing a trail all the way. "Jayden, you little shit! Use the fucking potty!"

Casey looked much smaller than I expected. She was a ball of matted fur, pressed tight against the carpet. Big, sad eyes looked out at me, ears flat to her skull.

"You're on a notice seeking possession already, Mrs Scott. Another count of anti-social behaviour will mean court action."

"You'll have to come back when my husband's home. It's his bloody dog. He's out, with our others. *This* dog don't cause no problems. *This* dog don't do shit."

"I've got witness statements to the contrary. I'm afraid this could lead to a full inspection, and police involvement."

Her mouth pursed tight, like a bright pink asshole. "They're fucking lying!"

I puffed myself up, putting on the most authoritative tone I could muster. "I've a duty to act on these allegations. You can let me take the dog now, and put a stop to the investigation, or I will be taking further action immediately. It's your choice."

Her piggy eyes flew wild. "Take my dog?!"

"I'll hand her into the local rehoming centre. She'll be well looked after."

"Who the fuck do you think you are?"

"I'm just doing my job, Mrs Scott." If looks could kill I'd be a dead woman. I held my stance, folding my arms tight across my chest, and still she didn't respond. I took a risk, all out of options, and reached inside my bag for my phone. "I'll make the call."

"Fucking hell!" she seethed. "You people make me sick. Take the fucking dog. It's a stupid, messy piece of shit anyway." She stormed off down the hall, and my heart lurched as Casey cowered from her, flattening herself against the wall. Janine grabbed her by the scruff, yanking her forward hard enough that the dog yelped. It was only when she shoved her towards me that I saw the full extent of the neglect. The animal was skin and bone, fur matted and filthy, and almost bare to the skin in places.

"Does she have a lead? A collar?"

Janine Scott rolled her eyes, like I'd asked her for a magic beanstalk. "Jesus Christ, you'll want the shirt from my fucking back next."

Casey looked terrified, eyes darting around the hallway. I placed my hand on her neck to stop her running, and she froze. "It's ok," I whispered, as though she would understand me. "I'm getting you out."

Janine returned with a manky old collar and a bit of twine. "Best I can do."

I slipped it over Casey's neck, praying to God she didn't decide to make a run for it, the twine would cut my hand to shit. Maybe that's what Janine wanted. "This will draw a line under the incident, I hope I don't have reason to call again." I turned away, pulling gently on the makeshift lead. "Come on, Casey, there's a good girl."

The dog responded in a flash, jerking into life and setting off down the corridor. I wrapped the twine tight around my palm, trying my best to keep her close. I waited for the lift to open, heart racing, and had only just stepped inside when I heard Janine's angry voice calling after me.

"How the fuck do you know the name Casey? Her name's Peaches!"

I jabbed for the ground floor like my life depended on it.

***

Casey moved like a wild thing when we got outside, lurching all over the place. Even with the twine biting my fingers I kept hold, leading her best I could back to the garages. The enormity of what I'd just done came crashing down. I'd broken every guideline. Fabricated complaints that didn't exist to make threats I couldn't enforce. I'd stolen a dog from a tenant, used my position as blackmail. Jesus. I was in deep.

"Casey!"

Callum Jackson's voice thundered loud on sight of us. I don't know who ran faster, him or the dog, but I was dragged without choice, in danger of toppling straight onto the tarmac. I let go just in time to avoid a collision, breaking to a halt as she flew into Callum's open arms. He dropped to the floor, slamming his knees onto the ground without the slightest care as the dog jumped all over him. Her tail was wagging so hard it shook her whole body, and she whined with such happiness I felt a lump in my throat, of the kind I'd only really experienced when watching soppy videos on Facebook. But this wasn't social media, this was a ringside seat, and it felt all the better for it. I stood and watched in silence, unashamedly voyeuristic as they lolled around in play. Maybe, just maybe, the savage had some humanity in him, after all. This was worth breaking the rules for, sure to God it must be.

When Callum Jackson finally looked up at me, the wariness in his eyes caught me totally off guard. "What happened?"

"Does it matter? They gave her to me, end of story."

"They just handed her over? Doesn't sound pissing likely."

My mood was suddenly crushed like a beetle under a boot, ungrateful piece of crap.

"A thank you would be appreciated..."

"I can't pay you anything..." he grunted.

My heart shrivelled. I'd felt a part of it—their beautiful reunion—as though in some weird way I was included in their happiness. But no. Of course not. I was nothing—just a nosey-parker estate manager, an intruder. It smarted hard, embarrassment burning.

"I didn't do it for money," I snapped. "I did it for the dog."

"She's grateful."

"And you?"

He removed Casey's crappy collar and cast it aside. "And me, yeah."

I took in Callum Jackson through fresh eyes. A twenty year old thug, dishevelled and wild. Torn jeans, tight to his skin, his baggy hoodie covered in dirt and blood and all kinds of shit most likely. His jaw was swelling, dark eyes sunken into his skull, but despite all that he was still absolutely fucking gorgeous. A gorgeous monster. A savage. An ungrateful, vicious, dangerous savage.

I adjusted my jacket, smoothed down my skirt. "What are your plans now?"

He shrugged. "Carry on like before. What's it to you?"

"How are you going to take care of her?"

He frowned. "Same as always. We stick together, me and her."

I folded my arms. "If you care about the dog, you'll let me take her for rehoming."

"*I'm* her home," he spat. "Ain't no one gonna be taking her anywhere."

"How are you going to feed her?"

"We'll get by."

"So, you expect me to rescue her from one bad home, and deliver her straight into another?"

"I don't expect shit."

"I think I should take her," I said, irritation making me brave.

He got to his feet, stepping forward with menace. "You can fucking try."

"You wanted the dog to be safe. I rescued her from the Scotts, and now she needs a proper home..."

"She's got a home, with me."

My senses reeled, neck bristling in fear, but still I couldn't shut it. "What about vet bills? Vaccinations?"

"I'll fucking manage."

"And I'm supposed to take your word for it, am I?"

He took another step forward, and I fought the urge to back away. "I'm good for my word."

"I should call it in, for the dog's sake."

His eyes were fierce. "Don't push it, estate manager. You don't know me."

Stand-off. I held firm until my adrenaline ebbed, fading away into nothing but jitters. "I just risked my job for that dog, and for what? So you can drag her back to life on the streets without even a thank you?"

"What you after? A fucking medal?" He stared at me, shifting from one foot to the other. My cheeks burned under his scrutiny. "What do you mean you risked your job?"

"I didn't follow procedure."

He dropped his eyes to the floor. "Don't normally have much to say thanks for. Not used to it."

"Is that your way of apologising?"

He shrugged. "Not much good with sorry."

"Nor with a decent thank you, seemingly."

He looked beyond me, to the buildings in the distance. "If you call the pigs I'll run, they'll never find us."

"So, why aren't you running?"

"Dunno," he said. "Maybe I don't think you'll call the pigs."

"Why wouldn't I?"

"You know she's better off with me. Else you wouldn't have rescued her."

"I did it for the dog," I maintained. "Nothing to do with you."

Liar. What the hell was I doing?

"Casey wants to be with me."

"She's a dog, she doesn't know what's best for her."

"She knows what love is. She knows better than most people."

My phone started buzzing. Office calling. Real life fucking calling. "Shit," I said. "I've got to take this."

He paced forward, and this time I did retreat, stepping backwards until I was cornered. He loomed over me, just like earlier, but this time he was so close I could feel the heat. "I don't want to hurt you, but I will. Don't think I won't."

I breathed in his breath, skin on fire. *Dangerous.* I was alone, out of my depth, threatened by someone with no limits, no restraint, no fucking safe word. His eyes weren't playing, no humanity staring back at me, not this time. I shifted against him, fighting the familiar thrill of being pinned.

"Go," I said. "I'm done here."

He released me in a flash, grabbing his holdall and walking away without a backwards glance. Casey followed, bounding along at his side like a different animal. Maybe he was right, maybe she did belong with him.

My phone was still ringing. I stared at the office number but it seemed so far away. Far away in a world of conformity and procedures and health and safety. I wasn't ready to go back there, not yet.

"Wait!" I called.

He didn't respond, didn't even slow down. I had to run after him, grabbing at his elbow without thinking. The savage spun on his heels, wild, ready to attack until he registered it was me. His fist paused mid-air. I put an arm up to block him.

"Thought you were Jones," he muttered. "What now?"

I don't fucking know. "The dog... I'll want to check up on her."

"Check up on her?" he growled. "What does that mean?"

"Just to know she's ok," I said. "I'll need your phone number."

"Ain't got one."

"Do I look that fucking stupid?"

"The number's 0791-mind-your-own-fucking-business," he sneered.

"I got your dog back, and I'll let you leave with her, but you *will* be giving me your number, or so help me God you'll have to knock me out just to shut me up."

He frowned for long seconds, then finally dug around in his bag. The handset was an old model, built like a brick. He scrolled through the numbers until he found his own, shoving it in my hand. I wrote it down on my clipboard, checking it once, twice, three times before I handed it back to him.

"Take care of her."

"Always." He pulled up his hood until his face was in shadow, and then continued away.

I watched him long enough to catch him turn back, just in earshot.

His words were simple, but they were sincere.

"I owe you, estate manager. I won't forget this."

Neither would I.

***

Chapter Three

Callum

Casey was nothing but bones, just like when I found her. I fought the red mist, ready to charge up to those cunting Scotts and make them pay, only I couldn't risk it. Not now.

Case stuck at my side, just like old times, ears pricked up as we headed for our dinner. The bin round the side of Al's fish and chip shop was usually packing with leftovers. I dug out some trays. Lucky haul—half a battered fish, and a couple of bits of sausage. I gave it all to Casey, every single bit. I'd feed her up again proper, just as soon as I sorted some cash. I'd have to hook up with some old acquaintances, let them know I was back in business.

My business was packages, but only the small stuff, taking them from A to B and asking no questions. They'd chuck me a bit of cash, a twenty here and there. The big money was in the harder stuff, but that wasn't my bag, not anymore. Too much jail time. She'd be dead by the time I made it out.

There ain't no real jobs for a guy like me, not even round the dregs in these parts. I'm too well known. Known by face and known by fists. It used to bother me, used to eat me up that nobody had a chance to give me. Got used to it, though. Life ain't never been kind, being older don't make no fucking difference.

"Alright, Case, easy girl." I sank against the wall, pulling her close. Nothing left of the haul but chip papers, and I didn't want her chewing on that. I got out my baccy, made a roll-up. Only a skinny one, had to make it last. My jaw pounded like a bastard. Tyler had got me a good one, asshole. His luck would run out one of these days.

Two of the little slags that live by Mam cruised on by, stopping to give me the eye. They laughed, all giggly and stupid, then huddled whispering. I used to be tempted, before I knew better. Dipped my wick in any tight little snatch that offered. I used to think it meant something, meant something about me, but all it ever meant was they'd fucked the bad boy, like a prize fucking medal.

They think it's a hard act, like I threw my manners out with the trash to be a cool guy. They're wrong. I never learned any to begin with, never learned how to be anything else. Maybe that's why nobody has a chance to throw my way.

I'm a loser. Born a loser, raised a loser, and I'll probably die a loser.

I just hope Casey goes before I do, so she's not alone.

My phone bleeped with a text. For a second I thought maybe it was her, *Sophie Harding*. Of course it wasn't.

"Nice lady saved you, Casey, didn't she? She weren't so bad for one of them."

Casey licked my face, giving me salty kisses. My perfect girl, my loyal girl. My only girl.

Well, maybe not quite my only girl.

"You wanna go and see Vick, Case? Shall we go and see Vicki?" She jumped up at the name, pawing me to stand. Clever dog.

I got to my feet, stomach still rumbling, but it didn't matter.

Casey was all that mattered.

***

The months hadn't been kind to Vicki. Her red hair was flat with grease, blonde roots showing. She'd come out in blotches her make-up couldn't hide, and she'd lost weight. She was nearly as scrawny as Case.

"You eaten?" she asked. "I could stick you a bit of pasta on. I got a few bits left."

"I ate already," I lied.

"It's good to see you, Cal." She pulled me into a hug, crushing me with bony arms. "What happened to your face?! That from the Scotts?"

I ignored her questions. "How's Slater?"

"So so," she shrugged. "He's with me mam. You'll see him in the morning, if you're still here. He grows so bloody quick."

"Two now?"

"Last month. Had a little party for him. Shame you weren't around. He loves you, Cal."

I smiled. "Love him too, little tyke."

"Haven't got a roll-up, have you? I'm gagging."

I sat myself down on the step and she perched alongside me. I'd been here so many times, hanging in her poxy little back yard, amongst Slater's scooters and charity shop cars. Case and me would bed down in her tiny little shed sometimes, when it got real cold. I handed her the roll-up.

Casey nudged her hand, looking for fuss. "How'd you get her back, then? Did you have to kick the door in?"

I shook my head. "Didn't go up there."

"How come?"

"Had some help."

She frowned. "Not from the Gabb boys? They'll want repaying big time."

"No. A woman, estate manager. Pretty, like."

"The blonde one?" she quizzed. "Posh old cow, with a bob haircut? She ain't pretty, Cal!"

"She sure ain't old."

"She is!" Vicki smirked. "Way older than us."

Vicki was older than me, almost twenty-five, but she didn't like to believe it. "She ain't even thirty, Vick."

"*Almost* thirty from the looks of her. Practically middle-aged. She acts like it, too, stuck up bitch."

"Got me my Casey back."

"What she do that for, then? Fancy you or summat?"

I shook my head. "For the dog. Animal rights and that."

Vicki was thinking it over, I could tell. She gave me a funny look. I can never read her funny looks. "Don't seem right to me, Cal, she must want something."

"I scared her."

"Scared her?"

"Pushed her into the wall, got all fiery. Couldn't help myself."

"Shit, Cal, she's gonna have the pigs right down your neck if you don't watch it."

"Don't think so. Took my number, said she'll be checking on Case."

"She does fancy you, then," she laughed. It was a funny laugh, though, one of those ones I don't like so much. "Don't you be shacking up with no posh bird. I need you here." Her eyes were nervous, shifty. My stomach churned and this time it wasn't from hunger. "I'm in some trouble…"

Wasn't she fucking always.

***

"Why don't you come inside? Stay tonight. We can talk in there." Vicki was edgy. Whatever trouble she was in had got her good.

I looked away. "Can't leave Case."

"She could stay in the kitchen? Just for tonight. I could clean up before Slater gets home."

I shook my head. "No, Vick. Ain't worth it."

Slater's allergic to Casey, has been since he was born. The kid don't have much luck, truth be told. He's allergic to everything, even milk, poor little bugger. Vicki blames herself, but it weren't her fault. Unhealthy pregnancy, she said, but she was shacked up with Tyler Jones back then, and life was even tougher. It's a wonder the kid was born at all, given the shit that bastard put her through. Ended our friendship dead in its tracks when I found out. He used to be a mate, grew up with him. Kicking about the block, up to no good. But no mate of mine punches his pregnant girlfriend in the stomach. Even I draw the line at that.

Vicki laid her head on my shoulder. "Sorry I couldn't keep her, Cal."

"Not your fault. Mam should've looked after her. Only thing I ever asked her for."

"Tyler probably twisted her arm. Anything to get back at you."

I changed the subject. "You still got my stuff?"

She nodded. "Everything you left."

"My paints?"

She smiled. "All still there. Some of them may have dried up, though, haven't checked."

I took a deep breath. It felt like the first in years. "Spit it out, Vick."

She pulled her jumper down over her knees, hugged her legs to her. She looked even more scrawny, like she'd blow away with the trash. "I got short of money. Owed Ben Brown a load from when Slater was ill last winter, and he wouldn't let it go. Didn't have any electric. Water was on my case. Didn't even have any clothes that fit Slay anymore."

"Shit, Vick."

"You were away, and Mam didn't have none to spare. Thought about going to Tyler, but couldn't risk it, not with the non-molestation order. Social services would be all over it."

"Where did you go?" My heart dropped through my stomach. "Please fucking tell me it wasn't the Stoney boys?"

She covered her face with her hands. "They were the only ones who'd lend."

"How much?" I rolled another cigarette, I fucking needed it.

"Seven hundred."

"Seven hundred?! Are you out of your pissing mind?"

"I was desperate!" she hissed. "I owed Ben Brown nearly five."

"How much now?"

"Twelve hundred last time I checked. You know what their interest is like. They want three of it by next Monday. I'm scared, Cal. Really scared. You heard what they did to Tina Ryan."

I pulled her hands away from her face. Tears. I hate tears, they make me feel weird inside.

"If they hurt me who's going to take care of Slay? Mam can't have him, not full-time."

"We'll sort it."

"How?" she cried, edging closer. "Not even you can take them on, Callum, they'll cut you up."

"We'll have to find the money." My foot started to twitch, adrenaline rising. No way I'd do that many small deliveries by next Monday, I hadn't even hooked back up with the circuit.

"I thought about turning some tricks... I know a couple of guys who'd have me."

I grabbed her by the shoulders, shaking some sense into her. She didn't fight me, just juddered in my grip. "Don't you fucking dare, you stupid cow. Think of Slater." I looked down at Casey, so quiet at my feet. So much for an easier life. "I've gotta go, Vick, get my head together."

Her hand was on my elbow, pulling me closer. "Sure you won't stay? I could do with the company."

I stood in answer, handing her a roll-up.

"Fine," she smiled, sadly. "I'll get your stuff."

***

Sophie

I watched Eric Fletcher stomp across the office, knowing by his trajectory he was heading straight for my desk. He scowled over at me, flustered and grubby, cleaning foam splattered over his maintenance overalls.

"One pissing night, that's all it took."

"Sorry?" I quizzed, pushing my mobile out of sight.

"Callum bastard Jackson. One night before he sprayed holy shit out the place. Don't know which fucktard let him out on early release, but I've a mind to have a word with them."

"Graffiti?"

"A shit ton of it. Must have been at it all pissing night."

"Definitely his?"

He shook his head, as though I was a bloody idiot. "CeeJay, same as always. Bold as pissing brass that one."

"Where this time?"

"Down by Al's chip shop and another on one of the skate ramps.

Oh, and a big old spectacle down the garage block by tower one of East Veil. Took pictures for the file. See if you can get community support on it, hopefully they'll lock him back up."

He handed me a digital camera and I flicked through the images on the previewer. The one by the chip shop was dark. Jagged bars hiding a hunched figure, his hands on his head, twisted in a way that reminded me of 'The Scream'. It wasn't like the other graffiti I'd seen around East Veil. Most of that was a load of names, garish and amateur. This was something else. I zoomed in on the signature in the bottom corner. CeeJay.

"Told you," Eric said. "It's Jackson alright."

I flicked along to the next.

A crime scene body outline had been sprayed onto the skate ramp. Cartoon-like but gruesome. *East Veil kills.* Again, there was the CeeJay.

"Quite good, isn't he?" I remarked, carelessly.

"Good? It's a bloody eyesore."

"No security cameras?"

"He knows them. Didn't catch a thing, even if they did, he wears a hood. Can't prove shit. Seen the spectacle at the garages? Can't make bloody sense of it, myself. Pissing vandal."

I flicked forward a few more, pulse racing at the memory of that place. My blood ran cold as I interpreted the images, guilt and embarrassment and something indeterminable crawling through me. The picture was of Casey. It had to be. A big black dog, in zigzag lines, frozen in mid-leap, tail curling into the sky. Red and purple script, the full height of the garage doors. *Thank you.*

Thank you.

Shit.

I could feel my cheeks burning.

Eric tutted. "Takes the fucking piss, doesn't it? That's going to take hours to clean up, budget's already tight for this quarter."

"Has anyone else seen these?"

"Not yet. Brought them straight to you. Hope you can take the little wanker down."

I smiled, a hollow mask. "I'll do my best."

I uploaded the first two scenes to the East Veil archives.

The third never made it.

***

I took a working lunch, catching up on my notes from my meeting with Hannah Jackson the day before. Her usual troutish bluster had been absent, leaving a chain-smoking husk of a woman in its stead.

He'll get me, she'd said, *he'll break his way in here and he'll get me.*

She'd said nothing of the dog, not one word. Only that her son was a monster, and had been since birth. As if children are ever born evil. Children are sculpted by their parents, I'd seen it a thousand times over on those estates. I'd battled with a whole host of questions in my time with her, all of them fizzing on the tip of my tongue. Questions about Callum, about the dog, about his prison time... I'd asked none, of course, bar those necessary to do my job.

I need security, alarms, extra locks. I need window bars on this place, and one of those fireproof boxes to catch the mail. You'd better get them for me, or I'll go to the papers!

I assured her I'd do my best. I was doing that a lot lately.

And you're sure he's a danger to you, Mrs Jackson?

He'll fucking kill me if he gets chance! I'll be dead! He's got a temper, that lad. A temper like you've never seen!

But I had seen it. Couldn't stop thinking about it. Couldn't stop thinking about *him*.

Hell, I needed a distraction.

I checked my Edgeplay login. Five new messages. A couple of idiots with one-liner chat-ups, some guy from Manchester, and someone I'd met once before. I flushed at the memory. A hotel room in Kensington and too much wine. He'd been good, but rough, and I'd been careless. I'd been reckless, in fact. Stupid. He'd given me a damn good fucking but left me bruised for days, requiring a trip down Accident and Emergency after an overly zealous fisting attempt. I clenched my legs at the thought. Fucking ouch.

He'd been good, though. His dirty voice, his edgy sadism... like Masque without the finesse... without the restraint, too.

Maybe...

My handset buzzed in my hand. Text message from Raven. Impeccable timing.

How's the hunt for Mr Dangerous? xx

I smiled as I replied.

One or two contenders. xx

She didn't leave it long.

Edgeplay? x

I screen shot his profile, attached it to my reply.

He's top of the list at the moment. x

Buzz.

Are you fucking mental? Craving some medical intervention? x

I'd been questioning that myself.

Pickings are slim. I'm contemplating my options. x

I spied Christine approaching, leaving me just enough time to read the last of Raven's messages.

Be careful, Missy. Don't you dare fucking go alone! x

"Not disturbing you, am I?" Christine sneered. "I'll hang around while you finish up on Facebook if you like."

"I wasn't on Facebook," I snapped. "I'm on lunch, anyway."

She pointed to the clock, two minutes past lunchtime. Pedantic bitch. I figured she'd come along for another moan at my lack of attendance at her meeting, but no.

"I just intercepted the strangest call, about *you*, Miss Harding."

"A call? From who?"

"Janine Scott."

I felt my colour drain. "Janine Scott?"

"These tenants try their luck, don't they? They must think we were born yesterday."

"What did she want?" I hoped my poker face was a good one.

"She had the most *incredible* story. It must have taken her hours to concoct the stupid thing. She claims you took a trip to her flat yesterday, and stole her dog."

"Stole her dog?"

"Quite. That's not the best of it," she smirked. "She only claims that you're in league with Callum Jackson. Apparently you stole her dog and gave it to *him*."

"Callum Jackson?"

"Yes!" she laughed. I'd hardly ever heard Christine laugh. I found it quite unsettling. "She was quite put out when I told her the scenario was entirely impossible."

I smiled. "I can imagine."

"She must think we're an office full of halfwits. I assured her in no uncertain terms there'll be trouble if she continues with this nonsense. Honestly, these people! Anything for sensationalism. Out for compensation, of course." She handed me a scrawled note. "Here's the detail. I haven't written it up."

"Thanks," I smiled. "I'll deal with it."

"Oh, and Sophie," she said, before wandering off. "Your mother called, asked that you call her back. Apparently you've been ignoring her messages?"

Yes. Yes, I had.

"I'll deal with that, too."

She rolled her eyes in a thoroughly patronising manner. "Seems you have a lot of things to be *dealing* with, Miss Harding. Best get to it. Chop-chop!"

Bitch! The note went straight in the bin, along with any intention to call my mother.

It could all wait, the whole sorry lot of it.

I had a date to arrange.

***

Chapter Four

Callum

"Got any more for me?" I whispered into the mobile, hiding my face from passers-by. "Need the work."

Jack Willis took his time answering, smoking a big fat joint, no doubt. "Not till next week. Next delivery's Tuesday."

I sighed. "Throw me some rope, Jack. Anything bigger?"

"I thought you weren't in the game for bigger parcels?"

Desperate times. "I could do one or two."

I heard him rustling papers. "Maybe next week, we can talk then. Best I can do."

Too late. Much too late. "Any chance of an advance, Jack, I wouldn't ask..."

"You know I don't do advances, kid. Sets a bad precedent."

"Yeah, yeah, I know."

I hung up, almost out of phone credit and feeling like a first class prick.

I'd made best part of two hundred quid the last few days, running myself ragged delivering packages across the city. Two hundred quid that could feed me and Casey like kings, but no. It was all for the Stoney's pocket. All that work and still it weren't enough.

Vick had scraped a couple of quid together, selling old toys on eBay, but we were still over a hundred short. Finding a hundred quid over the weekend wouldn't be easy. Not without robbing. Saturday morning, less than two days to go and out of options. We had nothing to pawn, nothing left to sell, no place left to turn.

Maybe the Stoneys would settle for two hundred, but I doubted it. They weren't the generous type. They'd take the two and give Vick a black eye for her trouble, probably even worse for me. Couldn't do deliveries with busted kneecaps, nor find food for Casey.

Vick had been crying every night. Sobbing on my shoulder like a little girl. Guilty, she said, but she needn't have been. It weren't her fault. She didn't ask for this life, where the money's too short to make ends meet, and we're all on a treadmill to nowhere.

The cash burned a hole in my pocket as we walked on past the butchers. What I'd give to buy a decent fucking steak. One for me, one for Vick and one for Case. Hell, we could do with it. I was still fit, but I was losing muscle, bulking up with extra layers so people didn't notice. They'd be on me like hyenas, some of them, if they thought they could take me.

My phone started ringing. I could hardly bear to look, hardly bear to break the bad news to Vick.

A number I didn't recognise. I'm wary of those, but I had no more credit to listen to voicemail, and maybe it was about some work.

"Yeah?"

A pause at the other end. A bit of a cough. "Callum Jackson?"

"Who's asking?"

"It's Sophie Harding. I rescued your dog."

Knock me down with a fucking feather. "I'm taking care of her."

"No, um, that wasn't why I called. Well, it is, but it's not."

"Why call then, estate manager?"

Maybe she'd seen my street art, seen the message I left for her. It felt stupid now.

"I need someone for a job. A one-off. I thought maybe you..."

I tried to hold back the relief, disappointment hurts like a bastard when you get your hopes up too high. "What the hell can someone like you want from someone like me?"

A pause. "It's a little... personal. I need someone tonight, someone who knows how to keep their mouth shut. Just for a few hours. Are you free?"

"What for?" I said, wary.

"I'm meeting someone, at a hotel. I need a man around, to keep an eye on things."

"Security, like? I can do security."

She sounded like she was smiling. "I thought you might be the man for the job."

"How much you paying?" I wanted to say I owed her one, clear that debt from my tab, but I needed the money too bad.

"One fifty? Cash? Is that enough?"

"One hundred and fifty quid?! What you want me to do? Mess someone up?"

"No!" she snapped. "Of course not!" I liked her voice, all posh like. Flustered.

"I'll do whatever you want for a hundred and fifty quid."

I weren't joking, either. I made a note of the address. A hotel in Kensington. Seven sharp.

And then I bought that fucking steak.

***

I skulked around the edge of Kensington Gardens. This place wasn't for me. Posh white buildings with posh white steps and all their posh fucking plants outside. Posh people inside too, no fucking doubt about that. I smoked a roll-up and kept my eye on the street, waiting for Sophie Harding to show up. She arrived ten minutes early and hung around the front of the hotel opposite. She didn't look like the woman I'd pinned by the garages. She was all made up, her hair all shiny and curled under her chin. More make-up on, too. Red lipstick, but not like the hookers round by East Veil. She looked good. Proper classy. Looked like she was planning on staying, judging by the suitcase she was pulling on wheels. She pulled her coat tight, looking back the way she came. Looking for me.

What the fuck did she want with someone like me?

I scuffed out my roll-up. Time to find out.

I wasn't expecting the smile on her face. "Thanks for coming. Where's Casey?"

"With a friend." I nodded towards the hotel. "What we doing here?"

She pushed her hair behind her ear. Nervous, like. "I'll go check in, meet me by the lifts."

The place was as posh inside as out. People stared but pretended not to, holding their bags a little tighter as I passed. Sophie wasn't long. I followed her into the lift and she pressed for the fourth floor.

"So?"

She did that hair thing again. "Not one for small talk, are you?"

"Nothing small to be talking about."

"You shouldn't need to do anything much. Just be there."

"Where?"

"In my suite, while I have a visitor."

"You buying a fat load of coke or something?" I nudged her suitcase with my foot. "Or selling? Don't seem the type, somehow."

She rolled her eyes. "Hardly." The lift dinged. "You know how to keep your mouth shut, right?"

"Ain't much of a talker. Sure ain't no grass."

"Figured as much." She opened the door with a credit card thing.

Fucking weird. "Do you want your money now, or later?"

"Not worried. Guess you're good for it."

I didn't know where to fucking put myself, everything looked too posh to touch. The room was fucking massive, with double doors that led through to another. I hadn't ever seen a four-poster in the flesh, looked like a king's pissing palace, this place. She sat herself down on a fancy chair. "I needed someone I could trust to keep their mouth shut. Someone who can be around... just in case."

"In case what?"

Her cheeks turned pink. "Have you, um... have you heard of BDSM?"

"Weren't born yesterday, estate manager. I've been around the block a bit."

"So, you know what it involves?"

"Whips and chains and all that kinky shit. Yeah, I know. Why?"

She smiled a bit, flicking her hair. Nervous and real fucking pretty. "Well, I'm, um. I'm... into it."

I hadn't seen that shit fucking coming. "You want me around while you turn into Miss Whiplash, go right ahead. Ain't gonna faze me."

She played with her nails. "It's the other way around, actually. I'm a submissive."

"Submissive? You like getting beat up?"

"Something like that..." She looked at me, and I saw something else in her. Something I'd never seen back there at the garages. A sparkle in her eyes, some clichéd crap like that. "I'm meeting someone here, in about half an hour. I just want you to stay out here, while we go in there." She gestured to the bedroom. "If I call for you, which is *very* unlikely, you come in and save the damsel in distress. If not, just sit here. Watch TV or something."

"I watch TV while some guy beats the shit out of you?"

"It will sound worse than it is," she said. "If he really is beating the shit out of me, believe me, I'll be calling for you."

"Fine," I said, only I wasn't so sure it was. My stomach felt fucked up. Not from the steak, either. "Who's the guy?"

"Just a guy."

I shrugged. "Fair enough. Likely to be trouble?"

"No," she said. "This is just a precaution. We try and play safe."

"We?"

"Players, in the BDSM scene."

"Who do you usually use for security? How come I got the gig?"

"I don't usually use anyone."

"So you are expecting trouble, then."

"Look, left to his own devices he can get a bit carried away. Knowing you're here, he'll behave himself. And you got the gig because I know what you're capable of."

"You're really into this shit."

"Yes." She loosened her coat, shrugged it off her shoulders. "Yes, I am."

This Sophie Harding was fuck all like the woman I'd first met. A red mini dress to match her red lipstick, and stockings, with the suspender bits showing. She looked hot. Really fucking hot. She checked her make-up in the dresser mirror.

"What's in this stuff for you?"

"Adrenaline, endorphins… the release… it feels good, to be out of control. Free, you know?"

"Where I'm from everyone's trying *not* to get beat up."

"This is very different."

"If you say so."

"It is," she said. "BDSM is about discipline and obedience, and heightened states. And sex. It's about sex. Violence through anger is something else altogether."

"I usually try and keep fucking and fighting separate." I smiled at her reflection, just a little bit. "Don't always work out that way, though."

She smiled back. "Fear and lust are a heady combination. It works for me."

"Whatever you say. I'll just sit here and keep me mouth shut."

I watched her reflection. For someone that looked as good as she did she seemed awful self-conscious, putting lipstick over lipstick, and messing with her hair. I had questions, shit loads of them, but none of them were any of my bastard business. Didn't even know her. I wondered what the man would be like, some posh arsehole probably, probably didn't even know how to hit. Just a bit of slap and tickle, that's all.

I changed my mind on that when she opened her suitcase. This shit didn't look like play-acting. Handcuffs, and weird gag things like you see in porn films, and a shitload of whips and straps and even a fucking school cane. I looked away as she started pulling out the dildos. Shit, man. You can't unsee that kind of private.

"I'll take these through," she said. "He'll be here any minute."

"What do I do if you call? Rough the arsehole up? Take him to the park and give him a kicking?"

"Christ, no," she smiled. "Make him leave, that's enough."

I doubted it would be. Not for me.

Sophie Harding went through to the bedroom with her bag of tricks, and I sat in that fancy chair.

My stomach felt more fucked up than ever. Maybe it was the fucking steak after all.

***

Sophie

I was more nervous around Callum Jackson than I would ever be around Roger. If Roger was even his real name, of course. I would have doubted so, but who'd ever make up a name like Roger? Whoever the hell Roger was he had money, enough to pay for this suite and its fancy four-poster bed.

My security guard was like a caged animal: dark eyes examining everything, examining *me*. I'd told him about the BDSM a hundred times in my imagination, and each time it became a little more sensational. He'd hardly reacted at all in real life. Maybe the slightest surprise, if you can call it that, a bit of shock that the prissy estate manager he'd faced off in East Veil was a kinky little bitch under her suit. He hadn't even reacted to the toys, nor the dildos. Nothing. Maybe he didn't give two shits about any of it.

What had I even expected? That the savage would pin me again the moment we were through the door? Growl that he was a secret dominant, skilled with a cane and Japanese rope bondage? And then what? Slam me and hit me and fuck me until I begged him to stop?

Of course not.

He'd come for the money. I'd do well to remember that. I *should* remember that. *Should* be relieved.

Finally, the savage sat down. He stared at the door, already on high alert. I made my way through to the bedroom, keeping him in view as I arranged my toys on the bedside dresser. I wondered what Roger had in store for me. Something noisy, I'd said, something that would make the neighbours talk. *Or Callum Jackson think.* The Savage jumped up at the knock on the door, eyes like daggers.

"Sit down," I said. "Relax."

He didn't sit. He backed up against the window.

I answered the knock, and a slickly-dressed Roger strode on in.

He kissed me on both cheeks before catching sight of the man in the room, then shifted awkwardly, eyes questioning.

"I didn't realise this was a party," Roger said. "He joining in?"

My cheeks bloomed. "He's just a friend."

"A friend?"

"Keeping a look out," the savage growled.

"I see." Roger smiled, but it was fake.

The two men stared at each other, opposites colliding. Roger was actually the thicker-set man, broader shoulders standing proud under his suit jacket. His chestnut hair was slick to his scalp, light eyes obscured by a pair of gold-rimmed glasses. His appearance only served to make Callum seem wilder in comparison. Wild, and tightly wound, ready to spring. I took Roger's hand, dragging him on through before the atmosphere bubbled to boiling point. I smiled at Callum before shutting the bedroom door, but he didn't smile back.

"What the hell?" Roger hissed. "Where did you find that animal? Looks fucking vicious."

"He's a friend."

"Really? I hope you know how to keep him on a leash."

"He'll be fine." I hoped it wasn't a lie.

Roger smiled. "Did it to wind me up, did you? A young bit of rough, all ready to jump in my place if I'm off my game..."

"Something like that," I mumbled.

"Bad girl. You'll pay for that." He examined my toys. "I'll give him something to listen to. On the bed."

I did as I was told, sitting down on the edge of the four poster, letting the familiar rise of adrenaline flood through me. Roger took some leather cuffs and a long length of chain, wrapping it tight around the thick carved wood of the posts.

"Maybe you'll be a better girl today, take my whole fucking fist without crying off. I'm gonna make you beg for it, so meathead out there can hear how much you want me."

Roger wasn't playing. He was inflamed by another man's presence, seething under his cool exterior. He stood over me, thick fingers under my chin, tilting my face up to him.

"You want him to hear you, don't you? Want him to hear what a dirty little slut you are. Maybe I should leave you tied when I'm done, let him come in for my leftovers. He's probably used to scraps." Roger yanked hard at my dress, forcing it down over my tits. "Has he seen these? I bet he'd like to?"

I shook my head.

"Good. He won't want them when I've finished with them. Hands behind your head."

Vicious smacks landing hard on tender skin, practiced enough to catch the nipple. I closed my eyes, arching myself into it. *Fuck yes.* This was it. This was what I craved. He twisted my nipples between his fingers, teasing them into a false sense of security before resuming his assault.

"Look at those sweet little tits, dirty girl," he whispered. "Now they match your fucking dress."

My flesh was rosy pink in his hands, he squeezed hard, until I squirmed. "More... please."

"Not yet. On the bed, show me that pretty white ass."

I moved into position, shuffling until my dress rode up around my thighs. Roger helped it on its way, giving my backside a thwack for good measure. It echoed around the room. Rough fingers forced their way between my legs, snaking inside the crotch of my panties.

"Just as I thought, sopping fucking wet."

"Please..." I hissed, craving the intrusion.

"You haven't earned it," he barked. I gasped as he withdrew, keeping my eyes shut as he rattled about on the dresser. I heard him slap his palm... with leather... a leather strap. He grabbed my wrists, pulled me up the bed until he could cuff me. Roger wasn't slack like Cain, the cuffs were tight, chains taut. He pushed my knees under me until my ass was in the air, groaning as he slid my panties down around my thighs. "Peachy fucking view from this end. Time for you to earn your pleasure."

There were no warm-up taps, no tickling with the strap. Roger got straight down to it, striking a heavy blow right across my ass cheeks.

"Yes... fuck..."

"Loud enough for you?" he growled, landing another. It *was* loud, really fucking loud.

"Harder... please..." I moaned, rocking back as the bite subsided.

"Dirty fucking bitch." He obliged, raining down perfect lashes, and the adrenaline spiked, ears ringing, breath ragged. Just how I love it. Roger leaned in close. "Beg for me, dirty girl, let that thug out there know how much you want me."

"More... yes... please..."

"Louder. Let him fucking hear it."

Shit. I was lost, coasting along on the rhythm... the beautiful pain...

"Let him fucking hear you," he hissed.

"HURT ME! PLEASE, YES, I WANT IT!"

"Good girl," he groaned. "You'll fucking take this." I squealed as he jammed his meaty fingers right the way inside me. Fuck. His modus operandi. I squirmed in my chains as his thumb tried to join his fingers.

"OW! Shit..."

"You're so wet for this, I'll bet he can hear your slurping fucking snatch through the wall." He wiggled his hand to demonstrate his point. "Spread your knees, wider."

I gritted my teeth and did as he asked, opening myself up for more. I arched my back, shifting position until his brutal fucking fingers hit the right spot.

"YES!" I cried. "There... please..."

"Hitting the sweet spot, am I? Oh, fucking yes." He wrapped his free hand around my thigh, finding my clit. "Let's make you fucking scream."

He had me. Endorphins peaked, careening me into subspace as I jerked in his grip. Months of frustration crested and subsided, and there was only submission, only the pleasure-pain salvation of his hand between my legs. I didn't fight it, didn't care, rocking back and forth, taking as much as my body could take.

"I should call him in," he growled. "You'd like that, wouldn't you? He could see how tight you are, how dirty, see me knuckle-deep in your horny little cunt."

"OW, FUCK... I'M COMING, FUCK, YES, I'M COMING..." I unravelled, jerking and writhing and grunting beyond care. It was everything I needed. Everything I wanted.

Not everything. My brain tried to hold fast to the man in the room with me, the man who's hand was pushing deep, but it wasn't him that sent me over the edge.

It was the image of Callum Jackson in the doorway.

Watching me.

Wanting me.

"FUCK. FUCK. FUCK..."

"Good girl."

I cringed at the sound his fingers made as they pulled out. I was soaking wet. Sore too, really sore. I collapsed flat on the bed, high in the afterglow. "Did you get all the way in?"

"Not even close," he said, reaching for my cuffs. He unbuckled them, set me free.

"What are you doing?"

"What does it look like?"

I stared up at him, confused. "But you aren't done yet."

He smiled. "I'm not a desperate man, Missy. I may be horny, but I'm not desperate." He leant in close, breathed in my ear. "It's not me you want, and you fucking know it."

Caught out, called out, humiliated and exposed. It felt fucking awful. "We could still..."

He stroked my hair. "Don't worry about it. This was fun enough, thank you."

"Shit, Roger, this is embarrassing." I sat up, eyes on his. "It isn't what you think..."

"It doesn't matter what I think." He checked his glasses in the mirror, brushed himself off. "Just make sure you know what you're doing. That's the most counterproductive security measure I believe I've ever witnessed. I'm almost scared to leave you with him."

I found I was smiling. "I'll be fine."

"I hope so, Missy. Maybe another time." He kissed my forehead. "I'll see myself out. Please save me if he pounces. I value my spleen."

I held my breath until I heard the main door slam, then sighed, relieved.

I wasn't sure how much I'd fancied his chances.

***

He'd been pacing, I could tell. He stopped as I entered, staring with dark eyes while I flicked the kettle on.

"I dunno about you, but I fancy a coffee."

"Don't do hot drinks."

"Something stronger? There's a minibar."

He shook his head.

I made myself a drink, taking my time to stir the milk in and trying to find words. They didn't come easy. "Thanks, for being here.

It must have been strange."

"Could say that."

"I'm sorry, if you heard anything..."

"Heard plenty."

My face flushed, along with the rest of me. "Sorry..."

He came closer, staring at me like I was some kind of alien. "Can't say I get it. You liking that."

"Hard to explain. You'd have to do it to understand."

"Did he really hurt you?" His eyes were dark fires.

"No more than I wanted him to."

"I heard what he was doing. You liked that?"

"Yes," I answered, simply. "I like the submission, I like to be taken. I like to feel out of control, with a man who knows how to command himself. A man who knows what I need."

"And he knows, does he?"

"Some of it." I stared at him, staring at me. Aware of the pink flush on my cleavage, my dishevelled hair, the heat between my legs. Aware of him, the confusion, the anger in his eyes, aware that he was reeling, brooding. Horny. He was horny. I could feel it, feel *him*.

He broke the connection, shut it down cold with one shrug of his shoulders. "We done here?"

I jumped up, reached for my bag. "Sure, yeah. Thanks." I counted the notes in front of him but he didn't watch. They were crisp and clean, straight from the ATM, but they felt really bloody dirty as I handed them over. He shoved them in his pocket, put up his hood.

"You alright if I leave?"

"You could stay," I said. "Sorry, I mean, not with me, I mean, I'm leaving..." I composed myself, daring to smile. "I'll start over. The room is paid for, if you wanted to stay."

"Nah, you're alright."

That was as much of a goodbye as he offered.

Chapter Five

Callum

I tracked back to East Veil, hood up and feet pounding the streets as it grew dark. I needed home, the closest, shittiest thing to it I'd ever known, with its stench and its trash, and its hopeless fucking desperation. My head was rammed, thoughts smashing into thoughts, and right through all of them was her. Sophie Harding. Her stockings under that red dress, the noises she made, her tits, her smell. She smelled so good, not like the women I'd known before. She smelled different, classy. She smelled so fucking good.

The cash felt dirty in my pocket. Dirtier than all the filthy cash I'd ever owned. My stomach turned. It made no fucking sense, none of it. She was one of them, one of the establishment. One of them that looks down on people like me. I shouldn't give a shit, not about her, not about her dirty fucking money. It don't pay to think and it sure as fuck don't pay to feel.

I slowed down as I reached the subway, the funnel of syringes and piss leading straight back to where I belong. I took out a roll-up as I came out the other side, cruised my way through the streets I'd grown up on. I wasn't ready for Vick's yet, not even ready for Casey.

Sophie fucking Harding.

Her stockings under that red dress, the noises she made. Her fucking smell.

Her blonde hair. Shiny, and soft looking. Red lipstick.

The hint of her tits, white flesh blushing red.

The noises she made...

I took out the cash, counted crisp notes in grubby fingers. I didn't want it. Not from her. I wanted to give it back, tell her thanks. Thanks for bringing my Casey back, thanks for keeping quiet, thanks for not putting me inside again.

Thanks for nothing.

I shoved the notes back in my pocket, as deep as they would go. I'd take her fucking money, be her fucking guard dog in the next room ready to spring if lover boy got a bit leery.

Her piece of fucking meat. Her trash.

She was trash. The noises she made. Her slutty fucking dress. The way she begged.

Fuck. The way she begged.

I hadn't had a fuck in months.

My dick was hard, balls aching so fucking bad in my jeans. I dropped into the shadows of tower two, stuffed my hand down where I needed it. So fucking hard. My balls were hot, tight, desperate to shoot my load. I needed pussy. Wet, tight, hot fucking pussy.

Her smell... posh perfume... and shampoo... and clean, soft skin... and sex...

I changed course, skirting back the way I came and detouring to Al's fish and chips. It was closed, and so was the off license next door, but the benches to the side were still live and kicking, a gaggle of tower one girls with a bottle of cheap vodka between them. A couple of Blades' gang members were kicking about across the road, but I'm good with Blades. Know them well enough to be on terms.

"You missed it," one of the girls said. "Closed half hour ago." I recognised her, Gemma Davies, brother's inside for arson.

I shrugged. "Ain't here for that."

I looked at her mates. A couple of alright girls amongst the rabble, one redhead, one with long dark braids. And another, facing away from me, giggling with a stocky little skank in pigtails.

"What *are* you here for then, Callum Jackson?" Gemma Davies smiled, hitched her skirt a bit. "Want a swig?"

I took the bottle. Tasted like paint stripper. "Who's your mate?"

"Which one?" she smiled. I tipped my head and she rolled her eyes. "So pissing typical. Lozza, get over here. Got an admirer."

The girl glanced back over her shoulder. Her blonde hair was just like Sophie Harding's. Face not so much. She was piggier, with a fatter nose, and her eyes were dark. My dick didn't fucking care.

"Hey," she said. "I know you."

"Most do," I said, taking another swig.

"Look pretty wired." She was smiling, twirling her hair. Drunk.

Gemma reached for the bottle. "How come she gets all the luck? How about it, Cal?" She pushed the bottle neck between her lips, eyes on me as she gave it fucking head. My fist clenched at my side, itching to ram it down her throat. I fixed my eyes back on blondie, on the way her hair curled under her chin.

"Wanna go for a walk?"

She smiled, feigned innocence. "A walk? Where you wanna walk to?"

"Around."

She flicked her hair, giggled at her pig-tailed mate. "Sure, I could do with stretching my legs. Just for a minute though, yeah?"

"No fair," Gemma laughed. "Come back after, eh? I don't do sloppy seconds, but for you..."

Lozza tottered over, unsteady on vodka legs. She was taller than Sophie Harding, but that would be the heels. Stupid high stiletto things she could barely walk in. She swayed along with me, taking hold of my elbow as we crossed the road.

"Where we going?"

"Around."

"We could go to mine, if you want. My mum'll be out all night, probably got some beer in the fridge."

I kept a pace, pulling her along until she stopped in the middle of the road, giggling like a retard. "Jesus, hold your horses, yeah? I can't keep up."

I stopped, turning to face her in the streetlights. Her hair glowed blonde, face dark in the shadow. "Not far now."

"I've heard about you, Callum Jackson. They say you're rough... maybe I should go back."

"Go. If you want."

She sucked her bottom lip into her mouth, staring up at me with drunken eyes. "They say you have tats. Loads of them. I wanna see."

I reached around her, slamming a hand onto her ass so hard it knocked her flat into me. "*I* wanna see *you*."

"Uh huh, where?" Her breath stank of fags and drink.

"Over there." I tipped my head towards tower one.

"You got a place?"

"Don't need one."

"Got a rubber in my bag... if you wanna..."

I grabbed hold of her arm. She didn't argue this time, just bounced after me, her heels clacking on the tarmac all the fucking way. I led her through the alleyway, slowing down as we reached the garage block. They'd already cleaned up my work, only the slightest hint of my thank you remained. I felt a weird relief.

"Ok, so what do you wanna do now? Talk a minute or something? Should have brought the vodka." She was more nervous off the main drag. The garages were dark, dim lights just enough to see by.

I didn't want to talk. Didn't want to think. My cock was throbbing like a motherfucker, straining for cunt. I turned on her, walking her backwards to the same fucking doorway I'd pinned Sophie Harding. My cock leapt at the memory, jerking in my fucking jeans.

"Wait," she said. "Just a second. I... I need to piss... and then we can talk... or whatever..."

She took a sidestep, squatting down beside me with all the grace of a fucking ape. Her knickers bunched around her knees, and she pissed like a horse. I could hear it splashing the tarmac under her, see it pooling in the half light, streaming its way across to my feet. Piss and fags and cheap fucking vodka. She was cheap, like me, cheap and fucking dirty, like everything else in this place. "Nearly done..."

I didn't give her a fucking chance. Need boiled over, springing my hands to life. I'd grabbed her in a heartbeat, rough hands on scrawny shoulders, yanking her to standing so fast her heels clipped the floor and sent her reeling backwards.

She squealed, trying to regain her balance, but I'd already pinned her. Pinned her tight, so much tighter than I'd pinned Sophie Harding. Her cunt was still dripping, but I didn't fucking care. I found the right spot, thumb tight against her filthy, piss-soaked clit. She moaned and spread her legs, wrapping her arms around my neck for balance. "Yes... fuck..."

She was warm and wet, and soft, real fucking soft. "You want it?" I grunted.

"Yes..."

"Ask nicely, you dirty fucking bitch."

"Yes... please..." she moaned. "I know about you... they say you're an animal..."

Two fingers went in easy, I spread them inside her. "Gonna open you up."

"Fuck yeah..."

She came in for a kiss, but I ducked my head, moving my mouth to her neck. She grabbed my hair, held me to her while I tasted her skin. Cheap perfume tasted nasty on her throat. I moved lower, yanking down her tight little vest top. Soft tits spilled out for me. Nipples like dark bullets. I took one between my teeth, sucked her hard.

"Yeah... like that..." she groaned.

Her tit tasted better than her neck. I sucked her in, cock straining in my jeans as her breath tickled my scalp. She was breathing fast, shallow. I pulled away so I could look at her. Her tits were nice, from what I could see, perky and pale. I wondered if Sophie Harding's would look like that. No, hers would be sweeter, smaller. Hers would fit in my mouth, her whole sweet tit in my filthy mouth. *Yes. I wanted that. I wanted her.*

"Feels so good..." Blondie's voice broke my mood. Ruined it. Her cunt was noisy, slurping like a slack-jawed mouth around my fucking fingers. I shoved another in, working that dirty little clit with my thumb until her hand was on my wrist. "Gonna come... shit..."

"Take it," I barked. That cunt's words through the door... his fingers in Sophie's sweet posh snatch... making her beg, making her take it.

"I'm gonna come..." Blondie hissed. "Yes..."

I let her, taking her weight around my neck as her legs juddered from under her. She moaned like the drunken skank she was, telling me how good it was, how fucking bad I was, such a fucking savage pounding her tight little pussy with my nasty fingers.

I didn't give her time to catch her breath on the come down. Her eyes widened as I attacked, spinning her and slamming her hard, her cheek pressed against the garage door, my hand around her skinny neck holding her firm. "Stay fucking still."

I reached down for her bag, fumbled around until I found a

rubber. I freed my cock, finally, tearing the packet in my teeth and sheathing myself ready. She'd stayed in position, bare tits tight against the metal of the door, shoulders goose-pimpled from the cold. I wrapped my arm around her neck, pinned her in a choke hold. Her hands came up in panic, trying to prise me off her, but I held tight, her soft blonde hair under my chin as I plunged my cock right the way in her snatch. I breathed in her hair, grunting in relief. She gulped for breath, her hands pulling at my wrist.

"Don't fucking fight me," I growled.

I fucked her hard, using her like the cheap hole she was. It felt so fucking good. I closed my eyes, listening to her desperate breath, loving the way she moaned and wheezed in my grip. She forgot the pressure against her throat, snaking her hands back to reach for me, fists on my hoodie, pulling me harder into her.

My thighs tensed up, balls ready to fucking go. Her pussy clenched, milking me, and I was gone in her, shooting my load and swearing like a fucking lunatic, lost to everything but her sweet, hot cunt.

I dropped her when it was over, and she rubbed at her neck as though I'd nearly fucking killed her, gulping in air and making a big fucking deal about it. Satisfied she could breathe, she turned to face me, piggy eyes glinting with excitement.

"They didn't lie about you, did they?"

I didn't say a word, tossing the rubber to the floor and shoving my cock back in my jeans.

"Fancy coming back to mine? We could get that beer, go another round."

I pulled up my hood, hiding my eyes from her. The cold wave of reality hit hard, and I felt dirty. Spent.

I looked at her through fresh eyes. She looked nothing like Sophie Harding. She wasn't even close.

"Gonna go now," I said. "I'll walk you back."

She looked disappointed but didn't grumble, holding out a hand that I avoided, gripping hold of her elbow instead. I slipped into the shadows the moment her friends were back in sight.

She didn't even have chance to say goodbye.

***

Casey jolted me awake. Barking then whining, spinning around on the spot, her tail tickling my nose as she went. I sat up, rubbing my eyes to adjust to the light. My stomach grumbled on instinct, the smell of toast making my mouth water.

Vicki poked her head around the shed door. She gave Casey a fuss with one hand, handing me a plate with the other.

"Sorry, only enough bread for one slice."

I took the plate, grateful. The toast was dry, with hardly any butter, but it went down a fucking treat. I threw the crust to Case. "Thanks, Vick."

She pulled her dressing gown tighter, rubbing the sleep from her eyes. I could hear Slater through the back door, singing along to cartoons at full blast. She took out a pack of ten fags from her pocket, handed me one. I lit up, taking one hell of a drag. "What time is it?"

"Eight."

I reached into my pocket, pulling out the wedge of notes. "One fifty, all there."

"She was good for it, then."

I nodded. "She was sound, yeah."

Vicki counted it, then slid it inside the top of her nightdress, hooking it into her bra. "What did she want?"

I shrugged. "Nothing much."

"Nothing much? For one fifty?" She raised an eyebrow.

"Just wanted some security, that's all. Was going out."

"Going out where?"

"Just a club."

"Just a club? Wanted just a few favours, did she? She make you frig her off or some shit? Do a little gigolo?"

"Don't be pissing daft, Vick."

She puffed her way through her cigarette and sparked another straight up. She was scowling, as well, proper pissed off. "Thought you'd be smiling, got the Stoney brothers off your case for a while."

"Yeah, thanks."

"What's up? Is it Slay? Keep you up, did he?"

"I was up waiting for you."

Guilt and anger brawled in my stomach, having a right old punch up. "Told you before, shouldn't be waiting up for me."

"Stayed up till three. You weren't back."

"Took a walk, after. Needed to unwind."

"Just a walk?"

"Yeah, just a pissing walk."

"Weren't off shagging Lozza Price, then?"

Anger won. "Fucking hell, Vick. Facebook? I hate that fucking shit."

"Gemma Davies put a status up last night. Said you were all over her apparently, snogging her face off, then fucked her by Al's chip shop and went back to hers for afters."

"Facebook's full of fucking bollocks."

"So, you didn't shag her?"

"Weren't by Al's, and I didn't go back to hers, neither."

She looked over the wall, over towards tower one. "Didn't think she was your type."

"And what's that, Vick?"

She shrugged. "Didn't think you even liked blondes."

"She was there, that's all." I got up, stepped out into the cold air. I took a deep breath, chasing off the sleep. Casey took a piss by the gate, then gambolled around the place, tail wagging. "Better take her out, wants a run."

"Coming back?"

"Later," I said. Only today I wasn't so sure.

"That Lozza looks a bit like that Harding woman, don't ya think?"

I felt my heart leap. I shrugged. "Hadn't noticed."

"You seeing her again?"

"Lozza? No."

"Good. She's a stuck up cow anyway, don't like her."

I opened the gate, smiling as Casey took off like a bullet. She waited at the end of the road, down on her front legs, tail going. "Gotta go, Vick. Thanks for the toast."

"Don't be late back, yeah? Can watch TV or summat."

She best not hold her breath.

***

Sophie

"Are you listening to me?"

I put down my fork, turning my attention to Dad. He was bleating on again, and no, I hadn't been listening. Roast dinner was surely never worth all this shit, and yet here I was, every bloody Sunday.

"Three months, I get it," I sighed. "But I've got initiatives running, a new estate to manage, I can't just up and leave. I guess the Hardings' grand entrance into the glittering world of showbiz will just have to scrape by without me."

"It's not *show business*," he snapped. "It's theatre, and art, and *culture*. But of course your *initiatives* for the drug addicts and reprobates far outweigh anything we have to offer."

"I like my job."

"Leave it for now, George," Mum said. "Not at the table."

The beautiful soundtrack of cutlery. I stared out at my parents' garden. You'd never believe this place was in London, not from the grounds. Money can buy just about anything, except decent family communication it seems.

"We don't need you, anyway," Alexandra chimed in. "The Southbank development is my baby now. Hang with the druggies all you like, I'll be hobnobbing with class. *Artists*, you know... and critics, and art dealers, and people from *Culture* magazine. You can come along to opening night and weep with jealousy."

Like that would ever happen. I've never been jealous of Alexandra once in my entire existence, despite her being the princess in the tower.

"Not the point," Dad barked. "We're a family business. *Family*. We should *all* be onboard."

We weren't a family business. A family business is like a twee family bakery, or having a family trade or some crap like that. Dad owns Hardings Property and Lettings, the largest but one agency in the country. He has over two thousand people working for him, including my snotty sister, so quite why it was so important that I, black-sheep Harding, should have to be on the payroll as well, mystified me. *Principle*, Mum said. He's so *principled*. So bloody pig-headed, more like.

I resumed my meal, picking at my peas while I waited for it. I thought I'd made it, that maybe for once he'd defy history and let it go until dessert, but no. Of course he wouldn't.

"Well, maybe it's time we spoke about the rent on your apartment, then..."

Oh how I love Sundays.

***

The thrill of defiance. A cheap thrill, admittedly, but nonetheless, signing out of the office before Christine's midday briefing was just the perk I needed on a Monday morning. Nothing like a super important, utterly routine estate walkabout to start the week.

I breathed in the dank, cold air of East Veil skate park, scribbling a note to call in maintenance. More syringes than usual. Must have been a real junkie smash up.

Some idiots had torn the benches apart, used one to smash the glass at the bus shelter across the street. A traffic cone covering a lamppost, and someone's old trainer wedged in the top. Give me strength.

Al Brown was already outside his fish and chip shop. He waved as I walked on by, sweeping broken glass from the doorway. *Dum Cunt* in big black letters, daubed over his windows — an irony if ever I saw one. Definitely not one of Callum Jackson's masterpieces. I kept a beady eye out, surprisingly excited at the prospect of finding one before clean-up had their way with it.

My legs felt a little seasick as I stepped from the alleyway into the tower one garage block, but the place was empty this time, no sign of life. Faintly, ever so faintly, you could still make out the top of the T where Callum's message had been. I skirted the edge of the garages for a better view, landing a heel straight into a used rubber. Fucking brilliant. My heel speared through, dragging it along the tarmac as I danced a jig, trying to shake the grotty thing off. Nothing says romance quite like a discarded condom.

Like I was in any position to pass judgement on romance. At least there *was* a rubber, a responsible choice about contraception if not about location. Can't have it all, I suppose.

I kept going, tower one pulling me like a ruddy grey homing beacon.

I was not looking for *him*, definitely, definitely not looking. He hadn't even crossed my mind, not once. Definitely not the first thing I'd thought of on arriving at the office. Certainly, absolutely not a factor when considering an estate walkabout. Callum Jackson could be anywhere for all I cared. Preferably on someone else's estate, fighting with someone else's tenants.

My heart leapt at the sight of a grey hoodie, but it was just a youngster, fourteen at most. Blonde, skinny.

Get back with the bloody plot, Sophie Harding.

I don't know how I found myself knocking on Hannah Jackson's front door, but it took her an age to answer, mumbling obscenities as she went.

"Not even ten o bloody clock yet."

I checked my watch. "Twenty past, actually."

She peered past me, to the lifts. "Ain't s'posed to come on your own, are ya?"

"That's discretionary on a case by case basis," I lied. "I thought I'd drop by again, about the security."

"Ain't got me new letterbox yet." She took the chain off the door, wandered back inside where I could follow her. I shut the door behind me, adjusting my nose to the stink. Stale tobacco and damp. She brushed a space on the sofa, dumping a load of fish and chip papers onto the carpet. "Nor the bars on the windows."

"Fifth floor isn't deemed an intruder risk, not for the windows. That might take some time, funding's tight."

"Fifth floor, tenth floor, won't bloody keep *him* out."

"Has your son made any threats towards you? Been in contact since our last visit?"

"Not since he got the dog back. Don't mean he ain't still coming after me, mind." She lit up a cigarette, blowing smoke in my direction. "Why d'you help him?"

Blood drained from my cheeks. "Excuse me?"

She smiled, and under her haggard appearance I got glimpse of the family resemblance. "Weren't born yesterday, love. People talk."

"I, um... did what I thought best for the animal."

"Which one of 'em?" Hannah Jackson laughed, rocking back on the sofa and blowing a fresh cloud of smoke over me. I tried to age her, placing her forty at most, although the years really hadn't been kind. She'd have been an attractive woman, minus the pitted face and sunken eyes; she was carrying a bit of extra weight, but carrying it well. She'd her own red-flag on our system, a much lower grade than Callum, but nonetheless cause for concern, yet I didn't feel the same intimidation in her presence. Maybe my bad, or maybe she wasn't showing her worst on a weekday morning. "You ain't the first and won't be the last."

"Sorry?"

She rolled her eyes. "Suckered by the looks. Prettiest damn thing I ever made. His dad was a pretty boy too."

"His dad?" The question was out before I could stop myself.

"Inside. Murder. Callum's got the same bad blood in him, too. Born nasty."

"I don't think violence is hereditary, Mrs Jackson." I met her eyes, challenging her with my own belief system.

"Believe what you like, love. Like I said before, kid's a monster, always has been. Loves that bloody dog and not much else."

I tried to hide my distaste, pushing it back behind a veneer of professional neutrality. "I'll submit a further request on the window security, although they may want to survey the balcony, establish any access points."

"He'll find a way up, if he wants in. Would scale the bloody wall in the right frame of mind."

"I'll do my best with the funding."

She stared at me, her face a weird mix of disdain and fascination. "You think I'm a bitch, getting rid of that dog."

"It's not my job to make judgement, Mrs Jackson."

"Think it was spite. It weren't." She stood, kicked her way through rubbish to the living room door. She pushed it closed, where I could see the back of it. It was clawed to shit, destroyed almost all the way through. She toed the carpet to show me the threads, torn up all along the edge. "That dog's got no place inside, couldn't control the thing. Ain't never had dogs, won't be getting one, neither. Ty was helping me by getting shot of it, though Cal won't see it that way. Hate each other these days."

"Tyler Jones?"

"Got his problems, I know. Good lad, though, under it all."

I pictured the Tyler Jones I'd seen in the garages, the Tyler Jones wishing Casey dead and landing his fist on Callum's jaw. "Again, it's not my place to make judgement."

"Don't be listening to that skanky ex of his, Vicki Pollock. Had a thing about Cal as long as I can remember, that one. She'd say anything to get a bit of sympathy. Ty may have raised his fists, ain't denying that, but that little bitch would have asked for it."

I knew of Vicki Pollock, ground floor of tower two, single mother of a young son, Slater, already on the at-risk register with Social Services. She had a direct link to the emergency services as part of the non-molestation order she'd been awarded against Tyler Jones. I'd seen her case file, met her numerous times as part of my initial tenancy visits. I struggled to believe any woman in her situation asked for that kind of violence, but I decided to keep my mouth shut in this instance. My pulse quickened, unease in my stomach. A stupid, ridiculous feeling.

"Are they together now? Your son and Vicki Pollock?" I raised my clipboard. "Background information for the funding case."

"Asking the wrong person, love. I dunno. Doubt it, though." I could almost see the cogs turning. "But then again... for the funding, like... I think he could be with her. She'll be hostile towards me, as well... my friendship with Ty... they could both be after me."

"I'll take that into consideration." I stood to leave, smiling as politely as I could muster. I made my way through to the hallway, craving the air outside. A door was open at the far end, revealing a tiny bedroom, walls a mass of colour and lines. I unconsciously took a step forward, straining for a better view.

Hannah Jackson followed my eyes. "Cal's room, not that he was ever here much." She paced on down, flicked the light switch. "Keep meaning to paint over it. Think I could get a decorating grant? For some magnolia?"

I joined her, pretending to consider it. The walls were alive; incredible, vivid scenes of horror colliding into each other. A portrait of Callum Jackson, crouched in the corner surrounded by flames. An urban landscape in greys and blacks, morphing into a crazy sunset. Some areas of the wall were much more rudimentary, biro scribblings of a child, most certainly, obscene language in jagged letters, faces with scribbled eyes. "This is quite something."

"Couldn't stop him. He'd paint with whatever he'd get his thieving little mits on. Painted in his own blood once when I took his pens off him."

"Did he study? At school?"

"Never went to pissing school." She lit up another cigarette, and her face lit up with it. "Tell you a funny story. When Cal was still a mite, eight maybe, I dunno, he got hooked up with old Jimmy Randall down Veil Parade. He loved it over there, went for years, learning all that bleeding spray painting. Anyway, one day he comes home, back to me and Rick, my ex, right as we was switching over to watch the soaps and that, and he sits down, proper serious like, and he says, hey, Mam, I'm gonna go to art college. Just like that, really bloody pleased with himself. He says, Jimmy says I'm good, says I can be an artist." She cough-laughed, a picture of pure amusement. "Me and Rick nearly pissed ourselves, we did. Art college! Bloody art college! Like a kid like him's ever gonna go to bloody art college. I said to him, I said, don't be such a stupid, gay bloody poofter. Only fucking posh twats and faggots go to bloody art college, who d'you think you bloody are? Leonardo fucking Van Gogh or summat?"

My stomach fell, all the way to the floor, twisting in horror at the heartless crappy mother in front of me. "What did he say to that?"

She let out a belly laugh. "Nothing much, stupid little shit. Stormed off all huffy and smashed up all his pens and that. Threw them off the balcony. Called him little Leonardo fairy boy for ages, we did. Rick had to give him a hiding in the end to put an end to the sulking."

I stared at the wall, trying to decipher the colliding scenes. "It looks pretty good, to me."

"If you say so," she laughed. "Try asking the pigs what they think of his art, been arrested for it more times than he's had hot dinners."

I forced myself away, while I could still hold my tongue. "I'll be in touch soon, when I've filed the paperwork."

"Make sure they gives me my window bars, won't you? Don't want him getting in here."

I didn't answer, already reaching for the exit. I was beyond done here. My hand was already on the latch as the door flew open, sending me thudding back into the wall. I steadied myself, shocked to find I was staring up into the face of a brute. The eagle on his head was even uglier up close, and his eyes were swollen red. Too much weed, and probably something else.

"Hey, Ty, I'll be getting them window bars. Miss washername was just leaving. Got all the paperwork together."

Tyler Jones stared down on me with nothing but venom in his eyes. "Dog weren't fucking dead, then, shame."

"The dog is fine, now, *thank you*," I said, despite myself.

He stepped towards Hannah, and I caught the way she smiled up at him. Lord have bloody mercy. He wrapped an arm around her shoulder. "Next time I beat the shit out of him I'll be sure to let you know. You can come watch again, tend to lover boy's wounds when I'm done with him."

Hannah slapped his thigh. "Watch it, Ty, she's with the housing."

"I know who she's with. It's written all over her. Ain't the fucking housing why she's here."

"Goodbye, Mrs Jackson."

I was out of that seedy, incestuous little shit hole as fast as my legs would carry me, only stopping to catch my breath by the main entrance. The rain started up, drizzle grey sky doing nothing for the appearance of the place. I leaned back against the wall, hiding out under the porch for the worst to subside, coat-less and umbrella-less and really bloody ill prepared.

I stared out over East Veil, over past the garage block to tower two, wondering where the savage was now. Was he dry somewhere? Holed up with Casey and Vicki Pollock and her poor little boy? Was he laughing with her, laughing about me and his stupid security job? The thought hurt a lot more than it should have.

The rain eased up after a few minutes, but kept me pinned long enough to find the answers to my questions. For as soon as I committed to move, several others did too.

Callum Jackson appeared from the shadows of tower two, hood up and pacing on a mission as he headed towards the garages. I could see him well enough that the ferocity in his eyes stopped my

breath, but this time he didn't see me.
   He didn't see me follow him, either.

***

Chapter Six

Callum

Three hundred quid could go a fuck of a long way for me and Vick. Could feed us for fucking weeks, pick us up some new gear, decent shoes and shit. Three hundred quid could buy me all the paint I needed, get some proper food in Casey too. It felt so pissing rough to hand it over to the Stoneys.

I'd have told them to stuff it, to fuck off and leave Vicki alone, but they'd only take me down. Me and then her. They don't fuck around, people like that.

I told Vicki to stay at home, lock the pissing door and let me handle them. Eleven sharp, they'd said, and I'd picked the venue. The garages round here are quiet, see.

I called Casey to my side, and she stayed close, eyes full of play as I rounded the corner. I saw the Stoneys approaching from across the way, but kept my head down until they'd closed the gap. It was Trent Stoney who'd come for his cash, a couple of his guys hanging back behind him. One was a big, tough old cunt, built like a brick shithouse. The other was small, and scrawny, nasty eyes. They'd both be packing, I knew that much. Blades for sure, if not bullets. Casey didn't like them, she kept well back, low to the floor with her hackles up.

"What ya got for me?"

"Three hundred."

"Said three hundred *minimum*."

"Everything I got." I handed it over, and it fucking pained to watch the bastard count it.

His coat was expensive leather, his fingers rammed with bling. Gold no doubt, the proper stuff. He shoved the cash into an inside pocket.

"That'll have to do, then, won't it? Same time next week."

"Next week?" I couldn't hide the fury from my eyes, the fucking panic.

"Aye, soft lad, next fucking week. They pack your brains with cottonwool while you were inside?"

"How much?"

"Five. This three only clears the interest. That little skank should count herself lucky. We don't normally come to terms."

I checked out the men at his back. No way I could take them, not even with the advantage of surprise. "We can't get five, Trent. I swear down."

"Maybe the little slag should come tell me that herself, ask me nicely, then."

I wanted to smash the smirk from his fucking face. "I'll get what I can."

"What pissing use is that to me?"

"I'll pay it back, Trent. Debt's on me now." My heart pounded in my fists.

"My kind nature ain't gonna hold up much longer, soft lad. That loan's overdue. Maybe I should go have a word, eh? Let her know what's at stake."

He made to leave, tipping his head to his sidekicks, but I was in his face in a flash, heading him off. "Back off her, Trent, yeah? Like I said, debt's on me. You'll get your fucking money."

The wanker smiled, slapped my shoulder. "Good lad. Guess she's got a tight pussy, eh? I'll keep that in mind."

I stepped to the side, letting him pass. Out of words, out of hope, out of fucking everything. He turned back before he crossed the street, a hint of a smile on his smug face.

"Say, Jackson, you've got some spark. Let me know if you wanna run with my guys sometime, maybe we could come to some arrangement."

My fists twitched, angry yet desperate. The Stoneys ran girls, and drugs. A nasty scene. Desperate hookers who'd do anything for an armful of smack. The Stoneys were brutal, into the hard stuff, slicing off noses and ears and anything else they thought would send the right message. It was Casey's wet nose on my wrist that brought some sense back to me. I needed to stay out, for her. I shook my head. "Nah, thanks, Trent. Not for me."

"Suit yourself. Same time next week, don't be late."

I wouldn't be.

I wasn't that fucking stupid.

***

I took a different route back, heading in the opposite direction from Stoney. We'd been so relieved, me and Vick. Now it was all for nothing. I had no phone credit to call Jack Willis and chase up any delivery jobs. I'd have to call round there later in person, but he didn't like that much. Case loped on ahead, as happy as I was to be away from those wankers. Her nose was in the air, tail high, turning back every now and then to make sure I was following. Fucking hell, now I had to break the news to Vick.

I stopped to roll-up, and that's when I heard them. Footfalls, down the alley behind us. They stopped when I did, meaning only one thing.

Seemed Trent weren't so happy with his three hundred after all. I weighed up which one he'd have sent for me. Hopefully the bigger one, he'd fall harder, run slower. I darted on ahead, veering off to the right to a connecting pathway. Casey changed course with me, and I sent her on away, waving my arms that she was free to run. The path opened up onto some boarded-up retail units, and I sloped down the side of them, into a little known alleyway that led to the bins at the back of tower two, and not much else. Casey lay down at the far end when she figured we were stopping, ears up.

I waited for Stoney's sidekick, fists clenched and adrenaline pumping. I'd need to take him quick, knock him down and shoe him good. My brain raced, but I blanked it all out. No time to worry about what came next, no time for planning. His footsteps were echoey, hesitant, lighter too. Shit. Must be the smaller guy, he'd be more of a springer, harder to take.

Casey started whining and I hissed at her to shut the fuck up. The footsteps stopped, and so did my breathing. I readied myself, determined at least to put up a good fight. He started up, coming closer, footsteps louder, closing the gap. The echo was loud, clackety... strange.

Heels.

My *tail* was wearing fucking heels.

I flung myself into the path regardless, fists high and ready, teeth bared and eyes wide fucking open.

Sophie Harding screamed and scurried backwards, catching a heel on a pothole and falling hard on her pretty little ass. Her paperwork scattered, landing in puddles like oversized confetti.

We stared at each other, breathing heavy.

"Jesus Christ!" she screeched. "You scared the shit out of me!"

"I could have fucking killed you." I was still wired, high on adrenaline, muscles on fucking fire. "What the fuck are you doing here?"

She grabbed the papers, soggy forms mushing together in one big mess. "I'm on an estate inspection. You know, doing my *job*."

"What you supposed to be inspecting?" I scoffed.

She waved her arms vaguely. "Here. Around."

"Round the bins of block two? Get fucking real."

She clambered to her feet, twisting to look back over her shoulder. "Pissing hell, I'm soaked."

"At least you're in one fucking piece. I talk with my fists first, mouth later."

"Nice."

"Truth." My arms were still twitchy. I reached in my pocket for my baccy, leaning against the wall as my heart slowed down. I whistled to Case and she came running, jumping up at my legs like I hadn't just seen her five seconds ago. "Why you following me?"

"I wasn't," she lied.

I rolled my cig. "Whatever."

"Who did you think I was? One of those guys back there?"

I narrowed my eyes, stared straight at her. "Do you ever mind your own fucking business?"

"This is *my* patch," she snapped.

"Yeah, well this is my *life*."

She stood in silence, and so did I, letting the tension ease off a little. Casey fixed her with curious eyes, tail twitching as though she hadn't quite made up her mind. Sophie watched her back, expression softening.

"She looks better."

"She *is* better, thanks."

She dropped on her haunches, hand out. "Hey, Casey..."

Case wasn't sure what to make of her. She looked up at me and I gave her the nod, sending her over to the woman who'd saved her furry ass. Casey sniffed Sophie's hand, then wagged her tail, satisfied Sophie was one of the good guys.

Sophie Harding smiled her lovely smile. "She's put on weight."

"A bit, yeah."

"That's good."

I watched her stroking the dog awhile, gentle little fingers. "Why were you following me?"

She shrugged, eyes still on Casey. "Saw you in the garages."

"Then came for a snoop?"

"I wanted to make sure you were good... after the weekend."

I sparked up. "Ain't told no one, if that's what you're pissing worried about."

"It isn't."

She smiled as Casey jumped up to lick her face, fussing her round the ears. It made me feel funny inside, hot and churned up. I looked at her as I smoked my roll-up, the posh little suit she was wearing, her clean white blouse. She looked so fresh, so proper. She didn't belong in this place. Didn't belong here, with me.

"Why d'you do it? This shitty job?"

She looked up at me, eyes soft. "To make a difference."

"Can't make a difference round here. Place is rotten."

"You can always make a difference, if you care enough."

"Dunno about that." I smiled a bit. "Be careful, estate manager. Nearly got yourself proper beat up back there."

"Those men. You gave them money. Why?"

I scowled. "Don't matter."

"Are you in trouble?" Her expression was well-meaning, but it pissed me off all the same. I ignored her, staring over her head until she got to her feet. "Fine. Sorry I cared."

She patted Casey goodbye and took off back the way she came, all haughty with angry little steps. This time it was me who leapt after her and grabbed her by the arm, spinning her so fast she lost her balance and toppled into me, slamming into my chest as Casey danced all around us.

"I ain't involved with those wankers, don't want nothing to do with them," I snapped. "I was helping a mate, that's all."

She didn't move, didn't pull away. She smelt so good again, so fucking clean. It made me feel like a piece of crap, still in the same tatty clothes from the weekend and well overdue a fucking wash.

"A friend?"

"A mate, yeah."

"Your girlfriend? Vicki?"

There was colour in her cheeks, same as in that hotel room. "Ain't got a girlfriend. Vick's a mate."

Her eyes were sparkly, big pupils. "Will you come with me again?" she whispered.

"Eh?"

"To the hotel... I'll pay you, just the same as last time."

My brain said fucking take it, but my heart weren't so sure. "I dunno."

"It'll be just like last time, I promise. I can relax when you're there..."

"Same guy?"

"Probably."

I pushed her away, keeping hold of her shoulders until she was steady. I wanted to say no, tell her to fuck off and find another chump to sit around and listen to her getting fucked, but I couldn't do it. Vick needed the cash.

"When?"

"Saturday. Same place."

I sighed, admitting defeat. "Aye, alright then."

She smiled, really fucking happy. It made me feel fucking sick to the stomach.

"I'll see you there."

She took off before I could change my mind.

***

Hot water felt so good on my skin. I soaped myself quick to save Vick's electric, but held on a minute longer, just to enjoy the heat. She'd raised an eyebrow when she'd put my clothes through the washer, questions heavy in the air. It was all drying now, on the radiator. Still looked shit, but at least I'd be clean. I stepped out, slinging Vicki's pink towel round my hips and wiping steam from the mirror.

My stubble was more of a beard than a shadow. I rooted through the cabinet until I found a razor, trimmed it back short.

"Ain't using them clippers are ya? Use them for me pubes," Vicki barked from the landing.

I opened the door a crack. "Hope I ain't caught your stinky fucking crabs."

She slapped my arm. "Ain't nothing wrong with my bits, Callum Jackson."

"Take your word for it," I smiled.

Vicki's eyes were all over me, following the line of hair down from my belly button. "Where's she dragging you to this week? The bloody Ritz?"

I shrugged. "Wherever she wants, she's paying."

"Wish you didn't have to go, Cal." She folded her arms. "She's after summat. A shag probably."

"Doubt it. Ain't likely to be her type."

"She's yours, though, ent she? Now you're into blondes."

I moved back to the mirror, checking out my reflection. Would have to do. I picked up a can of deodorant, sprayed under my arms as she watched. "It's a job. Stoneys want their cash."

She came inside, closed the door behind her. "I'm sorry, Cal, 'bout all this."

"We're mates, yeah? We look out for each other."

"Mates. Yeah." Her smile was sad. I hate that smile. I reached past her for my clothes, and she made no move to leave. "When this is all over, maybe me and you could go down Scotty's, get some more ink."

I turned my back to her, pointed to my shoulder. "I want a picture of Case done, here. Gonna draw one. Tribal, like."

"Sweet." She pulled her top down, showing me way too much tit. "I want something here. Draw something for me, yeah?"

"Yeah." I yanked a t-shirt over my head, then pulled my jeans on quick, showing her my ass but not much else. "Gotta go, Vick. Don't wanna be late."

I grabbed my hoodie on the way out.

"You look good, Cal," she smiled. "I'll see you later."

My stomach churned. Guilt. "Nah, Vick, don't wait up. Dunno how long I'll be." I pulled her into my side, ruffled her hair. "Look after Case, alright."

She grabbed hold of me, arms around my ribs.

I felt so fucking tight for pulling away.

✳✳✳

Sophie

I walked quickly, thoughts racing as the hotel came into view. My suitcase rumbled along the pavement, making it so bloody obvious I was coming.

I wondered if he was there already, watching. All week I'd been thinking about him. Literally, all fucking week. His eyes as he'd sprung from the shadows, so wild, like he'd tear me limb from limb. He could have done, could have snapped my neck in a heartbeat, thrown me to the ground and kicked the shit out of me. Or slammed me into the wall and... and... *fucked me... really fucking hard.*

I was officially crazy. Even Raven said so. I smiled at the memory, of her untangling the Roger-Callum threads over wine at hers.

Let me get this straight. You're using Mr Dangerous to bait Mr Super-fucking-dangerous? You're crazy, baby. Make sure this shit doesn't end in the wrong kind of tears.

She knew where I was headed, had extracted promises upon promises on pain of death that I'd check in when it was over. Taking address details, and times, and even bookmarking Roger's Edgeplay profile on her mobile. She'd be at Explicit, she said, phone close by, where I'd be too if I had any sense.

Roger had taken some convincing, not entirely game for another session after the washout last time. I'd offered to beg and no doubt he'd hold me to it. I owed him a good time, he said. I imagined he'd tan my backside good and proper for my cheek.

I waited outside the main entrance, eyes scanning the edge of Kensington Gardens. Callum Jackson didn't approach from that direction this time. He stepped out of the shadows at the side of the building, towering over me without warning.

"Thank you for coming." My voice was too bright, and way too professional.

"Same deal, yeah? We go up, he comes in."

"Yeah. Same deal."

He led the way in, skulking straight over to the lifts. I watched him as I checked in. He was so uncomfortable in this place. Can't say I'd be any different in his position.

We took the lift in silence, air heavy as I opened the door to our suite. He took the case on through to the bedroom, then he paced, slowly, eyes anywhere but on me.

I slipped off my coat, wishing he'd just fucking look at me. I'd dressed to impress... impress Roger, impress him... I wasn't even sure anymore. My dress had ridden high, barely covering my ass. I smoothed it down, checking my suspenders were still in place. I'd chosen purple this time, a deep, dark PVC, with buckles all the way up the front. I'd been happy in my apartment, happy that I looked the part and that maybe, just maybe, it would be enough to make an impression. Finally Callum's eyes landed in my direction.

"Do I look ok?" I chanced.

"Like him, do you?"

"No. Well... not like that."

"Why you here, then?"

"For the pain," I answered simply. "I like his hands a lot more than him."

"Fair enough."

Callum was straight to the door when Roger knocked. He blocked the way for what felt like an age, glaring before stepping aside. Roger shot me a look, raising his eyebrows before heading straight through to the bedroom. His expression was brutal, suit already straining with his hard on.

"Strip," he said. "All of it."

I reached for the first buckle, moving as gracefully as possible, but he shook his head.

"Out there."

"Sorry?"

"You heard me. I want you to go out there, take off all your clothes, and walk back in through that door naked. *Naked.*"

"Don't be stupid," I hissed. "Callum."

He smirked. "Get with the plot, sweetheart. I want him to see what tender fucking meat I'm feasting on. He may have come up trumps last week, but this is round two."

"Come on, Roger, let's play another game..." I stammered. "I'll do you a striptease, whatever you want."

His expression didn't lighten. "I'm the main act tonight, and I want that loser out there to know it."

Shit. My heart thumped, stomach churning. I thought about calling it off, wimping out and leaving them both to it. I could head over to Explicit, hook back up with Cain and drink cocktails with Raven. So what if Cain was slack with the bondage? Maybe it *is* better to play with the devils you know.

Roger waited, unflinching. My hand was shaking so hard I could hardly turn the door handle.

Callum was leant against the far wall staring right at me. I could barely get my words out, and when I did they were weak and flaky.

"Sorry... I'm, um... Roger wants me to..." I turned my back to him, darting a glance over my shoulder as I began to undress. His eyes flew wide, wild, just like they'd been in the alleyway. I kept going, freeing enough of the buckles that my dress dropped to the floor. "Just turn away or something."

He didn't turn away. I could feel him staring, eyes scorching my back. I unclipped my suspender belt, tossed it to the side, then stepped out of my heels, pulled my stockings from my feet. My panties came off last. I held my breath as I slid them down, shaking like a fucking leaf, then gathered my clothes up in a flurry and flung them onto a chair. I covered myself up best I could with my arms, a truly pathetic attempt at modesty.

"Sorry, Callum... I'm really sorry about this."

I dashed back to the bedroom, hissing out embarrassment as I closed the door behind me.

Roger had a cocky half-smile on his face. "Just as I thought."

He finished up taking my toys from the suitcase.

"What?"

"Wish you'd get that worked up when you stripped in front of me."

"I hardly know him."

"Hardly know me, either." He brandished a flogger. "Wake up to yourself, sweetheart. You're dripping fucking wet for him. Think I wouldn't know I'm being played?"

I watched the flogger, skin tingling in anticipation. "Punish me, then..." I whispered.

"I intend to." He closed the gap between us, spinning me around and slamming me against the door. "He'll hear *this*."

The flogger was vicious in Roger's hands. He swung hard, fast, curling the tails around my ribs to sting tender skin. I took it, all of it, breathing through the pain and rocking on my heels. Once he was done, he pressed up against me, slapping me hard on the ass with heavy palms. The force made the door rattle, and I groaned against the wood.

"I bet you want him in here. His scabby cock in your shithole. He'd probably tear you a new one, an animal like that, fuck you till you bleed. Maybe I should call him in, let him fuck you up. Maybe we could share you, him and me, plenty of holes to go around."

"Fuck, Roger... just fucking hit me..."

"My fucking pleasure, sweetheart."

He slapped me with everything he had, and I groaned at the burn;

the gorgeous tingle of skin as his palms coloured me pink. His arm was heavy across my shoulder blades, holding me tight against the door, the rattling catch the only barrier between me and the savage beyond. My tits mashed tight into the woodwork, the doorframe creaking with every strike. Roger dropped to his knees, slavering over my ass cheeks. I squirmed as he pulled them apart, burying his nose between my thighs.

It felt icky. Dirty. *I* felt dirty.

"Hurt me, Roger... the flogger again, please..."

He got to his feet, pressed his mouth to my ear. "No more flogger, sweetheart. Tell me you want me."

"I... just... more spanking, Roger, please..."

"You're a dirty fucking prick tease."

"I want pain..."

"I'll not be leaving with blue fucking balls again this week. I'm down two hundred quid for this fucking suite. Hot, wet cunt is the only currency I take." His laugh was grimy.

Reality raised its ugly fucking head and came up to bite me. Raven was right. Using Mr Dangerous to bait Mr super-fucking-dangerous was a stupid fucking plan. I'd been so busy thinking about Callum Jackson that I hadn't given a second thought to the sadist in the room with me. Hadn't thought whether I really wanted his cock in my ass, in my pussy, wherever he fucking wanted it.

I didn't want it.

I didn't want him.

So, why was I still fucking horny?

I eyed him over my shoulder, stomach lurching as I saw his twisted smile. "Give me that sweet juicy cunt you dirty bitch."

I heard him unbuckle his belt, pockets rustling. The tear of a packet, a grunt as he slapped his cock against my ass. I tried to back him up but he wouldn't shift.

"Roger... I don't..."

"You do..." His cock was slimy in my ass crack. "You want this, Missy. We both know it."

"He's out there... I could call..."

Roger's mouth on my neck, cock paused against my slit. "Take what you're given like a good girl. I know you like this shit... you told me, remember? *I need a guy who'll just take me... a guy who's not scared to take what he wants when he wants it.*"

I flinched at the memory, how hot the idea had seemed with a vibrator against my fucking clit.

I clenched myself against his intrusion, twisting away from the wet tongue in my ear. "It was a fantasy, Roger..."

"Open that hot little slit for me, dirty girl."

I squirmed against the door. "I could call for him..."

"It's *me* who's in charge here." He forced his fingers around my thigh, pinching at my clit. My knees juddered, my body betraying me. My legs opened for him, just an inch.

I whimpered, brain spinning, hating myself for wanting this.

"Call him, sweetheart. Call him or give me your filthy little fuck hole..."

I gasped, gripped in no-man's land, veering between outcomes.

But it didn't matter.

The decision was made for me.

✶✶✶

Callum

They both went fucking flying. That bastard, Roger, went further, crashing all the way back into the four poster, trousers round his fucking ankles, his cock bobbing. His glasses tumbled, bouncing to the floor before he could catch them. Sophie was down on her ass, rubbing her forehead where the door had smacked into her, but I didn't have time to give a shit about that right now.

I was on him in a flash, landing a solid punch right into his cheekbone. I got him good, and landed another, crunching my knuckles into his fucking teeth. He raised his hands, squealing like a fucking pig.

"Stop! For fuck's sake! It's a fucking game! A game!"

I kneed him in the ribs and he doubled over, sinking down to the floor as he gulped for breath. I went for Sophie, dragged her to her feet.

"You alright?"

She nodded. "Fine. I'm fine. Totally fine."

"Tell the stupid sonofabitch!" Roger wheezed. "It was just a fucking game!"

I lunged for him again, ready to kick him where it fucking hurts, but Sophie grabbed my arm. "Jesus, Callum, stop! Stop!"

I gripped her shoulders, spitting rage. "He was gonna fucking rape you!"

"He didn't! He wasn't..."

I shoved her backwards, soaking in the marks on her body. She was pink and white, dark lines curling under her tits from where he'd beaten her. Her thighs were rosy, they were wet too, she was fucking wet. I put my hands in my hair, reeling. "You wanted that? For fucking real?"

"No... yes... no!"

"She wanted it," Roger grunted. "She likes rape play. She's playing us both for bloody fools."

My eyes sliced into her. "That true?"

"In fantasy... shit." She stepped over Roger, darting to the bathroom for a towel. I stared as she wrapped herself up. "I said wait to out there! I said I'd call if I needed you!"

"Sounded like I was fucking needed!" I stalked over to the sack of shit on the floor. "Rapist cunt."

His jaw was already swelling, gums bleeding around his teeth. He turned to Sophie and I fought the urge to kick his fucking head in.

"Nice." He wiped his face with his sleeve. "This is what happens when you use dumb, fucking meatheads for security."

"Get the fuck out of here," I growled. "Before I tear your fucking dick off."

Sophie nodded, to which he shrugged and staggered to his feet, holding his ribs where I'd kneed him. He pulled his clothes back on, scowling the whole fucking time, then reached for his glasses, flinching as he sat them on his pudgy fucking face. I followed him out, watched him until the lift doors took him from view. Piece of fucking shit.

Sophie was perched on the bed when I went back in, face in her hands.

"I'm sorry..." she rasped. "This was a bad idea."

"Which fucking bit? Having him here or having me here?"

She moved her hands away, stared up at me. "All of it."

Her answer cut me way more than it should. "Fuck you, then. Find some other chump to be your fucking guard dog."

I'd reached the main door before she spoke again.

"I'm sorry, Callum."

I froze. Embarrassment burned, flaring in humiliation at the way I'd wanted her. Leaning up against the other side of that doorway, knowing she was just an inch away. My cock in my hand as I'd listened to the noises she made... the soft lace of her thong between my fingers, the gusset tight against my nose. The smell of her so nice. What the fuck was she doing to me?

She stood, towel hanging loose as she made her way towards me.

She stepped over the discarded scrap of underwear, so far away from the heap of her clothes on the chair.

"You were at the door, weren't you?"

"My cock's not fucking scabby, by the way. I'm not diseased, just fucking skint."

"Christ, you heard that?"

"Don't give a fuck what a cunt like that thinks anyway."

"He doesn't really think that. It was just talk."

"Don't give a fuck either way." I stepped back inside, away from the door. "Why d'you bring me here?"

"Just in case..."

"Bull-fucking-shit.

She stared over, eyes wide, mouth flapping as she tried for words. She gave up, sighed and shrugged. "I'm sorry about all this. Let me get your cash."

She fumbled around in her bag, pulled out the money. More clean, crisp notes ready for the Stoneys' fucking pockets. I hated it. All of it.

Her cash felt like shit in my hand. I stared at it while she grabbed her clothes, reaching down for her thong and scurrying on through to the bedroom.

"You can go now," she called. "He'll be long gone."

My fist clenched around the cash, crumpling it to shit. All I could see was that cunt, his smug fucking face, making her gasp and beg.

Jealousy grabbed me in a chokehold, frying my fucking brain. *My* name. I wanted her to scream *my* fucking name.

I flung myself into the bedroom with as much force as I'd knocked them on their fucking asses. Sophie Harding spun round in shock, eyes like saucers as I charged. I threw the cash at her, and the flurry of notes bounced off her sweet fucking tits.

"Don't want your fucking money."

She gathered it up, shoving it back at me. "Don't be crazy. You earned it. It's yours."

"You can't fucking buy me, not for this shit."

She shrugged, eyes defiant. "Just take it, will you? Spend it on Casey if you don't want it."

I forced her backwards, slamming my fist into the wall above her head. "Liked winding me up, did you? Wanted me sniffing your dirty fucking panties like a desperate fucking animal? Is that what you wanted? Hey? Wanted to make a fucking prick out of me?" I walked away. "You're a fucking joke."

"I'm not making a prick out of you!"

"Feels fucking like it."

"I'm not!" she screeched. She darted in front of me, blocked my way. "Jesus, Callum, I'm not out to humiliate you!"

"What then?"

Her flushed cheeks, the swell of her sweet, soft tits under the towel. She was more than I could take. I stared mute, tongue-fucking-tied.

"I.. I wanted... I want..." She closed her eyes, took a deep breath.

"What? What do you fucking want?"

Her fingers reached for my hoodie, latching underneath, freeing her towel to drop as she pulled me closer. "This..." she breathed. "You..."

My heart hammered. "This another fucking game?"

"What do you think?" Her hand reached for mine, guided my fingers to the heat between her legs. My cock leapt in my jeans, straining like a motherfucker.

"Don't fucking tease," I said. "It won't end well."

"I'm not teasing," she rasped. "Take what you want... anything..."

I balled her clit with my thumb, and finally she groaned for me. For *me*. It felt so fucking good. "I ain't gentle," I said. "Don't know how."

"I don't want gentle..." Her hands on the waist of my jeans, climbing up my stomach. "Whips... floggers... canes... take your pick..."

I grabbed her hair, yanked her head back until she yelped, eyes widening as they met the savage in mine. My fingers plugged at her slit, a growl escaping my throat as I pressed my mouth to her ear.

"...I won't be needing any of that shit."

***

Chapter Seven

Sophie

My fingers were frantic, jittering like crazy as they snaked under Callum Jackson's clothes. His abs were solid, burning up under his hoodie.

I pulled up his top, desperate for skin. He grunted, pulling his fingers out from inside me just long enough to yank his hoodie and t-shirt over his head. Shit. He was fucking gorgeous.

His chest was beautifully tattooed, taut flesh firm against my palms. Three skulls morphed into each other, a desolate tribal scene, marking out the ribs under his skin. The others were more abstract, slashes of colour in vicious lines down either side of his body. The designs met under his belly button, and fanned out to the toned V of his hips. I felt plain next to his colourful skin, really fucking plain.

When the beautiful savage clamped his sweet mouth onto mine his kiss was wet, messy, clumsy teeth bashing into mine. But it didn't matter. It was *real*. His tongue was so fucking hungry, plundering my mouth without mercy.

When he pulled away he was puffy-lipped, voice raspy. "Ain't no posh guy. Ain't got no fancy toys. Only me."

"I don't want posh," I hissed.

He brushed my bottom lip with his thumb. "Gonna feel so

fucking good to tear you down."

I gasped at his words. His tongue was hot against my cheek, slavering over my face. He moved his way down, coating my skin with the slick sheen of his spit, right the way down my neck. His teeth nipped, and I squirmed, arching my back as he sunk a bite into the soft flesh of my collarbone.

"Ow... Jesus..."

He yanked my head back, angling my chest up to him, vicious kisses heading down. "Gonna mark you. I like doing that."

He opened his mouth wide, sucking in as much of my breast as would fit. He looked so fucking hot there, dark eyes sharp as daggers as he slavered on me. I loved the way he sounded, his low grunts of pleasure. I tangled my fingers in his hair, coaxing.

"Please, harder..."

His teeth took my breath, clamping so hard the room began to spin. I held tight, for balance, soft expletives on my lips with no air to birth them. His fingers fucked me as he bit down harder, pistoning in and out in brutal rhythm. I squirmed into the lovely pain, flashes of light behind my eyes.

His teeth left deep red imprints in my skin. I ran my fingers over the grooves as the pain subsided, but he didn't leave me any reprieve, resuming his attack. I spread my legs, a part of me hoping he'd do a Roger and tear me open while I screamed.

Callum's eyes were glazed, lips swollen from sucking. "Your tits mark so pretty," he groaned. "Need to own your cunt now, mark you as mine."

My clit sparked as he pushed me back towards the bed.

"Don't need no chains," he growled. "You ain't gonna fight me."

He positioned himself between my legs, thumb brushing the thin line of hair I'd left there. He pulled my pussy lips apart so wide I flinched, closing my eyes at his scrutiny.

"Pretty cunt." He smiled at me. "Big lips. I like that."

He pressed his thumb against my clit, and I was already halfway there, fisting the bed sheets on impact. His teeth made me squirm; branding me with dark purple kisses, a chain of love bites across my thighs. I drifted for an age, writhing under his mouth as he finished his masterpiece.

"One left," he promised. "Crown jewel. Gonna hurt."

He kissed my pussy hard, tongue flat and wet against my clit, jerky movements until I was well on my way.

"Yes..." I hissed. "I want it... I need it. I so fucking need it..."

When his teeth clenched I howled the room down, shock and pain jolting me upright, but he was ready, arms prepared to slam me down. His hands reached up to clasp mine, mouth still latched on to my throbbing cunt. He stretched my lips as he pulled away, tender flesh held fast in his teeth. It hurt like fucking sin, and once he let go I strained for view, expecting blood and strings of torn flesh.

There was none, just hot, pulsing swelling. I groaned as I touched myself, checking for serious injury.

"Never been with a biter before, not like this."

"Wanted to hurt you, where he's been. Wanted you to feel me instead."

He crawled up the bed to me, and I was ready, reaching for him. Fingers frantic on his jeans. "Fuck me," I hissed. "Fuck him out of me. Please..." I pushed his jeans down and his cock sprang to attention: long, thick, and hard as hell.

He groaned at the grip of my hand on his cock. I looked up at the dresser, wriggled until I could reach a rubber. We tore the packet and slid it on between us, clammy hands desperate and clumsy. He was so big and veined, with a dark tangled mess of pubes around the base of him. His tattoos went all the way down, stopping just shy of his gorgeous cock.

He took my wrists, pinned them high above my head.

Then he fucked me.

Dirty.

Bad.

Savage.

Grunting and hissing and slavering at my mouth. His eyes in mine, dark as night, and vicious, really vicious. He made it hurt. Good hurt. Sore clit burning so hot as he slammed into me. He raised himself before he came, changing angle enough to grind my g-spot. Jesus he knew what he was doing. I arched myself, matching his grunts, jerking under him.

We didn't come together, but it was close. Close enough.

Hands gripped my bruised thighs as he shot his load, groaning in feral victory as I squealed beneath him.

He collapsed on my chest, spent and slick with sweat and panting like a dog.

I teased his hair with my fingers, enjoying his hot breath on my tits.

"Fucking hell, Callum, that was so good."

"You're bleeding," he said. "From my teeth."

I didn't care.

He got up from me sooner than I'd have liked, but I brushed it off, grabbing a towel and wandering through in a heady daze to flick the kettle on. He was dressed by the time he joined me. Eyes distant.

"Staying for a drink?" I asked.

He shook his head. "Gotta go."

"So soon?"

"Casey's alone, in Vick's shed."

"I see." The atmosphere was tense. Real fucking awkward. He hovered for ages, eyes on the floor, and it took me a while to realise what he was waiting for. "Shit! Your money! Christ, I'm sorry." I dashed into the bedroom and gathered it up, shoving it into his hands as he stared at me. "Count it, please. I'd hate if there was any missing."

His eyes didn't leave mine. "What's this for?"

I smiled. "You've definitely earned it."

His expression darkened. "Guess I did, yeah." He shoved the notes in his pocket. "See you around."

Fuck. He'd gone before I could even say goodbye.

***

"Jesus Christ, baby, you don't do things by halves, do you." Raven smiled, stubbing out her cigarette as the waitress delivered our coffees. "So, Roger is out, Savage is in?"

"Neither's in at the moment," I groaned. "Callum's gone totally bloody AWOL."

"AWOL?" she quizzed, perfect brows raised.

"Won't answer his phone, no sign of him on the estate." I sighed. "Avoiding me like the plague. He's painting, though, work's going ballistic about it, eating into next quarter's budget just to keep it under control."

"Is he any good?"

"Wouldn't catch the maintenance team calling it art." I handed her an envelope, stuffed full of photos I'd printed out at work when no one was looking. "What do you think?"

She flicked through the pictures, pausing on some for an age, eyes glittering. "He did these?"

"All of them, yeah."

"Boy's got skill," she said.

"You think so? I mean, *I* think so, but I'm probably skewed. Supposed to be filing these for prosecution, *vandalism*."

"*That's* the fucking crime, right there. These are fucking incredible." She turned a photo towards me, one of my favourites: a boy leaping, mid-flight, surrounded by twisted blades as he reaches for the sun. "Look at the lines... the colour..." She pointed to the swirls in the background. "That control, the care with which he layers the paint. Yet, it's jagged, rushed... clearly done at speed. You can feel the passion... the soul... I fucking love it."

I felt my cheeks burning. "Yeah, me too."

"Guess you found your Mr Dangerous."

"Found him and lost him."

"I'm sure he'll turn up. You're a hot chick, sassy as sin with a good head on your shoulders. What's not to love?"

I sipped my coffee. "I'm old. He's young. I live in my parents' ivory tower, he's on the street... do I need to continue?"

"Twenty fucking eight isn't old, believe me, I'm counting on it. Anyway, a guy loves an older woman, I'm sure you can break him in, teach him a few tricks."

"No need. He's been around a bit, that much is totally obvious."

"He's good, then?"

I couldn't hide the grin. "Rough, raw, dirty... really fucking good with his hands."

She handed back the photos. "That figures."

I looked her dead in the eye, girl to girl. "Shit, Raven, I'm losing the plot. I can't stop thinking about him."

"Crushing is hardcore. Maybe that's all it is."

"Hope so." I finished my coffee. "It's just a sex thing. It has to be. I mean what the hell would we ever have in common? And can you even begin to imagine me taking him home to the family? Parading him around at some property event? Can just imagine Dad's face if I dragged him along to the Southbank Art Centre opening, pissing on their snobby spectacle and blighting the family name. Alexandra would probably faint. Mum would probably cry."

"Hey, enough of that. He'd belong there more than they would. That place isn't just a fucking building, regardless of what your posh-arsed parents invested in it."

I smiled at Rebecca's passion. I love her as Raven, but I love her even more as Bex, bohemian art queen, tattoo artist extraordinaire. "Your stuff going to be on display at the opening?"

"Nah. I'm out the game now, don't get as much time for it now Cara's moved in."

"Shame."

"Not really. The girl's pussy tastes mighty-fucking-fine. I'd be lying if I said I'd rather be painting. Got the tattoo work anyway, keeps me busy."

"Cara's great. You two were made for each other."

"It was just a *sex* thing, once upon a time. I mean how could she ever take me home to the family, baby?" Rebecca winked, softening her snipe.

"Christ, Bex, I'm sorry. I sound like a real bloody snob."

"It's your parents talking through your mouth. Let it go, baby, let *them* go, live for you."

I changed the subject. "How's Explicit? How's Cain?"

"Come back soon, will you? With or without the savage in tow. We're all missing you."

"How's Cain, Bex?" I grinned. "Seriously, spill the beans. I'm cool."

"He's giving it another go with Diva. They've been on each other like a rash since you left. Sorry."

"Don't be," I laughed. "I'm happy for them. All of them... even Cat and Masque."

"Even Cat and Masque?!" Raven's mouth was set in a mischievous line, eyes sparkling as she stared at me. "You weren't joking, were you, baby? Boy's got you really fucking good."

Damn fucking right he had.

***

Callum

I'd never been so glad to offload cash as I'd been to hand that filthy fucking money to the Stoneys. They weren't happy, of course. Never fucking would be. Not until that debt was fucking done for. Another three hundred, all my fucking work for the week. Diving from here to there with shitty little parcels, handing them over to any fucking low-life skank who was buying. Hated it. Hated my fucking life.

Hated being paid for sex more than any of it.

Didn't want to take it but the Stoneys had us in a corner with nowhere to fucking move.

Vick was grateful, I know. But there was more to it than that. She was trying too hard again, just like she was before I went inside. Sitting too close, smiling that smile. Telling me how good I was with Slay, how much he fucking loved me. I'd skulked away like a sewer rat, bedding down with Case at the old King's Road maintenance huts. Licking my wounds with just a twenty left to my name and some loose scraps of change. That and my paints. I'd been painting every fucking night, my only escape. Taking more risks these days too, hanging off the subway by a bit of tatty old rope, heart fucking racing. I had a letter in my pocket, just in case. A note to her, Sophie Harding, asking her to take care of Casey. She could hand her into one of them rescue homes, maybe she'd find a good family after all.

I'd seen Sophie looking for me on her estate visits. Eyes darting around the place, heading down alleys that led to nowhere. Even watched her check around Vicki's place, sticking a brave head over the fence to the yard. I'd kept out of sight, one step ahead. Just watching. She'd tried calling too, from several different numbers. Hadn't answered. Too fucking ashamed. Angry too.

The Stoneys would be after me again in a few days, wanting another instalment I didn't have. I had one-eighty owing from Jack Willis, barely enough to show my face with. I'd come away with a black eye next time, maybe a couple of smashed ribs. Fuck it, who fucking cared anymore.

Friday afternoon hit hard. My paints were in dregs after my latest mural, black clean out and red not far behind. No money to get more, no fucking hope in sight. I stashed my paints in Vicki's shed when she was out at her mam's, then broke my twenty on a cheap bottle of vodka and a tin of food for Case. Sophie Harding was a fucking nightmare, charging helter-skelter round my brain. Her soft blonde hair, her pretty eyes. The way she smelt so fucking clean. Her sweet little pussy so wet for me. She'd cried my name like I meant something. Like I was *someone*. She was wrong. So fucking wrong. I'd put paid to that by taking that cash off her. My last tenner bought me an underground day pass, and I headed down Islington way, over to Baker Road. I knew the housing office was based down there. Mam had dragged me enough times when I was little, harping on about rent and benefits and the poxy fucking neighbours. I found it easy enough, pressing myself into the shadow of the shoe shop opposite to keep an eye out. I just wanted to see her, that's all. Watch her for a little while.

Case settled down, resting at my feet as I drank my way through the vodka. I'd almost finished by the time the housing shut up for the day, staying out of sight as they spilled out the place, suited up so fucking smart. Sophie was amongst them, laughing and smiling as she went. A group of them stopped at the pub down the road, Bay

Leaf Inn. I watched her through the window; watched her talk, watched her smile.

She looked happy. Pretty. Just a normal woman on a Friday night, oblivious to the freak outside waiting for her. I picked about in the ashtrays, smoking a load of scabby leftovers. My tobacco was down to the crumbs, papers almost out too. I stuffed a couple of skanky fag ends in my pocket for later and left before she did, heading back across the street to watch her leave. It was dark by the time she came out, tottering on down to the tube station. I kept my distance, shushing Casey to stop fucking whining, while I followed her all the way. She got off at Canary Wharf. I'd heard about this place. The buildings were fucking crazy, tall glass space towers of fucking money. So, she was from here. Richer than I'd fucking thought, made of fucking money. The thought made me bitter and I closed the gap in a rage. She heard Casey before she heard me, spinning at the sound of her whining, only to find herself up against me as I grappled for her arms. She recoiled, shocked, squeaking as I yanked her down the side of the nearest building, dog jumping all around us as I smashed her into the wall.

She looked angry, angry and scared.

"What the hell are you doing here?!"

"Followed you," I grunted.

"Followed me? Why?"

I shrugged. "Dunno."

"Could have just answered your phone, or, I dunno, stopped fucking avoiding me." Her mouth was so pretty when she was angry.

I gripped her cheeks in my fingers, squeezing her beautiful lips into a pout. "You should be careful, out on your own."

"I don't usually get followed. This isn't East Veil, Callum."

"This where you come from, rich girl?"

"I rent my apartment from my parents. Only lived here a couple of years."

"Nice rich mammy and daddy looking out for their princess."

Her eyes narrowed. "It's not like that."

"What's a little rich girl like you doing round East Veil? Like a bit of rough, do ya? Need dirty rough cock in ya to feel good?"

She tried to shove me away but I didn't budge. "You're drunk."

"So?"

"So, don't be such an arsehole. I'm from money, big fucking deal. I have a nice apartment, whoopy fucking do, Callum."

"Liked paying me for it?" I sneered. "Hope my cock was worth the money."

She shoved me again, harder this time. "Is that what it was to you? A fucking job?"

"That's what it was to *you*," I snarled.

"Of course it fucking wasn't. I was paying you for the shit with Roger, for your *time*."

"Didn't want it!" I thundered.

She stared at me in shock. "Why take it, then?" she snapped. "I was trying to be nice. If you were so fucking offended, why not say so?"

"Needed it," I spat. "Needed your filthy money! Fuck you, rich girl!"

I walked away, scrabbling for one of those scabby fag ends and ignoring her attempts to call after me. I hadn't gone far before I realised Case weren't coming along. She was still with Sophie, getting her ears scratched. I stomped back to grab her, but Sophie wouldn't send her away.

"You're being a prick," she said. "I'm not going to cower away from you, handling you with kid gloves. If something's up then fucking say it, don't just sulk off like a big fucking jerk."

"Don't like being bought."

"I don't like being ignored."

"Both fucked then, ain't we?"

She sighed. "Fucking looks that way." She rolled her eyes. "I live over there. Why don't we go inside, talk it out properly."

"Talk?"

"Talk, fuck, whatever. Don't worry, I won't even offer you a coffee this time."

I pressed up against her. "This ain't no place for me, I don't belong here."

"Neither do I," she said.

"Where do *you* belong, then?"

"Do you actually want to know? Seriously?"

I nodded. "Not taking no money again, though. Don't want it."

"This place doesn't mean shit to me, it's just a nice apartment, handy for work." She reached for my hoodie, cold hands burying inside. "Meet me tomorrow, if you're serious. No money this time, just because you want to."

I weighed it up, drink slowing my brain. "Where?"

"Soho. I'll meet you at Tottenham Court Road Station. Eleven PM."

"Got nowt to wear."

"I wouldn't worry about that," she smirked. "You won't need it."

***

Chapter Eight

Sophie

I'd missed Explicit much more than I realised, underestimating its importance in my emotional equilibrium. Friday night work drinks had only reinforced that point. Laughing with my vanilla colleagues had taken effort, far too much concentration. I'd tried my best to be one of the crowd, but they cared about too much shit that meant nothing to me; gossip, and fashion and what's on TV. I was all out of fucks to give, craving instead the embrace of my freak show friends, *my* people. Excitement ran through me, reinvigorated anticipation.

Only this time would be different.

I'd gone all out. Satin underwear under a sheer lace mini dress. Elbow-length gloves in black velvet. No stockings this time, only boots. Stiletto heeled leather to the knee, so tall I felt precarious. I liked the feeling.

I'd hidden it all under a long cardigan. My choker was the only giveaway, the unmistakable O-ring a tell-tale sign for anyone in the know.

Callum Jackson didn't appear to be in the know. He was waiting when I stepped from the tube, trademark hoodie paired with black jeans I'd never seen him in. I checked him out, nodding my approval.

"Best I could do," he grunted. "Ain't got nothing else."

"You look great."

He didn't respond to the compliment. "Where you taking me? Some swingers place or summat? Ain't getting it on with no old cougars if that's your thing."

"You'll see."

He followed me across to Soho, shoulders hunched as his eyes scoped out every shadow. Explicit's double wooden doors were unmarked from the street, no hint at the crazy awaiting inside. I put a hand on Callum's arm as they swung open, smiling my usual welcome at the security guys. They eyeballed my guest, but let us pass with nothing more than a 'good evening'. Callum kept his eyes on them until we were out of sight, muscles tense enough that I could feel them under his clothes.

"I'm Missy in this place," I said. "We all use a club name."

Dark eyes pierced. "Why?"

"Privacy... atmosphere... some people like the allure of a separate persona." I handed my cardigan to the metal-studded girl at reception, and watched the savage take a step back. Outfit success. "Pick a name, Callum, any name..."

He swallowed, eyes on the line of my panties. "Am who I am. Fancy name makes no odds."

"I quite fancied you as a Blake, or a Wraith, or a Steel..."

"Fancy you as you are. Don't give a fuck about stupid names."

That put me in my place, I only hoped he'd continue the momentum upstairs.

The Explicit crowd were out in force. I eyed Rebecca—*Mistress Raven*—in an instant, perched on a high stool at the bar with a possessive hand on Cara's backside. They were laughing with Tyson and Trixie, Sergeant, Lilith and Devon, too.

"Know these people, yeah?" Callum grunted.

I nodded. "I've been coming for two years, I know pretty much everyone."

"What shit goes on here?"

"It's a BDSM club. This here is the main floor, where most of the hanging out happens. Main stage gets a bit of action, if couples want to play for the crowd. There's a chill-out room behind, but, really, it's not so chilled out." I pointed to the far corner. "Toilets are over that way, men's, women's and anybody's. Oh, but be careful... there's a wet room there too, but I, um, wouldn't recommend you venture in there."

"Why not? People all nude, like?"

"People are nude pretty much everywhere in this place," I laughed. "But the wet room is something else altogether. It's, um, popular for piss play."

"Piss play? Like actual piss? For real?"

"For real." Memories of Masque flooded my senses, his filthy fucking tastes dancing through my mind. "It's not really my bag. Some people here are into it, though."

"What is your bag?" he asked, eyes still fixed in the direction of the wet room.

"I like to play in scenes, general pain play, stuff like that. Down to the left are the play rooms. They're full of equipment; racks, and benches and suspension hooks, that kind of thing. People use them in couples or groups, whatever they fancy. Most rooms are open for public viewing. They have windows, so you can play or watch, join in sometimes too if people are up for company. Playroom four is private, the only private space in the club. We can start there if you like? Later, I mean."

I had his attention. "You want us to fuck? In here?"

"I was hoping you would too."

"Shit." He brushed his hands through his hair. "I dunno. Never been nowhere like this before."

I risked stepping closer, wrapping an arm around his waist. "I want you to fuck me here, Callum, this is my place. I belong here."

He was weighing it up, I could feel it. His arm landed on my shoulder, fingers trailing down my skin. "See how we go, yeah? I wanna fuck you, just ain't sure about here."

I smiled. "No rush. Let's get you acquainted."

I led the way through the club, soaking in the familiar ambience. No sign of Masque. No sign of Cain or Diva, either, but the night was still young in Explicit terms. I took a breath before leading us up to the bar. The neon lights leant everyone an electric blue glow, making them appear even more striking in their fetish ensembles. Cara nudged Rebecca and she spun on her stool, smile wide. She looked fucking awesome, as usual, a crazy mane of red-black curls tumbling down her back, cat-flick liner full and dark around her eyes.

"Baby!" she pulled me in for a kiss, full on the mouth. "I'm so fucking glad you came."

"This is Callum," I smiled, stepping aside for introductions.

Her smile was warm, without reservation. "I'm Raven, heard so much about you." She pulled Cara close. "And this little minx is my girlfriend, Cara. Glad you could make it. Missy's been away too bloody long."

She held out a hand, bright red fingernails poised in mid-air. Callum took it reluctantly, giving her a solid shake before stuffing his hands back in his pockets. I saw his eyes hover on Raven's arms. She was inked from wrist to shoulder, swirls of birds and flowers and brightly coloured stars vying for attention.

"Nice tats," he said.

"Thanks. Work at a studio in Camden, Black Hearts. My ex Jaz runs the place."

"You an artist?" I watched his eyes light up in a way I'd never seen before. It made my stomach flutter.

"Ever since I was big enough to hold a crayon in my fingers. Canvas before skin, mainly skin now, though."

"I paint. Street."

"Reputation precedes you," she grinned. "I'm involved in the scene, a little. Run some of the street art tours round Camden in the summer. Ain't a lot of it that's a patch on your work, though. "

He stared at her like she'd grown wings in front of him. "You seen my stuff?"

She nodded in my direction. "Missy showed me. You got skills, kid. Fucking loved the blades with the sun, seriously fucking awesome."

He looked at the floor, scuffing his battered trainers. "Ain't nobody usually says much about it."

"Then you've been hanging with the wrong people, baby." Raven's eyes were so warm, so genuine. I died a bit at the way she handled the man at my side, the way she gripped his wrist without hesitation or concern. "You're an artist, kid, if ever there was one. Believe it."

"Just paint what I feel."

"Your work's got soul, baby. Beautiful soul."

I made to offer him a drink, but he was a million miles away. "Designed my own ink." He pulled up his top, just a few inches, showing her a hollow-eyed face on his hips. "Don't know if it's any good or not. Just drew it, like."

She raised her eyebrows, reaching out a hand. "May I?" He nodded, staring at his shoes as she uncovered his stomach. "Fucking hell, kid. You should be in the studio. It's a fucking travesty if you're not." I considered whether Raven was being polite, putting him at ease on my behalf, but the set of her mouth was deadly serious. She reached into her bag, pulled out her cigarettes. "You smoke?"

He nodded. "Aye."

"Then I'll show you the balcony. Missy can get the drinks in." She winked at me on her way past, leaving just a trail of vintage Poison in the air. I watched the savage follow her, hot on her heel, as though she were Moses leading him to salvation itself. Jealousy nipped, but I choked it dead. It was fucking Raven, *Raven*, my *friend* Raven, who's awesome to everyone in the universe.

Cara sidled up to me, chocolate brown eyes smiling. "She says his art's the real deal. Been gushing about it for days, even in bed."

"About Callum?" I ordered four vodka and Cokes, doubles.

"Yeah. Spitting fumes, about them covering up his work. You know what she's like about censorship."

I smiled. "Suppression of art by the establishment. I know. I'll rue the day she ever meets my parents, she'll want to tear my dad a new asshole. His approach to the Southbank Art Village isn't going to impress her much."

Cara's eyes twinkled. "I rued the day she met mine. She *did* want to tear my dad a new asshole, and it was quite mutual."

"Your parents are part of the establishment, I take it?"

"Super well off, yeah. Contract lawyers, got their own firm." She pouted. "Wanted me to be one too."

"And you didn't?"

She grinned. "Hell no. Wanted to be a dancer. Teach kids ballet now, so I guess their investment in my extra-curricular activities paid off, just not how they'd like."

"They not so happy with your career choice?"

She took her vodka, stirring it with a neon pink straw. She was cute, really bloody cute, tapping her foot against her stool as she smiled at my question. "A lot happier than they'd be if they knew what other dance I specialise in."

I smiled. "My parents hate what I do. They think it's a pointless shitty job with no prospects."

She patted my shoulder in sisterly solidarity. "Nothing like being the family disappointment, hey? Wouldn't change it, though. Life's about following the heart, right? Even if it does tempt us freaks to the dirty bad wrong side."

I raised my glass, heart already calling loud and clear. Calling after the dirty bad savage on the balcony outside.

"I'll fucking drink to that."

***

Callum

I'd never seen a woman like Raven before. She walked like she knew she belonged in this world, like she had a place, a purpose. Never seen much of that round East Veil. Everyone round there's always scraping in the dirt, head low, looking for the next deal to scam. Not Raven, she was different.

She led us out to the balcony. It was empty; just a glorified roof terrace with a view over nothing but an empty yard. Outside wasn't nearly so posh as the inside, with its fancy lights, and its fancy seats and its fancy strange people. Raven gave me a cigarette, it was black, out of a bright gold box, nothing like you get down the off-license. I said my thanks and lit up with her, staring at the way her mouth moved. Her eyes were on me, taking me all in, but there wasn't anything judgey about it, no challenge.

"How long you been painting, kid?"

My mouth was moving before I even noticed. "Long time. Met this guy, Jimmy, when I was a littlun. He used to paint, on the street. Loved his stuff, would follow him everywhere, watching. Was probably a pain in the pissing arse." I grinned. "Let me have a go once and that was it, like. Fucking hooked."

"Nothing like the zone, is there? Finding your groove and letting the muse steal you away."

"Only thing that makes me feel right." I looked away, feeling stupid. Like I'd said too much.

She took a step closer. "I get it, kid. Art was my only thing too, for a long time. Only thing that felt like it had soul. World was so bloody dark, but it didn't matter, not with a paintbrush in my hand. It was like bleeding my pain onto the canvas, you know? A purge."

My heart started pumping, mouth clammy. "Yeah. Just like that."

"You have a gift. You see what other people don't, the rhythm behind the grey, the colour in the dark. You take what's in here." She put her finger on my heart. "And you put it out there, for the world. Your mark in time. The stamp of your soul. That's why you're here."

"People say it's mindless shit. Scrub it off as soon as they get to it."

"People are ignorant fucks. Gotta find your own kind, baby, or you're a ship lost at sea."

"Mainly found arseholes and backstabbers and liars so far. Well, and my dog, Casey."

"You've been looking in the wrong place, kid. I know East Veil. Well, I know places like it. Grew up in Croydon, the Kenny Estate. Heard of it?"

I had heard of it, gangland central. Ain't even the Stoneys that'd venture round that place. "Aye. Heard enough."

"Not the best environment for a lonely teenage freak who didn't know her place in the world. Had some scuffles, but I came out the other side."

"How?" I knew I was staring, but I couldn't stop. Most people flinch when I stare like that, look away, but not Raven. She stared me right back.

"Lucky break. Got involved in youth art, met a guy with a gallery in the city, he liked my stuff. Coached me on, gave me a leg up and I never looked back." She took a long drag, and blew out a perfect smoke ring. "I met my girlfriend, Jaz, a few years later and she got me into the tattooing. Another lucky break. Still friends now, owe her a lot."

"I ain't never been lucky. Could jump into a well of gold and come up holding some other fucker's shit."

"Think your luck might just be changing, kid." She squeezed my wrist again, and it felt nice. "Missy's a good girl. Loyal, and smart, and kind. Kinky as fuck, but that's par for the course with us lot." Her laugh was like a cackle. It suited her really fucking well. "You'll get used to it, this place. If you're planning on sticking around, I mean. Give us a shot, and we'll give you one right back. We're a good crowd."

"Dunno what I'm doing," I admitted. "Feel like a fucking idiot messing around with all them whips and shit. Don't get me wrong, I like it hard. Like playing rough. It's in my blood. Just don't know how to put it together, don't wanna fuck her up, neither."

"There's violence and there's violence, baby. Depends on the motivation." She stubbed out her cigarette and offered me another. I took it, grateful. "What we do here isn't temper, or rage, or violence taken too far. BDSM is sexuality without judgement. We play safe, sane and totally consensual. We look out for each other, too."

I scuffed my trainers on the ground. "Sophie told you about me? I ain't like other people. Bad blood, Mam says. Got a short fuse, and used to using me fists before me brain. Kept me alive. Don't know what someone like Sophie's seeing in someone like me."

"She sees soul in you, baby. I see it too."

"See something in her. Never met anyone like her before." I looked away. "Ain't much of a talker usually. Dunno why me mouth's suddenly running."

"Talking's good, enjoy it." She looked back towards the door. "Say, maybe I'll have to take a trip down East Veil one of these days, take a look at your work."

I tried to keep it cool. "Sound, yeah. Got some left they haven't reached yet. Been going higher these days."

"I'd like to see them."

"Can't miss some of 'em." I dropped both my fag ends in the ashtray and buried my hands back in my pockets. "Gonna give this place a go, for Sophie."

"Good choice." Her eyes were sparkly, like the night sky. I tried to remember, so I could paint her one day. "We'd better get back in, they'll be wondering where we're at."

"Aye."

I went to open the door but it was already swinging our way. I stepped back, adrenaline spiking on instinct, clearing some space between me and the huge motherfucker heading our way. I heard Raven squeal, and got ready for trouble, but it wasn't that kind of squeal.

She flew at the man as he stepped outside, jumping up into huge arms that lifted her clean off the floor. The man was wearing a mask, a dark leather thing covering most of his face. He was half naked too, like a bloody gladiator, muscles ripped and tanned, with a fucking massive piece of ink all the way across his chest.

He was a fucking beast.

And he was heading my fucking way.

***

"Masque!" Raven squealed. "Didn't think you were coming, baby. You're so fucking late." She dropped from his arms, and dragged him a few steps over. "This is Callum. He's here with Missy. He's got the most amazing fucking ink, designed it himself."

The big bastard gave me the chills, made the hair on the back of my neck stand on end. He looked tough, not tough like the Stoneys, or me, or Tyler Jones, though. He looked like he'd walk into a bar fight without even breaking a sweat. Calculated and tough. Tough but not hot-headed. Hard to explain.

Was trying to work out whether I needed my wits about me, but he smiled and held out a hand.

"Missy's a fine girl, congratulations on the guest status."

I took his hand. It was firm, like the rest of him. "Cheers."

"Must have some fine ink to get compliments like that from our lovely Raven. She's quite a talent herself." He stepped forward into the balcony light where I could see him better. "She designed mine."

His tattoo was fucking awesome. A huge black beast, bit like a dragon, two heads, though. It curled around his back, touching almost down to his hips. "That's some cool ink, man."

"Chimera. One body, two beasts. Resonates with me." He turned back to the door as it creaked on its hinges. A girl followed him out, tall and pretty. Long dark hair and the craziest green eyes I'd ever fucking seen. Looked like a fucking lynx or something. Raven did another squeal, then more hugs, more kisses, gushing about her tan. The beast turned his attention back to me. "Sorry, we just got back. Holiday."

Green eyes headed over, threaded a dainty arm through his. "Hey. Who's this?"

"Missy's guest."

The way she looked up at him sent shivers down my back. Her pretty eyes were so wide, smiling like he was God himself in front of her. She offered her hand, and I took it carefully. "I'm Cat. Pleased to meet you."

Name kinda figured. "Callum."

"Always nice to see a new face," she smiled. "Especially a pretty one."

I was glad it was half fucking dark out here, so she didn't see me burning up. "You got ink too?" I asked, thinking of summat to say.

She shook her head. "Not yet. Raven's working on it."

"You'd look so fucking hot with ink, baby," Raven said. "And so fucking hot in my chair getting it done."

"Don't ask," Cat grinned. "Masque and Raven are conspiring to decorate my most intimate of places."

"Yes, we are," Masque said. "Say, Callum, you'll have to check out our little show in a while. You can give Cat some feedback on whether she'd suit some tattoos or not. You'll see enough of her to form an opinion, that's for certain."

She seemed to swoon at his words, all giddy, like. I wondered what fucking skills the guy had to make her act like that. Hung like a fucking donkey on steroids, probably.

"What show?" I asked.

"On the main stage," Raven explained. "Quite an eye-opener." She winked at me, and my stomach went all funny.

"Will we see you later?" Masque asked. "After the scene?"

I didn't really know what a fucking scene was. Not really. I shrugged anyway. "Yeah, likely. I'll be around."

"We'll catch you then, chat more about that ink," he said.

I watched him leave, watched the way his girlfriend melted into his side, like she really belonged to him.

I jumped at Raven's hand on my arm, but she was only offering me another cigarette.

"Masque and Cat," she said. "They're quite a couple."

"Seem like it."

"He's good. Knows his shit, knows how to control himself."

"Looks like he'd walk into Hades and not break a sweat."

"You'll like him," she said. "And he'll be a good person for you to know, quite enlightening."

"Yeah? How so?"

She nodded, eyes twinkling again. "You'll see, baby. You'll see."

***

Chapter Nine

Sophie

"Nice choice. Lad's definitely got potential."

My body leapt on instinct, heart rate notching up a gear or twenty. Masque looked more Godlike than ever. His muscles had browned to a sun-kissed bronze, skin so taut he rippled like steel under satin. The dark lines of the beast on his chest called to me, baying for adoration. I wrenched my eyes away before I slavered, looking up instead to the shadowy pools behind his mask. I forced aside the memories of the man's mouth on mine. On me. All fucking over me. Forced aside the memories of him tearing me apart, of his greedy tongue forcing its way inside, insatiable for the taste of pain.

Masque leaned over the bar to my side, ordering two large reds and a pint of water. I smiled inwardly, knowing exactly how his filthy mind was playing out. He turned to offer, but I pointed to my fresh vodka, smiling thanks. Masque didn't leave with his drinks, just stared me out, waiting for my response.

"You met Callum, then?"

"Raven seems to have taken a shine to him."

"Yes, she does."

"And how about you, Missy? Are you feeling a shine too?"

"I don't know about that, Masque." I paused, but he didn't fill the gap. He rarely does. "It's very new, we're very different. And he's young... and, well, I'm not."

"You didn't answer my question."

I felt myself flushing. "That's usually *my* line with *you*, Mr Evasive. How was your holiday?"

"Perfect. Thank you." His bloody attention burned right through my skin. "The lad has it bad for you."

"How on earth do you know that? He's only been on the balcony twenty minutes. Did you put him in chains? Beat him until he confessed?"

"Maybe would have, if I swung that way," he smiled, a filthy fucking smile. "Would you like that, Missy? Does the idea make you wet?" He laughed gently. "I didn't need to force a confession, the situation is crystal clear. He's uncomfortable here, edgy, but still he stays."

"And?"

"There's a reason for that. I'm confident I'm looking right at her."

"I think he's more into Raven than me right now."

"Raven just speaks the same language. He's here for you, Missy. Mark my words."

"Don't I always mark your words, Masque?" My voice was softer than I intended, more playful. *Oh God, how I'd served him.* I crossed my legs, clenching myself tight to appease my thrumming clit.

"You mark my words *very* well, Missy. I remember it fondly." The corner of his mouth twitched deliciously as his dark eyes roved over me, lingering so long at the juncture of my thighs that it fucking burnt. "I hope he gives you what you need. A pretty little cunt like yours deserves a man who knows how to own it. Like I said, there's potential there. I can see it in him."

"It's just sex," I protested. "Nothing more could ever work."

"So, he's just a cock to you?"

My heart thumped at my breast, defying me as I formed my response. "It's a bit of fun."

"I see." He shrugged. "In that case you won't mind if I borrow him. I want to shake things up a little for Cat, new experiences. He'd be perfect."

I felt every drop of blood draining from my face, pooling in my horrified stomach like a rancid lake. He took his drinks, but didn't even flinch as I yanked him back by his elbow. "Wait... I... um..."

The beast that is Masque leaned down over me, so close I could feel his heat on my face. I held my breath as he brought his face down to mine, exhaling as he planted the softest kiss on my forehead.

"That's what I was looking for." He smiled, warmly. A smile so warm it sent tingles through my tits. "Do you trust me, Missy?"

I didn't need to weigh that up. "Yes, I trust you. Of course."

"Then let me help."

"Help? How?" I quizzed, but he was already leaving.

"Remember that trust," he called.

I was all set to follow, but my time was up. Cat's green eyes smiled at me as she reached his side, taking up her pint of water like the good little sub she is.

I sat back in my stool, waiting for the jealousy.

But it didn't come.

***

I watched Raven and Callum approach from across the dance floor, only letting my eyes linger for fleeting seconds, so as not to appear too interested. Raven was alight with expression, and Callum followed mutely, hanging on every single word she was saying. Cara's dainty arms snaked around my waist, and I leant back against her shoulder, waiting for her verdict.

"Two arty peas in a pod," she whispered. "That's cool, isn't it?"

"Yes," I said. "I think so."

"She's a great judge of character."

I kissed her on the cheek. "Clearly."

"Shit, I didn't mean it like that," she blushed.

"I know you didn't. But she is, it's true."

Callum's dark eyes met mine, and for that one moment something clicked. He was still edgy, hands thrust in his pockets in an attempt to appear nonchalant, but his expression said it all. My stomach fluttered, hands itching to reach out and touch him, drag him into one of the playrooms and fuck his brains out, but it wasn't to be.

"They're on," Raven said, grabbing her drink and downing it in one. "Showtime, baby," she squeezed Callum's arm. "Here's your initiation, kid, the best of the best."

Sure enough, the lighting changed on the main floor, and the ripple of excitement spread like wildfire, a bustling of bodies making their way to the stage. Raven led the way, gripping Cara's hand possessively en route, and smiling back at us over her shoulder to make sure we were close behind. The spotlights lit up, fixing their glare onto the shackles hanging from the ceiling. The stage was empty, but not for long.

I twisted my arm through Callum's and he squeezed it close to his side, leading me along after Raven without coaxing. Raven secured us a bench in the shadows, a clear view from the far side of the dance floor. We were just in time to watch Cat make her appearance, stark bollock naked apart from knee high boots. She had the ghosting of bruises across her perfect thighs, the faint remnants of whip lashes across her ribcage. Their holiday had been fun, no doubt about that.

I cuddled up to Callum, daring to rest a hand on his thigh. I smiled inside as he wrapped his arm around my waist, resting solid fingers against the slope of my thigh. *Please enjoy this. Please God.*

The room turned silent as Cat prepared for the shackles, holding her wrists high in the air and taking slow, deep breaths, oblivious to the roomful of eyes on her body. I gripped Callum's thigh as Masque stepped onto the stage. The man in the mask moved with purpose, solid steps as he closed the gap between him and his submissive. Cat shuddered as he took her wrists, hands limp in his grip as he fastened her into the chains. My mouth turned dry, thighs clenching involuntarily. Callum must have felt it, as his fingers teased my skin, splaying out to press against me.

I moved my mouth to his ear, whispering just loud enough that he would hear me. "Watch closely. Maybe you can do the same for me sometime."

He didn't respond, but I'm sure I felt his breath hitch just a notch.

Cat tested her bonds, lowering her weight into the chains to ensure she was secure. She was. Of course she was.

"Spread your legs," Masque ordered. His voice had taken on its trademark low growl, thick with lust. She did as she was told, shifting her feet apart without hesitation while Masque took up a flogger from the side of the stage. He swished it in the air by her head, close enough that she flinched. I felt Callum flinch too.

"Don't worry," I whispered. "He knows what he's doing. She really wants this."

He grunted in response.

Masque took hold of Cat's hair, wrapping it around his fingers for grip. He tipped her backwards to the edge of her balance, until her limbs were straining in their restraints and her thighs were taut with the pressure. She moaned as he draped the flogger down over her shoulder, dancing the tails across her stomach and up over her breasts. He snaked it with expert precision, then let go of her hair long enough to wrap the whip around her throat. I took a breath, twitching in my seat.

She didn't fight him, melting seamlessly to his body as he pressed himself up against her.

"Take it for me, Cat, take all of it."

Her lips parted, expression glazed in rapture, as though Masque was God Himself. I knew that feeling. It unfurled in my stomach like a flower, dancing right the way down between my thighs.

"You're so fucking beautiful." He secured her flogger choker in one hand, sliding the other around to her breast where he twisted her nipple until she groaned. "That's it. Hurt for me. Show me your pain."

His grip was so fucking harsh. Her next groan was choked by the restriction at her throat, it came out raspy and desperate.

"That's right, good girl. Let's see how much you want me."

His fingers weren't gentle, splaying her pussy to reveal her glistening clit to the crowd. She was soaked, her pussy lips like dewy petals, wet and wanting. Wanting him.

I had to choke out my own whisper. "See how good this is for her?"

I felt Callum nod, and my own clit started tingling, hot with its own need.

Masque smiled against Cat's cheek, perfect lips tight against her skin. "That's my girl, Cat, my beautiful, sweet, perfect girl. I want to hurt your pretty little cunt, Cat. You'll give it to me, won't you?"

She groaned, nodding her head in spite of the pressure at her throat.

"I'm going to hurt you so bad, Cat, so the whole room can share your beautiful pain. I know you want them to see how good you are for me."

Another nod, the slightest choke.

"And then they can watch me fuck your tight little cunt until you scream. They can watch me love you, Cat... love you with pain... with beautiful fucking pain..."

I twitched in my seat, itching to jill myself fucking crazy regardless of who was around to watch. I forced myself to keep calm, resisting the urge to drag Callum away from this place and beg him for cock. Not yet, I wanted to watch, wanted him to watch this too.

I kept my eyes on Cat, on her pliant body, so fucking wet for him. Masque took the flogger from her neck, giving her a moment to regain her balance.

"Get ready."

She straightened up, took hold of the chains, muscles tense in anticipation.

He didn't go easy with the first strike. The tails of the flogger curled around her ribs to bite the soft underside of her breast. She cried out, head lolling back, then prepared for more. The next lash caught her around the thigh, hard enough for her to jerk to the side. She resumed her position without being asked, trained to perfection.

I watched Masque watching Cat, the way his eyes were all over her body, taking in every twitch, every movement, every little gasp from her mouth. He timed his stokes perfectly, stringing her tight on the edge of her tolerance. His punishment became more brutal, increasing with the spike of her endorphins. Slowly she stopped jerking, letting the chains take her weight as she submitted entirely to his will.

He pushed her so fucking hard, and she was so beautiful for it. Eyes big and pretty, her gaze soft and willing. And then tears. They welled up slowly, pooling in the corners of her eyes. She sobbed so softly, spilling her pain in sweet release.

Masque's demeanour changed, his strikes placed further apart, giving her time to cry between each flash of pain.

"That's my perfect girl, Cat. My beautiful girl. Tell me what you need."

My heart leapt in memory of those perfect fucking words.

"I need more pain..." she begged. "Please, Masque, please..."

He closed the gap between them, pulling her face to his for the deepest fucking kiss. He kissed her like he loved her, like there was nobody but them, like she'd given him the biggest gift a person could give.

And then he licked up her tears. Slowly but surely he licked them all up.

A moan escaped my throat and Callum's fingers responded, dancing ever so slightly closer to the heat between my thighs. I willed him to continue, willed him to touch me, but he stayed put. I looked at him in the shadows, finding his eyes as transfixed by the stage as mine had been.

Masque moved to Cat's front and I knew what was next.

"Your tits are so beautiful, Cat. They'll mark so fucking pretty."

Pink slashes across her skin turned red. Dark red. He was a picture of composure as she cried before him, choosing the perfect moments to unleash the torture. Her eyes never left his, never faltered. The room had disappeared for her, lost in subspace with only that beautiful fucking beast in her thoughts.

The last stroke made her scream, an animal howl as the tails caught her nipples. She croaked for breath as her legs went from under her, body racked with sobs as she cried out in torment. And he was there, at her side. His arms around her, whispers in her ear. I could only imagine what he was saying, but it didn't matter. The adoration in his expression said it all.

He lifted her to standing, peppering her skin with gentle kisses, and she twisted towards him in her bonds, craving his skin on hers. I knew that feeling, too.

"You may speak," he said. "Tell me."

"Love me..." she hissed. "Please, Masque, please love me."

"Always, Cat. Always."

My heart fucking keeled over, stopping in my chest as I fell over the precipice of hot fucking need. I could barely fucking swallow, lost to everything but the tingles between my legs, begging for fucking deliverance.

I took Callum's fingers in mine, shifting in my seat to convey just how fucking desperate I was for contact. How much I fucking needed him to touch me. I lifted my leg, hooking my knee over one of his to spread myself in invitation. I could feel his eyes boring into me, his breath like fucking flames on my cheek. He took the bait, pulled me further into his lap, my throbbing pussy aching as it pressed into his thigh.

And that's when I felt it. The ridge between his legs. The strain of his excitement.

I flushed with sheer fucking delight.

The savage had a hard on.

Maybe, just maybe, we weren't so different after all.

***

Callum

My dick was fucking aching, twitching like a motherfucker. My thoughts were fucking smashed too, torn to pieces, unable to work out what the fuck was going on. Or why I found this so fucking exciting.

The man on stage, Masque, was an even more brutal motherfucker than I'd expected. The way he hit the girl in chains, so fucking hardcore I could barely fucking watch. But she loved it. She really fucking loved it.

I'd never seen someone want something as bad as she wanted him. The way she looked at him, like he was God, no... fucking *bigger* than God. Like the sonofabitch would pummel God's puny ass into oblivion and not even break a sweat. He was mean, twisted, fucking violent as shit, but she wanted it. And he wanted her. He fucking loved her right back.

I didn't fucking get any of it. But my dick did.

My dick got it loud and fucking clear.

So, this was the shit that Sophie craved. I could feel it too, she was beside her fucking self. Breath ragged, and desperate, legs twitchy. Fluttery fingers coaxing me without words, aching for me to light the fuse. God, I fucking wanted to. I pressed my face against her neck, breathing in the sweet scent of her, her soft hair so fucking nice against my cheek.

My fingers gave in to her demands, teasing a path up her clammy thighs to the heat of her. She bucked against my chest, hissing as I brushed her clit through her thong.

"Please..." she breathed. "I can't stand it."

I yanked the scrap of fabric to the side, no longer caring who the fuck saw us. She jerked in my grip as I teased her, fingering her swollen cunt so fucking softly that she squirmed for more. Then I stopped. Stopped fucking dead.

She inhaled and made to grab my hand but I pushed her away. "No," I growled. "I fucking say when. *Me.*"

She responded to my words, body turning limp like the woman on stage, flopping back against my chest like a ragdoll. I kept my fingers pressed against her clit, but kept them still, barring her from release.

I was in charge. For real.

It felt fucking good.

The scene on stage was shifting gear. Masque's hands were softer on his woman's body, tracing where he'd hurt her like she was a piece of art. She was his canvas, a living, breathing, horny fucking canvas. The tools were his paint, pink, and red and sweet dark purple in living colour. My cock responded to the parallel, pulsing so hard it set stars off behind my eyes.

Sophie Harding could be *my* canvas.

I could paint her skin with the pain she wanted. Make her cry my name.

Then I could fuck her, and she'd want me. She'd want me so fucking bad.

I watched the woman in chains, fixated on her eyes.

I'd never fucking wanted anything more than I wanted Sophie Harding to look at me that way.

Masque fucked as hard as he hit. He lifted Green Eyes clean off the ground, holding her by her hips as she swayed in the chains. She gasped when he jammed his cock inside her, wrapping her legs behind him to take her own weight. His fingers worked at her clit, and it drove her fucking insane. Rasps and grunts and seedy fucking gurgles spilled from her throat, more animal than human. I'd been right; he *was* hung like a fucking donkey on steroids. She loved it, too. Begging him for more, harder and harder and fucking harder.

His voice again, so fucking commanding.

"You feel so fucking nice, Cat. Your cunt is so fucking wet for me, I hope everyone can hear those perfect fucking slurps you're making."

"Yes!" she screamed. "Fuck me, please, Masque, fuck me... fuck me!"

Sophie stared at them, mouth open, no longer begging for my touch. Her breathing was shallow, so shallow. One flick of my thumb could ignite her, I knew it, but I stayed still.

Masque drilled Green Eyes good, his jaw locked dead in

concentration, fingers working her ragged. He knew when she was cresting, knew just when to let her fucking fly.

"Come for me." His words were so simple, but they worked. They worked fucking perfectly.

The girl in the chains didn't hold back, squealing and jerking as she came. Masque kept his expression deadpan, kept his thrusts steady, playing with her juicy little clit until she was spent. He lowered her to the floor and uncuffed her in a flash, working his donkey dick in his hand while she dropped to her knees, mouth wide and hungry for him.

I heard Sophie gasp again, straining forward for a closer view, and I was too, craving to know what the fuck was about to go down.

Masque looked less composed now, cock all fucking veiny like he could shoot any fucking second. He jammed the whole length down Green Eyes' throat, so hard she coughed and retched and spluttered all over him. She didn't pull back, though, didn't fight.

He fucked her face like a doll, until her eyes were streaming and her throat gurgled soft and wet. Finally, he let fly, burrowing until her neck swelled thick with the length of him, bellowing as he shot his seed down her pretty little throat. Her eyes bulged wide, lungs fighting for breath, hands twitching behind her back as she fought the inevitable, but it was no use.

She sicked up all over his filthy fucking cock, but the dirty bastard didn't care.

He dropped to his knees beside her and kissed her sicky mouth like his life depended on it.

And I nearly jizzed in my fucking pants.

***

Sophie made to get off my lap but I held her still while I willed my hard on away. The lights were changing again, the room much brighter now the show was over. Raven and her girlfriend untangled themselves from each other.

"Hot in here, or what?" Raven laughed. "I think I need some air after that little performance."

"Air... nicotine..." the girl at her side said. "Go get what you need. I'll get myself a drink."

"Good girl, Cara, good girl."

Sophie turned her head to me, eyes still glazed as her breathing calmed. "You coming to the bar?"

I couldn't face it. Not yet. I needed to clear my head.

"Think someone needs a cigarette," Raven smirked. "Come with me, kid."

Sophie's face was questioning but she didn't argue. She raised herself slowly, and smiled as Raven took me by the arm.

"Won't be long," I grunted.

The cold air was welcome. Raven grinned as I jumped from foot to foot, trying to change my headspace.

"Liked it, then?"

"Dunno," I lied. "Feels fucking weird. And the puking, man. That's fucking hardcore. Weren't expecting that."

She leaned in close, fluttering dark lashes, like she was telling me a secret. "That wasn't sick, baby, not really. He makes her drink water beforehand. It's that she brings up. He likes the rush on his cock."

"Still fucking hardcore."

"*He's* fucking hardcore, baby." She grinned. "Good though, right?"

I felt the beginnings of a smile on my mouth. "Aye. Yeah."

She handed me a cigarette. "Masque's so good because he knows how to push boundaries without ruining the scene. He reads his subs perfectly, knows exactly where they're at and what they need. Even if they think they don't need it. Make sense?"

I shrugged. "She looked like she was enjoying herself enough."

"Want to go there, you think? With Missy?"

Her words smashed into my senses, but with her I didn't mind, didn't clam up like usual. "Hope so." I took a long drag. "Want to, ya know?"

"If you can dom her even half as well as Masque doms Cat, she'll be putty at your feet, baby. I promise you."

"I want her to look at me like that. Like Cat looked at him."

"That's the rush we all crave, that reverence in someone else's eyes. Knowing that right then you're everything... their master, their lover, their fucking God."

I stared at the woman in front of me. "You're a dominant then? Same as Masque?"

"I'm a switch, but you'd hardly know it," she smiled. "Yeah, you could say I'm a dominant."

"Cool," I said, lost for any more words.

"Yes it is, baby. Yes it is."

The balcony door creaked, and once again the bulk of the beast filled the doorway. I stepped aside so he felt free to speak to Raven, but he called me back.

"I'm here to see you," he said. His voice was back to normal, friendly like.

"Me?" I retraced my steps. "Oh shit, yeah, the tattoos. She'd look good with ink, yeah."

"Not about the ink, this time," he smiled and my heart thumped fucking faster. "Did you like the show?"

"Aye."

"Think it's for you, this scene?"

I shrugged, tongue-tied, and Raven saved me, placing a hand on Masque's chest and leaning in close to him.

"It's for him," she smiled. "Most definitely."

I felt my face burning, and toked on my cig, awkward.

"You ever done anything like this before, Callum?" he asked.

I shook my head. "Nah. Not like this. Been rough, like, but not like what you did, in there."

"Missy is a good girl, she'll take what you give her."

"Dunno what I'll give her, yet," I admitted, staring out beyond them to the yard below.

"Maybe that's how I can help," the beast said. "I have an offer for you."

***

My nerves were all over the place, but still I fucking followed him. Right through the club I followed him, right over to the bar and right into the flustered gaze of Sophie Harding.

"Callum is coming with me awhile." Masque had that tone again. The don't fuck with me tone.

Sophie looked up at him, and her eyes were like Cat's, full of adoration. "He is?"

"Yes. He is."

Her eyes darted to me and I didn't know where to put myself. I looked at the floor until I felt her attention leave me, turning back to the man at my side.

"And me?" Sophie asked. "Can I come?"

"No," he said simply. I could've fucking died. "You'll stay here, won't she, Callum?"

I found the words but they felt hollow. "Yeah, stay here."

She didn't argue, but her face was white, panicked like. I wanted to say something, tell her it'd be alright, but Masque was already leaving. I shrugged and followed, where to I didn't fucking know, but

I followed anyway. He led me down a packed out corridor. People were watching through windows, jerking off to the sight of hot, naked bodies. I kept my attention ahead, watching only Masque's muscled back as the onlookers parted for him. He opened a door at the far end, one of the rooms with no windows.

Cat was waiting there. She was standing in the centre of the room, still naked, eyes on the floor with her head bowed. She didn't acknowledge our presence, made no move at all. My stomach flipped, heart in my fucking throat.

"This is no place for Missy," Masque said. "She's your submissive in this place, and a submissive has no business being involved in what's about to occur here."

"What's that?" I said. "What we doing here?"

He smiled, and patted me on the shoulder. "Call this a helping hand. If you want it, that is?"

"A helping hand?"

"I want to show you the ropes. I think it should help."

"With Cat?!" I asked, eyes wide as fucking saucers.

"This isn't sex, Callum. I'm not that presumptuous, nor that generous." His mouth twitched into a grin. "BDSM is a complex interplay of dynamics. The way you read your submissive is critical. She needs to feel dominated, but she also needs to feel safe, secure in submitting her will to yours. A dominant's role may seem all about their own pleasure, but it's far from it. While you are in play your attention should be entirely on your sub, how she's reacting, how close she is to her limits. Becoming a skilled master can take years of practice, I just want to help you along the way."

"Why's that?" I said, curious. "Why d'you wanna help me?"

"I like Missy," he said. "She's a good girl. And I like you, Callum. I see a bit of myself in you. Untamed potential is the fuel for the flame, my friend. I'm just here to help you harness it. Point you in the right direction. Is that acceptable to you?"

I looked at Cat, at the way she was so still. Waiting on his command, listening to every word he said.

"Aye, that's what I want. I wanna do what you do."

He clapped his hands. "Excellent. Over the bench, Cat, hands flat."

The bench in the room was padded, bright red leather on black wood. It looked the fucking part. Cat folded herself onto it without a sound, hands flat to the leather and arse in the fucking air. She shifted her legs apart, no prompting necessary. Masque took position at her side, smoothed his hands over the soft skin of her butt cheeks.

"A submissive's ass is a fine canvas for pain, Callum. It blooms slowly, eases quickly. Well, sometimes eases quickly," he smiled. He reached down to Cat's knees, marking a line with his finger just above the fold. "Here upwards is safe territory." He stroked his way up her legs, and over her arse, until it dipped down into the curve of her spine. He made another line at the dip of her hips. "Safe until here. The lower back is off limits, unless you know exactly where you're hitting. It's too dangerous, you can hit the wrong spot and fuck up someone's kidneys. Bottom of the ribs is painful but generally safe for whips, and the chest and shoulders make excellent targets for floggers. It goes without saying to be careful of the neck and face, arms too."

"Aye," I said. "No kidneys, no knees, no neck."

"That's about it," he agreed. "I'm not going to teach you to suck eggs, I'm sure you're perfectly capable of reading a woman's arousal. You'll know when she's hot enough to play."

He pulled Cat's ass cheeks apart, and groaned as he saw how wet she was. "I think you have a fan," he laughed. "I think my dirty little Cat is enjoying this." She shuffled in his grip, breath speeding up. "You want Callum to hurt you, don't you, Cat?"

She nodded, groaning.

"Answer me."

"Yes, sir, please, sir."

"Good girl." He gestured behind me, and I turned to find a rack full of fucking toys. Canes and floggers like the one I'd seen on stage. Flat wooden shapes too, that looked a bit like ping pong bats. "I think we should start with the paddle," he said. "Good for close contact, easy to read the sub."

"You want me to hit her with that?"

"Only if you want to."

"If you're sure, like." I took it from the wall. It was heavier than it looked. The handle felt nice in my hand, like it was made for my grip.

"If you're playing nice, with a decent build-up, you want your submissive's ass to be well adjusted. The longer the warm-up, the easier she'll manage the pain. Ever heard of the frog in a pan being warmed slowly?"

"Heard that, yeah."

"I'm not sure whether the frog would sit it out that long, but the analogy works. Of course there are times you may want a quick, sharp punishment. The rules are there to be broken, but it helps to know them." He slapped Cat's arse, steady thwacks over and over. "See the way her skin blooms, Callum? Isn't it fucking beautiful?"

I nodded, lost for fucking words again.

"Come over here, she doesn't bite."

I shuffled over, still unsure, like he'd flip out any second and swing for me. "Feel how warm her skin is."

I reached out slowly to her arse, brushing her skin with my fingers. My dick fucking jerked, and I stepped away quick sharp. "Yeah, nice."

"Are you ready for some proper pain, Cat?"

"Yes, sir," she hissed. "Please, sir."

"I think you should be asking Callum, not me."

She turned her head over her shoulder, gorgeous green eyes on mine. My dick twitched again.

"Please, Callum. Please hurt me."

Masque moved away, gesturing that I should take his place. I approached slowly, warily, out of my fucking depth but really fucking horny. I wished this was Sophie, wished it was her asking for pain. Soon. It would be soon.

I took a breath, looking again to Masque for confirmation.

"Short, sharp smacks," he said. "Feel her pain, Callum. Her body will show you what's right."

Shit. My knuckles were white around the paddle, heart like a fucking steam train. I was too fucking gentle with the first thwack, it hardly made a sound. I didn't make the same mistake with the second, and she flinched under me, breath heavy.

"That's it," he said. "Feel when she's ready for the next, her body will tell you."

When I felt her relax at my side, I hit her again, harder this time, and she clenched her muscles, letting out a groan. I found my groove, watching and feeling, and landing that fucking paddle on her skin whenever she felt ripe for it. She rocked against me, breath fucking ragged, the softest fucking moans from her lips.

"Harder," Masque said. "She's not made of glass."

I did hit her harder, and this time the thwack was fucking loud. She yelped, and it got me straight in the dick, the scent of her pussy teasing my fucking nostrils. Her groans encouraged me, instinct taking over. I hit her fucking good, listening to her breath, feeling the tension in her legs as she jumped under the paddle.

It felt fucking awesome.

I felt like a king.

"Make her beg," he growled. "You're in control here, Callum, let her know it."

"Beg for me," I grunted. "Now."

"Please..." she hissed. "More, please..."

I gave her more, so much fucking more. I felt myself burning up, stopping just a moment to pull off my hoodie. My hands on her ass, feeling the heat, her scent knocking me, the soft swell of her pink fucking ass threatening to knock me out of kilter.

"Focus," Masque barked. "Read her body, Callum, read her."

I reined myself back in, concentrating on nothing but her, the twitch of her legs as I landed her punishment, the moans from her throat. I could feel it, feel her. Feel when she was ready, when her ass was bared for pain.

And I knew, I knew what to do.

"Spread your legs," I rasped.

She obeyed without question. Fuck, it felt so fucking good. I slapped her thighs, and she hissed in pain. I knew where to strike, I knew when to stop, I knew before she did. She softened, yielding, her breath shallow, legs trembling, and then she moaned, the softest little mewl. I gave her one for good measure and stopped to catch my breath.

Masque was at my side, a strong hand on my shoulder.

"Well done," he said. "Nicely timed."

My heart fucking bloomed, and it felt weird. Felt like I was a kid again, when old Jimmy told me I could paint good. *Well done, lad,* he'd said, *you're a natural. You'll be an artist one day.*

"Thanks," I grunted.

Cat didn't move, just lay there, breathing softly. Waiting. She was waiting.

"I think Cat wants to ask you a question," Masque smiled.

"Please..." she said. "Please may I touch myself?"

I waited for Masque's answer but he deferred to me. I moved to the side, giving her space before I answered.

"Yeah," I said. "You can touch yourself."

I could hardly watch as she reached between her legs. She bit her lip, teasing herself to orgasm without a care for who was watching.

"Tell her she can come," Masque whispered. "Now."

"You can come," I said.

She did. She came fucking hard.

And I loved it. I really fucking loved it.

I was silent as she caught her breath, too fucking aware of the bulge in my jeans and the blood racing round my fucking body. She raised herself from the bench and shot me a smile. A warm smile, full of thanks.

"That was great," she beamed. "You were great. Thank you."

"No bother," I grunted, self-consciousness returning to bite me in the arse.

Masque was waiting for her with open arms, holding her close as he instructed me further. "There's another aspect of BDSM that may come into play. We call it aftercare in the scene, although I call it common sense. When a submissive comes down from the zone she may feel a little unsteady. It can be a big endorphin crash for the body to take, an adrenaline crash too. She may feel disoriented, shaky, maybe even cold. Physical contact can be good for that, a safe pair of arms to hold her tight until she's back in control. You'll know what's right for the situation." He led Cat to the doorway, turning back with a smile on his face. "Remember, Callum, the paddle was just one tool. You can use as many as you want, or none at all. The magic is in *you*, in your manner, in your composure. Find your own groove, use your imagination, and you'll find your own way."

I nodded, brain still reeling.

"We'll send Missy in," he said. "I think she'll be keen to see you."

I fucking hoped so.

***

Sophie

My heart leapt as Masque and Cat arrived at the bar, but Callum wasn't with them. Masque ordered their drinks, pretending to be oblivious to my questioning stare. I had to reach for him, pulling him close with more urgency than I'd intended.

"Where is he?"

"In playroom four," he said, simply. "Waiting for you."

"What happened? Why couldn't I come?"

He stared at me, and it was right about then that I realised how fucking nervous I was, how jealous, how fucking sick to my stomach. "A submissive has no business seeing her dom when he's exposed in that way, Missy. I showed Callum a few pointers, and he took to them. I'm sure you'll appreciate the result."

"Did he... um... did you...?"

His mouth curled into a smile. "There was no sex, if that's what you mean. Nothing of the kind. Please give me some credit, Missy."

I could hardly contain the relief, it washed over me in a wave. "Callum knows I'm coming?"

"Of course. I've a feeling it will be a little explosive."

"Why did you do it?" I quizzed. "Whatever you did, I mean."

"Maybe I'm getting sentimental in my old age," he laughed. "Or maybe I just felt like it."

I stood to leave, excitement burning, stopping only to plant the softest kiss on his jaw. He took my hand in his, squeezed it tight.

"He's a good lad, Missy. He'll make a fine dom. Don't lead him on, though, if he isn't what you want. If you aren't the one to give him the chance he needs, just do him a favour and walk away."

"I'm not playing him," I said.

"I know you're not. It's not your style," he pressed his forehead against mine, just for a moment. "Just be sure, or let him go."

I had no answer for him, and he didn't expect one either.

I left them to it, Cat and Masque and Raven and Cara, and everyone else I knew so well in that place. My heart was already out of there, beating only for the dirty bad savage in playroom four.

He was pacing the room, hands in his hair. His hoodie cast aside, his t-shirt too. His beautiful skin was flushed, and he was hot, frantic, burning up. The room smelt heavy with the scent of sex and sweat, and him. I closed the door behind me, feeling so exposed that my legs started to shake. He had that wild glare in his eyes, the one that had driven me crazy, right from the beginning.

His gaze fell on me, and stayed there.

"Masque said to come in..." I stammered.

There was something different about Callum Jackson now. He looked taller than before, head high and shoulders back. His jaw was set like concrete, lips thin and deadly. Like Masque. He looked like Masque. Shivers danced up my spine, and I was nervous, really fucking nervous.

When the savage pounced I was unprepared. He took me by surprise, lunging without warning, clammy hands on my neck, his mouth hot and wet over mine. His lips suppressed my gasp, tongue forcing its way inside my mouth to wrestle mine into submission. He pushed me backwards without breaking the kiss, and I let him dance me across the playroom. The bulk of the flogging bench stopped me in my tracks, but Callum was prepared for that. He flipped me in a heartbeat, bending me with so much force that my cheek slapped hard against the leather.

"Hands above your head," he barked.

I did as instructed, wriggling to help as he yanked my dress up and over. He unclipped my bra, wrenched it out from under me, then yanked my panties down until they were bunched by my knees.

His spanking was merciless, the heavy thud of his palm jamming my thighs into the bench with every strike.

"Oh God..." I wheezed. "Yes. Like that!"

His hand plunged between my thighs, finding me so fucking wet for him. He slid his thumb inside, fingers curling round to grind my clit.

"Yes, please!"

"Shut up, Sophie, shut the fuck up," he growled. "I say what, I say when, I say fucking how."

He resumed my spanking, and I stayed quiet, gripping the side of the bench as he landed his palms all over my ass, my thighs, even the swollen wet lips of my pussy. I didn't care where he hit, slipping into subspace like a soft, warm bed. Its endorphin-high glaze cocooned me, swallowed me whole.

I didn't notice Callum take up a paddle, not until it landed hard on my ass. I arched my back, wheezing out my breath.

"Yes," he barked. "Fucking take it."

I nodded, not trusting my voice.

Callum Jackson was brutal with the paddle in his hand, but he was polished. Way more so than I'd expected. He read me with surprising ease, aware of the arc of pain as it crested and eased. He kept me on the edge, until my breathing was frantic and my skin was raw, and then finally, he cast the paddle aside and pressed the weight of his body tight onto mine. His t-shirt sailed across the bench, the heat of his chest so nice against my back. I wriggled underneath him, spreading my legs without reservation.

"Fuck me," I hissed. "Please, Callum."

I felt him shake out of his jeans, relieved to feel the swell of his cock against my burning skin. "Gonna take you in the ass," he grunted. "Gonna take you fucking hard."

My stomach lurched, nervous of the intrusion, and I was right to be. He spat on his hand to lube me up, but it was fucking tight. I squirmed under him, letting out a yelp as he pressed the head of his cock inside.

"You're so fucking tight," he groaned. "You're gonna milk my fucking cock dry."

"Do it," I rasped. "Make it hurt, I don't care."

"I hope you fucking bleed."

I was pretty damn sure I would. It hurt like fuck, a searing pain right the way through me as he forced his entry.

"Do it!" I screeched. "Fuck me, Callum, just fuck me!"

He hissed and spluttered and ground his hips against my ass. Then he fucked me. Hard. It hurt so fucking bad, but it felt so fucking good.

"You wanted this," he groaned. "You fucking wanted this."

I had no breath, no words. Just pain. Glorious fucking pain.

"Gonna come in your dirty fucking hole," he grunted. "Fuck, I'm gonna come."

He wrapped his hand around my thigh, thumb circling my clit as his cock jerked in my ass. It was enough. Enough to send me tumbling, exploding in beautiful release. My knees went from under me, and only his weight kept me from falling. He pulled out slowly, hands under my thighs to support me as I found my feet.

He spread my ass cheeks, grunting at the view.

"I can see inside you," he growled. His fingers stretched me open, straining bruised flesh. "Your arsehole is fucking ruined, you're gaping so fucking wide."

"It's fucking sore. I'll be walking with a limp for a fucking month."

He let me go, and I rose slowly, flinching at the pain. His eyes were on mine as I turned around, softer this time.

"You alright, Soph?"

I nodded. "I'm great."

"Sure?"

"Deadly."

"What d'you wanna do now?" he asked, reaching for his t-shirt. I stroked his chest before he covered it from view, but he didn't allow me long. His mood had changed, I could feel it, feel the shutters coming down.

"Go home," I said. "Sleep. Rest my poor battered asshole."

"You need a lie down? You know... aftercare and shit?"

I smiled. "I'm fine, thank you. Nice thought, though."

He shuffled on the spot. "Ain't no good with this small talk shit, dunno what to say."

I reached for his hand, stroking his knuckles with my thumb. "You don't need to say anything. Just don't leave."

"Ain't going nowhere," he smiled. "Not if you don't want me to."

My stomach did the dance again, the one packed with butterflies on speed. I didn't want Callum Jackson to go anywhere.

***

Chapter Ten

Sophie

I squeezed Callum's thigh, but he didn't respond, staring blankly out the taxi window at the city lights. When the car turned onto East Veil he pulled his hood up, wrapped himself that little bit tighter.

"My stop," he said. "Thanks for the ride and... you know."

The driver pulled up on a side street by the East Veil subway, and Callum slipped away without any more words, raising his hand only briefly before disappearing into the night. He moved quickly, like an alley cat, keeping close to the shadows of the buildings with his head down low.

"Canary Wharf, Miss?"

I met the driver's eyes in the rearview mirror. Willed myself to say yes.

"Follow him please. Catch him up."

Shit.

We caught up with Callum Jackson as he crossed the street by the old retail units. I wound down the window, beckoning him over.

He leaned down, his face right next to mine. "What you forgot?"

"You," I said. "Come home with me. Stay."

His face was a picture, eyes wide with shock. "Stay?! With you, like?"

"Yes. With me."

"Can't," he said. "Gotta get back for Casey."

I could feel the pulse in my temples. "Bring her."

He smiled. "Ain't no good indoors. She'll mess things up."

"So, we'll cope."

His expression turned dark, lost in bewilderment. "You shitting me? This some other game...?"

"No," I said. "No game."

He looked into the darkness towards tower two. "Shit, I'm not sure, Soph. She'll trash the place."

"We'll keep an eye on her."

"Yeah, but..."

I looked at the meter, at the driver's amused eyes in the rearview. "Forget Casey for one second. What do *you* want to do?"

He shifted awkwardly. "I...um... ain't really stayed over before. Nowhere. Not for the night."

"Do you want to?" I knew I was pushing him, but the moment was passing us by.

"Yeah," he answered. "Yeah, I'd like that."

"Then, we'll get the dog," I said.

***

It cost me a small bloody fortune to have the dog in the taxi, but I'd shrugged aside Callum's protests. I simply couldn't care less. Casey bounced around my feet as we entered my building, provoking raised eyebrows from the reception desk. I glared them down, reminding them without words whose fucking parents owned the building. Tenancy terms and conditions can kiss my sore arse.

"This a pissing hotel or summat?" Callum asked in the lift.

"Just posh. Residents pay through the nose for it."

"Fair enough."

"You asked," I smiled. "My wages would never cover it. Like I said, I rent from my parents."

"And they don't mind? You having it cheap, like?"

"Money and property are two things they have in abundance. I don't imagine they give it much thought. Not unless they're trying to blackmail me with it, that is."

"Blackmail you?"

"Dad wants me to work in their property business. I don't. We go round in infuriating circles with it, mainly every Sunday lunchtime."

The lift dinged, and my heart leapt as I put my key in the door. This shit was getting real.

Callum's eyes sparkled like dark jewels as he looked around my place. Open plan, minimalistic, like every other apartment in this block. It was nice, though, light wood, and glass, and computerised fucking everything. I stepped into the kitchen, pulling out a bottle of wine from the cooler.

"Want a glass?"

"Aye, cheers."

I watched him as I uncorked, skulking around the place with his hands in his pockets, careful not to touch a single thing. Casey wasn't quite so considerate, she gambolled about, spinning in excitement at her own reflection in the balcony doors, and charging headlong into the coffee table.

Callum jumped a mile as she sent a couple of candles flying, but I only laughed.

"Shit." He picked up a chipped tea light holder. "Sorry, Soph."

I handed him his wine. "It's only a trinket."

"Guess you've got enough of 'em."

I followed his gaze, registering, as he was, that candles were my only real personalisation of this space. Everything else was standard, mirrored in the apartment opposite and identical in the one downstairs, but candles were my thing. I like the light.

He stood to check out a piece of art above the dining table.

"It's a print," I said. "Don't even ask me who by. I expect we might be getting a compulsory refurb now my parents are getting all arty, though." I smiled to myself, I could just fucking imagine it.

"Your parents are artists?"

That look again, the same one he'd given Bex. "Hell, no. They're just developing that fancy new Southbank complex. You must have heard of it?"

He shrugged. "Dunno."

I smiled. "You don't know if you've heard of it or not?"

His eyes met mine. "No. Ain't heard of it. Ain't from your world, Soph, ain't heard of none of this fancy shit." He stood up, chasing after Casey who was jumping up at the worktops. "Shouldn't be here," he snapped, flustered. "Don't belong."

"The dog's fine, let her be."

He brought her back with him, pushed her into a sitting position between his knees, but she sprung up again, regardless. "You don't understand. She gets food anxious. That's what they call it. Used to being hungry so she takes what she can get. She'll find it, too. Tear your fucking kitchen apart if you don't watch her."

"She'll be fine." I laughed as she jumped up to shove her nose in my face, her tail wagging so hard it wiggled her whole body with it.

"Won't be saying that when she's trashed all your shit."

"She'll learn. She's sharp."

"Not in one night. She ain't that quick a learner."

"Not in one night, no." I left it at that, unsure of what I even meant by that statement. I changed the subject, subtle as a freight train. "Did you enjoy Explicit?"

His smile rocked my world. "Aye. Liked Raven, Masque too.

Sound, they are. Raven said she'd be on down, to East Veil. Check out my art and shit."

"She's really good. She knows what she's talking about."

"Dunno why she's so bothered. Ain't nothing much."

"I don't believe that, and neither does she."

He shrugged, and I felt him prickle, awkward again. "What you got me here for, Soph?"

Nothing like a direct question. "I can enjoy your company, can't I?"

"You mean sex?"

"No. Although I can enjoy that too, I hope."

"That shit in the club. I liked it." He stared at the darkness beyond the balcony windows. "Didn't know if I would, but I did. I liked it there."

"I hoped you would."

"Why?"

"Jesus, Callum, isn't it obvious?" I stroked Casey's ears, looking into happy doggy eyes. "You really want me to say this? It's late, I want bed, I want sex, I want to go to sleep with a sore pussy to go with my sore arse."

"Just wanna know where we're at."

"We're here. Doesn't that say enough?"

"Maybe for you."

I reached over to twist his fingers in mine. "Come to bed with me."

A gentle squeeze as he downed his drink, then a shrug, conversation over. "Alright, Soph. Whatever you say."

***

Callum

I'd never been in a bed before, not like that one. Sophie's bed was fucking massive, a big fucking hulk of a thing, all fucking posh, with white sheets and too many fucking pillows. I felt dirty in it, even though I was clean. Well, clean for me, anyway. I stared up at the ceiling, feeling so fucking naked even under the covers. She'd stripped my clothes off me, all of them. Ditched them at the bottom of the bed and dragged me in with her like I was someone. Like I deserved to be here.

Someone like me don't deserve this shit. Was born for the streets. Born for cold fucking nights and scrabbling for food. Fighting, and stealing and surviving best I can, not for this. Not for someone like her.

Casey was still whining her head off in the hallway, scratching at the door. I told her to quiet again, settle down like a good girl. She didn't know what to do, bless her. Not her fault, neither. Still, I couldn't have her in here, dirty paws all over Soph's white sheets. Felt bad enough for dirtying them up myself.

Sophie edged closer, snaking a hand across my stomach. I rolled onto my side, awkward, getting as close as possible to the edge. She followed me, stalking me under the duvet like she was on a mission. I felt her breath against my back, her leg wrapped over mine. It felt so fucking nice.

"Comfy?" she asked, in a lazy voice.

"Aye."

"You sure? You're right on the edge."

"Aye. I'm alright."

"Night then, Callum."

"Night."

I closed my eyes, trying to drift off. Couldn't stop thinking, though. Of Sophie, of Explicit, of Raven and Masque and all the things I'd seen. Couldn't stop thinking of the Stoneys, either, and Vicki back home. Sophie's breathing deepened, long exhalations on my skin. I listened to her sleeping, wishing I could follow, but the minutes ticked by and still fucking nothing. I was careful not to wake her when I got out of bed, lifting her arm so softly that she didn't feel a thing.

I went to the window, pulled back the drapes to look at the city outside, but it weren't a window, it was a door. I turned the key quietly, stepping outside as naked as the day I was born. The balcony was high, looking right over the Thames. It was a great view, London lights twinkling on the skyline. Not lights like East Veil, proper lights. Could see the London Eye from here, loads of other shit too. I leaned over, breathing in the river air. Breeze on my face felt good. How the other half fucking live, eh?

Soft footsteps padded out to me. Sophie's warm arms around my waist. "Can't sleep?"

"Sorry. Didn't mean to wake ya."

She kissed my shoulder, and it made me cringe, wanting her so fucking much it hurt. "Come back to bed."

"Can't sleep, Soph."

"I'll help you sleep." She grabbed for my wrist, pulled me back inside, her hands all over me, over the tats on my chest. "Relax. It's alright."

"Why d'you want this?"

"Stop talking, Callum," she whispered. "Stop questioning it."

"Why d'you trust me here? I can't even trust my fucking self." I pulled away from her, hands in my hair, stomach in fucking knots as Casey whined away outside the door. "I fight, I steal, I hurt people. I eat from fucking bins, Soph, like a fucking sewer rat. I ain't got no money, no fucking home, no nothing."

"Stop it," she said. "That isn't what I see."

"What d'you fucking see, then, eh? Cos I don't fucking see it."

She wouldn't stay away, pressing up against me like I weren't a fucking monster, like I couldn't choke the breath from her for a cheap fucking thrill. "I see you. Not your past, not your problems, not your pissing credit status. Just you."

"Why are you so fucking nice?" I relented, resting my chin on her head, breathing in her sweet fucking scent.

"Born perfect, I guess." I could tell she was grinning, felt her lips against my chest. "Come to bed."

"Told you, can't sleep."

"Who said anything about sleeping?"

***

This time it was her in charge. There was something desperate about her, primal. She pushed my head back into the pillows, straddling me like a rodeo horse, yanking her satin slip off and grinding against my crotch like a bitch on heat. I gritted my teeth, cock fucking hungry for her. She took my hands and pinned them over my head, her weight on her arms as she leaned forward to kiss me.

She found me ready. I slammed my tongue in her mouth, claiming it as mine.

I tried not to think about the men who'd already been in this place. The rich men, the smart men, the men with prospects. Even more, I tried not to think about the men who'd be here after me. The man who'd make her his, for real.

Tonight, at least, Sophie Harding was fucking mine.

"Fuck me," she hissed. "Take me. Hurt me. Use me."

"No," I growled. "*You* fuck *me*."

She rubbed her perfect little tits in my face, and I sucked on her so hard, coaxing her nipples until she groaned. I could feel her excitement, the clamminess of her sweet cunt against my cock. I twitched under her, wanting nothing more than to bury deep in her juicy snatch.

"Fuck," she rasped. "That feels so good."

She let go of my hands, leaning over to rummage in the bedside drawer. Again my heart fucking dropped. A stash of rubbers, ready for whoever was sharing her bed. Tonight it was me. Maybe tomorrow it wouldn't be.

She tore open a packet and rolled it on, dainty fingers so fucking nice. Then she rode me, groaning like a whore as she leaned back, hands on my knees as she circled her hips, round and round and fucking round, her tits bared to the ceiling, the dainty curve of her waist so inviting.

I grabbed hold of her, gripping her tight and forcing her in wider circles. She moaned as I encouraged her efforts on my cock.

She felt perfect around me, tightening in all the right places. I closed my eyes in concentration, trying to delay the inevitable, but she felt too fucking good to resist for much longer.

"More..." she hissed. "Please..."

I didn't need asking twice. I bucked against her, slamming my cock all the way inside, and she jerked and she jiggled and she moaned my name, diddling her little pussy while my hands mashed her tits.

"Fuck me, Cal. Fuck me!"

I rammed in and out like a fucking piston and her eyes rolled up into whites.

"I'm coming," she breathed. "God, Callum, I'm fucking coming..."

I wasn't far behind, grunting and groaning and pumping my

spunk right into her as she shuddered. My heart was pounding, breath frantic, chest clammy with sweat as she collapsed onto me. I smoothed her hair, landed kisses on her face as my cock slipped from her sopping cunt.

"That was so good," she whispered. "Really fucking good."

"Didn't hurt you, though, thought you needed that shit."

She slid to the side, head on my chest as she snuggled up against me. "So did I," she said. "I guess we've both learned new something new tonight."

This time around sleep found me quick, and it felt fucking sweet.

***

Sophie

I was used to being woken up by an alarm clock, not a wet nose. Certainly not a wet nose in my face on a Sunday morning. I opened my eyes straight into Casey's dark brown stare. She whined her approval, licking at my face before I could stop her. I giggled, trying to fight my way out from under my furry assailant.

Callum bolted upright, eyes startled as he adjusted to his surroundings. It took him a moment to get his bearings, but once he did he grabbed for Casey, shunting her off onto the floor.

"Jesus, Soph, sorry. Don't know how she got in."

I pointed to the open bedroom door. "I guess she learned how to work the handle."

"Too smart for your own pissing good," he said to her, ruffling the fur on her neck.

He slipped out of bed, taking just a second to pull his jeans on. I admired his skin and the tightness of his ass in the morning light, the muted sun through the windows casting him in a beautiful glow.

"No need to get up yet," I said. "It's a Sunday."

"Gotta check on Case, see what she's been doing."

I followed him, wrapping myself in just a satin slip as I padded my way through to the living room.

Callum stood rigid in the hallway, hands on his temples in mortification. The place was a tip. A cushion from the sofa shredded across the coffee table, some torn up letters from the dresser by the main door. The worst was in the kitchen. The bin lay fallen, lid off and the contents strewn over the floor. She'd been in the cupboards, too, judging by the torn up cereal boxes and the scattering of cornflakes and Cheerios.

"I guess we're having toast for breakfast," I smiled.

"She's had the door," Callum said. His expression was heavy, really bloody horrified. I followed his gaze, and sure enough the living room door had been lacerated, strips of paint missing from the woodwork, the bedroom door hadn't fared much better. "Must have shut herself in and panicked."

"Oh well, now she's learned to open doors I don't imagine there'll be much more scratching."

"Your glass always this half full?"

"Only on mornings when I've had a great fuck the night before."

He smiled. "I'll remember that."

"Hope so."

I stepped over the kitchen carnage, flicking on the kettle for morning coffee. Callum began sorting the living room, and I couldn't help laughing as Casey jumped in play, trying to wrestle the cushion stuffing from him. He was angry at first, shooing her back, but she persisted, lying flat to the floor with her tail wagging, big brown eyes fixed on his.

I watched his expression soften, eyes filled with affection for his furry companion.

He dropped to all fours, charging her, and together they wrestled, rolling around in doggy-human bliss as they played. Casey broke away and took off, charging around the room, racing past just out of his reach as he lunged after her, round and round in crazy circles. It was quite a game.

"She loves you so much," I said. "She really does."

"Love her, too," he said. "She's fucking awesome."

I agreed with him, despite the mess. The dog was really something.

"Black fur ain't so good with your white sofa," he commented. "Got a hoover or summat?"

"I'll sort it later," I said. "Don't worry about it."

That seemed to knock him, and his shoulders hunched a little. "I'll get my stuff together."

"You haven't even had coffee yet."

"Don't wanna outstay my time, you know."

"You're not." I held out a mug, and he hesitated before he took it, but only for a second.

I dropped some kitchen roll onto a puddle that looked suspiciously like dog piss, and pulled the bin back to standing. Callum stared, dark eyes heavy with something. I couldn't read him again, couldn't fathom what he was thinking, or what he wanted.

"What now?" he said. "Want me to help clean up?"

I pondered awhile, excitement dancing up my spine.

"Say, Callum Jackson, have you ever watched the entire Alien Quadrilogy back to back?"

Sunday dinner with the parents was officially cancelled.

***

Chapter Eleven

Callum

I raced over to Jack Willis' place, Casey running at my side all the way. I was late, really fucking late. Only half hour left until the Stoneys showed up and I hadn't a fucking quid to my name. Not yet anyway.

I bashed his door like my life depended on it, sighing in relief as movement showed inside.

"What the pissing hell you doing here, lad? It's a bleeding Monday morning."

"Need me cash," I said. "One eighty I'm owed."

"One fifty you're owed," he said. "Only cash I got in the place."

He was a lying cunt and we both knew it, but I couldn't risk an argument. Stoneys would tear me a new arsehole if I turned up empty-handed. I left him to it, heart racing and not 'cause of the exertion. Stoneys don't play nice and one-fifty was a pisstake.

I didn't have time to drop Case with Vicki, only just making it to the garages in time. Trent was already waiting. The usual big cunt was with him, but my hackles spiked as I saw the other piece of shit alongside.

"What the fuck's he doin here?" I grunted.

"Jones is one of our lot now," Trent said. "Offered you the gig first, remember?"

"No place for that piece of shit in your running, Trent," Tyler scoffed. "He's a fucking weasel. Good for nothin'."

"Watch your fucking mouth," I seethed. "Don't give a fuck who you're running with, you're still a fucking cunt, Jones."

"Ain't got time for all this crap," Trent snapped. "Where's me money, lad?" I handed him over the notes, stomach sinking as I watched his expression turn sour. "And the rest? Where's the fucking rest?"

"All I got," I said. "I swear down. Been a slow week."

"Heart fucking bleeds, lad. It really fucking does."

"I'll get you more," I said. "Next week."

"And what kind of message does that send, soft lad? Show up with half for the Stoneys, they don't fucking care. Soft touches them lot."

"Won't be telling no one, Trent. Don't talk, don't grass."

"Don't matter, lad. Principle, like." He gestured to Jones and the other big cunt, and I bared my fists as they headed in my direction. "It's a shame you got such a pretty face, lad, shame to mess you up." His laugh was hollow and full of pissing spite.

Adrenaline hit, pulse loud in my ears. I knew the smart move. Take a beating, shut my mouth, let them prove their point. Live to fight another fucking day. But I couldn't do it.

"Not gonna make this easy," I hissed. "Better be prepared for a scrap."

"Gonna fucking enjoy this," Tyler said.

I heard Casey's growl, yelled at her to stay back, but I was out of time. Tyler lunged, missing me on the first swing, but coming back for seconds. I landed a decent smack to the side of his face before the other cunt grabbed my arms, and even then I managed to throw my head back, landing my skull on his nose. He cursed blue murder, staggering back as his blood poured. I laughed as he red misted, then jumped into action kicking and punching and flailing for all I was worth. Think I caused some damage before they got me cornered, they were breathing fucking ragged enough, anyway.

Casey was barking her head off, circling low to the ground. I ordered her away again but she wouldn't listen. Case ain't no small dog, but she weren't bloody big enough to take a couple of arseholes like them.

Big cunt pulled me into an arm-lock, wrenching my wrists so hard I hissed out all my breath. Tyler waited until Trent gave the nod, and I watched his piggy eyes fill with joy as he landed his fist in my stomach. He didn't have time to land another. I struggled for air at the sight of Casey hanging off Jones' wrist. Her eyes were wild, growling low and dangerous as she clamped her teeth in his flesh. He bellowed in rage, kicking out at her, but she was too fast with her feet.

I heard Trent laughing. "Shake the fucking thing off, ya bloody idiot. It's only a fucking collie."

I lunged forward in spite of my predicament. "No, Casey, run!" I rasped. "Just fucking run!"

She didn't run. Not even when Tyler cracked his fist down on her skull. She held firm as he tried to shake her, and he bellowed again as she adjusted her grip. "Get off me ya fucking shit!" Tyler boomed.

"Run, Casey!" I screamed. "Go!"

Tyler caught her good next time. She loosed her bite as she yelped, and stumbled around dazed. She came to her senses quick enough to dodge his next assault. Narrowly avoiding a boot in the ribs.

"Gonna fucking kill that fucking shit!" Jones screeched.

"Go, Casey!" I tried again, and this time she listened. Her eyes on mine broke my heart, she was so fucking sad. She weighed up going for Tyler again, I could tell, but I kicked out at her myself this time, just to get her to leave. "GO, CASEY! GO! FUCK OFF!"

Her tail was on the floor as she skulked away, shooting me a pitiful look. At least she was safe.

I breathed easy, thanking my lucky fucking stars she'd gone away.

Jones' wrist was bleeding badly. "Better get that looked at," I sneered. "It's your wanking hand, ain't it?"

"Don't need no pissing wanking hand, Jackson. Got your mam's dirty cunt to see me right." He checked his fingers, clenching them easily. No major damage done, unfortunately. "Dog's a fucking menace. Scotts should'a finished her."

"Scotts got no business with her. You, neither."

"Got business with you, though, Jackson. So much fucking business. Gonna fucking love this."

His bloody fist landed right on my cheekbone. My ears rang, pain pounding through my temples. Didn't make a sound, though, didn't wanna give him the satisfaction. I took another couple from him, on the jaw this time. His tubby knee cracked me right in the ribs, and I fell forward heaving. I was struggling for breath when I heard voices, stars behind my fucking eyes.

Casey's bark sounded loud again and my heart fell. Please God, no.

"What the pissing hell's going on here?"

I knew that voice. My eyes opened in time to see Raven light up a cigarette, hand on her hip. She looked different in daylight. Fuck-off big boots and combat trousers, leather jacket too. Her hair was up in a high pony, hanging down her back to her waist. Her make-up was the same, though. I struggled for words, but I still had no breath in me.

"What's it to you, girly?" Trent scoffed. "Got a thing for him, have ya?"

"Got a fucking thing for his money," Raven said. "Who the fuck are you people?"

Trent's expression turned sour and I flinched inside. "I'm Trent fucking Stoney of the Stoney brothers, who the fuck are you?"

"I'm one of Ash Rixon's girls," she said. "So, you'd better back the fuck up. Kid's ours."

I watched Trent's eyes flare wide, but Tyler carried on oblivious. "Don't give a fuck who you are," he raged. "Gonna fucking pound him."

"Stop, you stupid dumbfuck!" Trent yelled. "This is one of Ash Rixon's girls. ASH FUCKING RIXON, comprende?" Trent approached Raven, hands out. "Look, lady, we ain't got no beef with Rixon, this little shit just owes us cash, alright?"

"You'll have to get in line," she said, cool as cucumber. "Owes us first. Drop him, asswipe."

Trent nodded, and I was on the tarmac, coughing and spluttering and wrenching my arms back into position. Casey was at my side in a flash, licking my face as I caught my breath.

I listened to the conversation happen over me, keeping the hell out of it.

"How long til we can have him back?" Trent asked. "We need paying too. Maybe I could speak with Rixon, explain what shit's goin' down?"

"Rixon's got no time for you." I watched her stub her cigarette out. "You'll have to wait a month."

"Month's an awful fucking long time."

"Best you're getting." Raven stared him out. "Come anywhere near him before he's paid off Rixon and we'll be coming after you."

"You'll get your pissing month," Trent said. "Any longer and Rixon'll have to come down here himself, though. Got me?"

"Think we're clear," she hissed. "Now fuck off."

Tyler's eyes were bulging with rage. He gripped his bleeding wrist, on the edge of red misting.

"We're off," Trent said. "Now." Tyler didn't move, just stayed staring. "NOW, DUMBFUCK!"

I could breathe again when they were out of sight. I rolled onto my side, pulled my knees up, ignoring the pain in my ribs.

"Stay down," Raven hissed. "Until I know they're pissing gone."

She stalked to the edge of the garage block, only returning when she was satisfied.

"What's all that shit about?" I said. "Who's Ash pissing Rixon?"

"From the Kenny estate. Croydon," she said, yanking me up by the elbow. "Hardest bastard in London, one of the hardest anyway. Serious shit."

"You're one of his girls?" I quizzed. "Jeez."

She smiled. "Of course not. Just know him. Do his tats."

I stared up at her in admiration. "You've got some shiny fucking brass balls on you, ain't ya?"

"Just as well. Saved your bloody arse, didn't it?"

I accepted her hand up, holding myself against the wall until I was steady. "How'd ya know I was here?"

"Your friend," she said, reaching out for Casey. The dog leaned into her side, accepting the fuss. "She was frantic, like something from one of the Lassie films, barking and running, barking and running. Knew something was up so I followed her, figured she might be yours. Sophie told me about the big, grand rescue mission," she smiled, crouching down to kiss Casey on the head. "And she told me all about you, Casey, told me what a cute ball of fluff you are."

"Thanks," I said.

"Don't mention it, kid, all in a day's work. Keeps the adrenaline pumping."

"What you gonna do if that Rixon guy finds out you used his name?"

She smirked. "Don't you be worrying about that, baby. He owes me."

He weren't the fucking only one.

∗∗∗

Sophie

Three missed calls from Rebecca. I watched my mobile flashing away on my lap under the table, itching to get the hell out of Christine's crappy briefing and find out what the urgency was. *Callum*, my brain screamed, it had to be about Callum. My skin was still blooming at the thought of his name. Sunday afternoons with the Savage weren't supposed to be that good. Time with him was supposed to be about edgy sex, nothing more than the pounding of his vicious flesh against mine. My pussy ached with the echo of him, battered from his invasion, but my mind ached more. Oh, how it fucking ached.

"Anything to add, Sophie?"

I looked blankly into the faces around the table. "Sorry?"

"East Veil, any update on how we're handling the graffiti epidemic?"

"A one pissing man epidemic," Eric muttered. "Hope they lock the animal back up, save what's left of our pissing budget."

"Still a work in progress," I said. "I'm on it."

"And, what avenues are you considering?" Christine was so bastard snooty. I felt my hackles rise. "Surely the police are working with you on this? They do have a history with Callum Jackson, after all, a *lengthy* history. What's their take on the situation?"

My mouth turned clammy, but I pasted on my professional face. "Actually, I'm only going to utilise the law as a last resort. I'm planning on tackling this using education and opportunity, rather than enforcement." A wave of scathing amusement rippled through the room, and I felt my temperature rising, tongue itching to run riot. I let it fly. "Graffiti, or street art, is an attempt to express oneself creatively. East Veil has no youth program, no effective outlet for artistic expression. It's a boiling pot of frustration and apathy, and the crime rate is symptomatic of this, as is the lack of community cohesion. The graffiti is merely one face of a much larger problem. I'm planning on tackling *that* problem, not singling out one individual and treading him down. Others will merely spring up in his place, it's firefighting, not a solution."

Eric slammed his notepad on the table. "It's not pissing art, it's an eyesore. Locking him up's the answer. Not this embracing hippy bullshit."

"It's not hippy bullshit," I said. "Look up anything you like on youth crime. The statistics speak for themselves."

"What you planning on doing, then?" he scoffed. "Taking some felt tip pens down the old youth club and have them all do some bleeding colouring-in for half an hour every bastard Friday? I could tell you how well that's going to work, don't need no bloody statistics."

"That isn't quite how I'd choose to frame it," I hissed. "But yes. An outlet *is* needed."

"I've heard it all now," Eric snapped. "No wonder this place is going to the dogs."

"I think we're done for today," Christine concluded. "Keep us informed, Miss Harding, everyone here is keen to see the situation resolved. It's why you were brought in, after all. Your expertise spoke volumes when you were assigned this patch."

Spoke, past tense.

I shifted in my chair, meeting her eyes with a confidence I wasn't feeling. "I'll let you know when I have an update."

Don't hold your fucking breath.

***

Rebecca buzzed me again as I was on the way out of the office, and I answered with a sigh.

"Finally!" she exclaimed. "Thought you'd bloody emigrated."

"Work shit," I groaned. "What's up?"

"We need to get Cal off the street. Kid's way too good to be wasting his talent on garage blocks and subways round that shithole."

My stomach lurched in agreement. "Getting a shitload of heat from the office, they want me to bring in the police, get him locked up again."

I waited for it. "Your colleagues are asshole fucking idiots, Sophie, *idiots*. Kid's a bloody star. His skill, baby, holy mother of God, his *skill.*"

"They don't see that, Bex. They think he's a nuisance, nothing more."

"We'll see about that when Callum's on the front of *Urban Life* magazine. Narrow-minded cunts."

I smiled. "I'd love to see their faces."

"Oh, you will do, if I have anything to do with it."

"I don't know what I can do, Bex, my hands are tied and the heat is on. I can't get him a property through allocations, he's not even on the waiting list. I checked."

"We need another solution, then. What about your place?"

I groaned. "As if. Parents would go bloody spare if they caught wind of it. Had the dog there this weekend and even that raised eyebrows. All that art stuff would be a serious no-no."

"Maybe it's time you jumped out of their pockets. Bit long in the tooth to be leaping through Daddy's hoops, don't you think, baby?"

"Don't start," I sighed. "Not today."

"Sorry," she said. "Just feeling the frustration."

"You and me both." I pondered awhile. "No room at yours? I know your fondness for taking in waifs and strays."

"Room's stuffed full of Cara's shit. Haven't got space for my own work, let alone someone else's. Breaks my heart, baby, I'd have him there in a flash if I could swing it."

"I know," I said. "I'll get my thinking cap on."

"Get it on swift, baby. Kid needs a break. He needs it quick, too."

There was something in her tone, something heavy. I felt it in my stomach, a low rumble of dread. "Has something happened?"

She paused too long. "Nothing for you to worry about, baby. Think hard, think fast. I'll be doing the same."

"Won't be thinking about anything else. He's got me bad, Bex. So bad it's scaring the shit out of me. I can't even explain it, this *thing*. He's electric, driving me insane."

"I feel you," she laughed. "Enjoy the ride, baby, got a feeling it's gonna be a white-knuckled fucker."

She wasn't the only one.

***

My thinking cap didn't have too long to work its magic. Call it fate, the universe, or pure bloody coincidence, but my break came out of nowhere, dropping in my lap on Wednesday afternoon without even a hint of warning. I'd been itching to call Callum, itching to have him in my place again, in my bed, in my pussy. I'd held back, a scaredy cat to my own emotions, but my resolve was buckling, my fingers darting to my phone with increasing urgency.

Christine's expression was twinged with disapproval as she

announced I had a visitor at the office.

"Miss Headley," she announced. "34 Haygrove Park, insists she needs to see you."

I knew Helen Headley well, a carer for her elderly parents on the Haygrove estate. I knew them all well, in fact, regular attendees at my resident coffee mornings back in the days when I was good at my job. I missed Haygrove so bloody much.

I greeted Helen warmly, ushering her into a meeting room with a genuine fondness. She sat at the other side of the table, clutching paperwork in white hands. Her mousy hair was scraped back in a ponytail, her skin sallow and sunken. My heart dropped.

"How are you?" I said. "How are your parents?"

Her lip trembled, and instinct forced a lump into my throat. "I'm sorry," she said. "I know I should go to the new estate manager, Veronica whatever-her-name-is, but, you know. She's not you, Sophie. I needed to see you."

"What's happened?"

"It's Dad," she said. The tears welled up in a flash, and my own threatened to join in. "He, um, had another stroke last week. He… I'm afraid he didn't make it."

Real grief knocked me sideways. His cheerful grin as he helped with the Community in Bloom initiative, his willingness to muck in and help with the estate. "I'm so sorry," I said. "So, so sorry."

She waved thanks and took a breath. "I need your help, with the tenancy stuff. I've sorted out Mum's stuff with the benefits, I just need the tenancy transferred to her sole name."

"Of course." I took the paperwork, flinching at the copy of the death certificate.

"And the garage," she said. "I've cleared out his tools, as much as I can, anyway. Mum can't face it. You know how he loved that place, his little workshop."

I smiled sadly. "I know. I'd always find him down there."

"He liked the quiet," she said. "Helped him think. Away from Mum's nagging, he used to say."

I smiled along with her, trying my best to keep it together. "You want me to end his tenancy?"

"Please."

I took the key. "I'll sort out the paperwork. You don't need to worry about it."

"Thank you," she said. The tears dropped from her eyes freely and she made no attempt to brush them away. "He liked you," she smiled. "Said you were a good lass. We all miss you, Sophie, it's not the same without you."

"I miss you all too," I said. "I'm on East Veil now, not so far away."

"Maybe you could call in sometime. We've got the young mum's support group up and running now, meets on a Tuesday."

"I'd love to."

"I'd better let you get on," she smiled. "Hope we see you again soon, under happier circumstances."

"Me too."

I broke protocol completely by pulling her in for a hug. I held her tight for long moments in the meeting room, and she sobbed onto my shoulder like a broken child. My eyes were wet with tears when she pulled away, and I struggled for composure as I waved her off. I sat at the desk in that poxy little room and cried. Cried for Derek Headley, for Helen and her mum. Cried for Haygrove and my old job. Cried for me, too, cried for something I couldn't place, some deep-seated fear of missing out on life, on not seizing the fleeting gifts that life offered up to me. Life is short, and fragile, so fragile.

Then I went back to my desk.

I stared at the garage tenancy screen, hovering the mouse over the terminate button. Derek had been renting the garage for ten years, rent always paid on time, in cash, with no client visits necessary.

I gripped the garage key in my hand, taking a moment in remembrance of Derek Headley and his happy smile.

"Only live once," he'd said to me, after a ten hour stint in the community garden. "Gotta make it mean something, else what's the point?"

I made it mean something.

I put the key in my handbag and got the hell out of there.

I got the tube down to East Veil and wandered round in a daze, ignorant to all its dangers, its rabble of violence and seediness, and drugs and fear and hate. I passed unhindered and unnoticed, until I found Callum Jackson.

He was rolling a cigarette outside Al's while Casey tucked into a piece of old fish by the bins. He didn't see me at first, not until I was practically in his arms.

"Soph?" he managed to mutter before I was on him. I wrapped my arms around him without care, barely registering the cackles from the crowd on the benches down the way. He flinched as I gripped him, but it only took a heartbeat before he held me back, his lips on my hair as I cried into his hoodie. "Jesus, Soph, what's happened?"

I shook my head, unable to find words. He didn't push me, just held on tight until I was ready to speak. "Missed you," I said. "Come home with me. Please, just come home with me."

"Now? For the night, like?"

I nodded. "One night, two nights, ten nights, forever, don't fucking care."

"You fucking serious?"

I looked up at him through watery eyes. "What do you think?"

"I think you're upset."

I blinked away the tears, and that's when I saw his face. His jaw was swollen, eyes black and blue. "Fucking hell! What happened to you?"

He shrugged, looking away. "Don't matter."

"It does matter!" I hissed. "Who did this to you?!"

"Leave it, Soph," he said. "Don't matter."

I reached up to touch him, turning his face so I could see better. It made me suck in all my breath. "My God."

"Said it don't fucking matter!" he snapped. He looked down the road, scowling at the crowd gawking at us. "Let's just go, yeah? I'll stay one day, ten days, don't fucking matter to me, Soph. Just wanna be where you are."

I took his hands in mine, and they felt so alive, so real, so warm. "Just want to be where you are, too," I smiled. "That's all I want."

He whistled for Casey.

***

I lay with my head on Callum's arm, stroking his chest in the darkness. I was careful, staying away from the bruising on his side, just wishing he'd open up and tell me what the hell was going on, but he wouldn't say a peep about it.

I'd told him about Derek Headley, told him more than I'd ever told anyone about my job, about Haygrove, about the people, about all the things I'd done there. My parents had scoffed when I'd brought any of it up, and I'd learned to stay quiet, downplaying my achievements like they meant nothing.

Callum's voice sounded so loud in the room when he spoke.

"I lost someone," he said simply. "Years ago, like. Still hurts, though."

"Who did you lose?"

"Old Jimmy, guy who taught me to paint. Thought he was fucking awesome."

"You knew him a long time?"

"Long enough." I knew he was smiling at the memory. "Helped me out, he did, when I had no one. Shoved a spray can in my hand and let me help. Fucking loved it, best feeling in the world."

"What happened to him?" I said, propping myself up on an elbow.

"Liked taking risks, stupid old cunt. Know the multi-storey down on Acer Street? One you can see from tower one?"

"Yeah, condemned, right?"

"Aye, but it weren't back then. Used to go on about it, how he could do a fucking masterpiece up there. Would laugh that no fucker would be able to cover that shit up, not even with twenty men." He laughed gently. "I weren't there when he did it, probably arguing with Mam or some shit. He went up there, off his face, I reckon. Dangled himself from the railings but didn't secure it properly. End of him."

"He fell?!"

"Long fucking way. Instant, they said, wouldn't have felt nothing."

"Shit, I'm sorry." I shuddered at the thought.

"He'd have wanted to go that way, ya know? Died for his art, like."

"That must have been rough on you, how old were you?"

"Thirteen, summat like that. Could'a been me up there with him. Could'a saved him, maybe."

"Or maybe not. Maybe you'd have fallen too."

He squeezed me into his side. "Maybe."

"You won't ever take risks like that, will you?" I said. "Promise me."

He laughed, louder this time. "Jesus, Sophie Harding, what's this? Proposal, like?"

"I want you alive."

"I'm alive with you," he mumbled. "Weren't alive sometimes before."

My pulse quickened, hedonistic urges racing. A need for life, to feel something, to feel fucking real.

"Make me feel alive," I whispered, inching my leg over his. "The way I need. I need to *feel*."

His body responded in a heartbeat, his breath turning shallow. He took my hand, squeezed my fingers round his cock. "Feel that," he groaned. "That's for you."

"Alive..." I whispered. "I need to feel it... make me..."

He got out of bed, hissing at the pain in his side, but he recovered quickly, yanking me out and up onto my feet. He pulled the drapes aside, unlatching the balcony door. The breeze hit my naked skin, sending shivers right the way through me. He stepped out, his shadowy body beckoning me. I followed, nervous, pussy begging for his touch. "I'll show you alive," he rasped. "Trust me."

I didn't have time to respond before he shoved me forwards, jamming me into the railings with such force I folded over the edge, hands flailing for grip. He kept pushing, and I squealed, panicked, head swimming with vertigo. I gripped hold of the bars from the wrong side, head lolling and eyes fixed on the ground such a long way below. My centre of balance was precarious, tiptoes my only contact with solid ground. His warm hand between my thighs made me cry out, his bulk pressing tight against my thighs.

"Heart racing," he growled. "Brain fucking spinning... hits you in the gut, don't it? The fear. Knowing you could fall, any fucking second, just one tiny slip." He pushed me forward further still and my toes lifted, I cried out, petrified, but he pulled me back in, just enough. "Wanna feel alive, Soph? Ain't nothin' feels more alive than the fear of death. Nothin'."

"I'm scared," I cried. "Don't let me fall."

"Ain't gonna let you fall," he groaned. "Trust me."

I tried. I really tried, but my lungs were screaming in my ribs, gulping for air. His fingers found my clit, and found me wanting in spite of my predicament. I moaned and it sounded so weird, so fucking loud in my head.

"Don't fight," he growled.

His hands moved to my waist, arms folding around me as he lifted my feet from the floor. The railing cut into my stomach, taking my weight as I teetered on the edge. This was crazy, fucking stupid, but still I spread myself for him, groaning in the back of my throat as he slammed his way inside.

"Yes," I hissed. "Take me."

"Ain't got no rubber, Soph," he growled. "Fucking sorry 'bout that. Just wanna feel you."

I didn't fucking care.

My tits bounced, nipples freezing cold as they bashed into the metalwork. I gripped the side as hard as I could, blood rushing to my head. He fucked me so fucking hard, growling and cursing and slamming his way into me. Adrenaline and endorphins hammered the shit out of me, and I was a hot mess of fear, my pussy on fire as he pounded me from behind. I closed my eyes, the breeze around my ears as my hair flew limp.

"Let go," he groaned. "Let go of the fucking railings."

"I can't," I choked. "I fucking can't."

"Let go," he barked. "I'm fucking telling you to."

His voice shocked me into submission. A strange cry came out of my mouth, almost a sob, and I let go, senses reeling in fear. My hands dangled in the air, scrabbling for nothing, until finally I clenched them into fists and let them be. His cock was savage, thrusting so hard it hurt. It took me a few minutes to realise I was crying. Tears streaming from my eyes with only my frantic breath as accompaniment. It was cathartic. It was cleansing. It was really fucking beautiful.

He pulled me back before he came, laying me flat on the cold balcony floor with my legs pinned high. I groaned as he slammed back inside, hands in his hair.

"Come with me," he hissed. "Wanna see you coming."

His warmth was a relief, the bulk of his body the anchor I needed to unravel. I let myself go, bucking underneath him to get my fill, groaning like a whore as his hips ground hard against mine, mashing my clit between us.

"Fuck..." I cried. "Now... yes..."

"Come," he barked. "Come for me..."

"Fuck... please... hard..."

"Want this, yeah? Want this fucking hard?" he raised himself on his arms, gritting his teeth with the pain as he fucked me raw. "Fuck, Sophie, your fucking cunt is so fucking sweet."

I cursed as I exploded, a flash of light behind my eyes. It was intense. So fucking intense. He grunted as he came, pulling out enough to shoot his load over my tits. He rubbed his hot seed all over me, eyes wild as he marked me as his own.

"Mine," he growled. "Never had no one I wanted before. Want you though, Soph. Ain't gonna let you fucking go, neither."

I reached for his fingers, guiding them down my body, still wet with his release. "Yours," I said, forcing his fingers inside my pussy.

His eyes widened, feral, like the savage I met. "You fucking mental?" he rasped.

I nodded. "Something like that, yeah."

***

"Are you fucking mental?" Bex didn't bother with niceties, and I didn't expect her to. Her heels clacked across the street by Haygrove tube station, dark ringlets flying in the breeze. Confessing my stupidity by text probably hadn't been the best choice.

"Callum asked the same thing," I said. "I sure felt a bit fucking crazy last night."

"You want to get knocked-up or something, baby? I mean, seriously, I know the hormones can really fly, but this really isn't the way to go about it."

"No, of course not. I don't know what the hell came over me. It's him, I think. He makes me crazy."

"No shit," she smiled. "Don't know this side of you, darling, it's news to me."

"News to me, too."

"You should watch that shit, seriously. The first Explicit baby, hey? Thought it would be Masque and Cat."

"Christ," I said. "Enough of the baby shit. I'm not planning on getting knocked-up anytime soon."

She leaned down and pressed an ear to my stomach. "Hello, little Savage, meet auntie Raven."

"Knock it off, Bex," I laughed. "I'm serious, I lost my fucking mind, alright? That's all, won't happen again."

"What you doing here, anyway? Called in with morning sickness already?"

I rolled my eyes. "I called in with a migraine. Needed some space. Haven't called sick in about five years, I think one day is forgivable."

"Why the summons, then? Want to talk baby names with me?" I frowned in irritation and she cackled her very best laugh. "Ok, ok! I'll drop it. Why am I here? Jaz nearly blew her top when I asked her to cover me."

"Sorry, but this is pretty urgent." Her eyes widened as I took the garage keys from my bag. "Wanted to get started, Studio Jackson is in motion."

She lunged forward and kissed my lips, her hands on my cheeks for long moments. "You're a fucking superstar," she said. "Knew you'd sort it."

"Tenant passed away," I explained. "Really sad. We should have a while with the property before it gets flagged. Better make it count."

She smiled. "Best take a fucking look, then."

***

Callum

"Don't like surprises," I said. "They make me edgy."

I followed anyway, dragged along by Sophie on one arm and Raven on the other. Casey was having a fucking field day, bouncing from one to the other. Least they was all having fun.

"You'll like this one," Sophie said. "Promise."

My stomach lurched. Happy lurched. Being around Soph was too good, too sweet. It made me nervous. Don't hurt to lose something you never had, but losing something like her scared the shit out of me.

They dragged me all the way down by Haygrove, past the King's Road maintenance huts and into the garage block. Place was like a ghost town.

"And?" I said. "This party ain't really digging."

Sophie put a key in the door to one of the units, springing the catch and lifting it open. Took me a minute to get with the plot.

"Surprise!" they squealed. "Studio Jackson is open for business."

They had paints, whole fucking racks of them. The ones I liked too, the whole range. Must have cost a fucking fortune. They had big white sheets of canvas, like I'd seen in the art stores. They had a bench, and some brushes, and turps and mixer and a tray full of pencils.

"Shit." I put my hands in my hair. "What's all this?"

"For you," Raven said. "Call it a joint effort. Soph got the garage and I arranged the materials. Christmas is here early, kid. You're welcome." She smiled so fucking bright, eyes all shiny.

I looked at Sophie and she looked nervous as she stared at me. I didn't know where to put myself, didn't know what to think, what to feel.

"Don't you like it?" Soph asked. "Have we got the wrong stuff?"

"Got the right stuff," I said. "It's fucking mint, like."

Her eyes searched mine. "What is it, then?"

I was pissing on their parade and I knew it, but I couldn't help it. "Can't take this," I said. "It's too much."

"Hey," Raven said. "Listen up, baby. It's a gift. Don't make a pity party out of it. Doesn't suit you."

I tried to smile. "Ain't making a pity party, just can't fucking take all this shit. Can't pay it back."

She took my arm, so hard it fucking pinched. "Look at me," she said. "This isn't a loan. It's not charity, either. It's a gift, from people who believe in you. From people who give a shit about you and your art, alright? We cool on this?"

I nodded, but my throat felt weird, all thick and swollen. My head was spinning, tears springing up like a fucking pussy boy. I turned away, coughed them back. "Fucking hell," I said. "Dunno what to fucking say."

"Thanks is the standard response," Sophie said. Her smile was so pretty. She was so pretty, prettiest thing in the world.

"Ain't much good with thanks," I smiled. "Thanks, though, this is crazy mint. Crazy."

"Don't mean to pile the pressure on," Raven said. "But I've got someone waiting to see your art. A dealer, same one who launched me."

My brain whizzed like a spinning top. "A dealer?! They ain't gonna like my shit, Raven. Ain't nothing like as good as yours. Shit, man, they're gonna laugh me out the fucking park."

Her smile was like the sun, eyes twinkling again.

"He's already seen your shit, baby," she said. "The paint is from him."

***

I painted and I painted and I painted some more. Lost in time, in space, lost to everything but the colours on the canvas. It was bliss in that place, with Casey at my side and Sophie in my life. It don't get any fucking sweeter than that.

Case liked it down there, garage door open, catching the sun. When it'd rain she'd come inside, curl up at my feet and snooze without a care in the world.

She'd taken to sleeping on the bed at night, too. Dog didn't know herself these days. She was still trashing the bins, mind. Tearing the kitchen apart every time we weren't looking. Soph didn't seem to care, though, didn't seem to care about anything apart from getting her ass slapped red and getting a good pounding. Guess that's what she liked best about me, that's what I figured. Sure weren't me talking skills, but I was getting better at that. I was tryin'.

I'd been at Soph's nearly two weeks when I decided to get some of my shit from Vick's. I'd been avoiding her, hiding my bruises where she wouldn't see. She'd only feel bad, and I didn't want that. They'd taken an age to go, especially the swelling on my eye. My ribs still hurt, but she wouldn't know that, not now my face didn't give it away.

Vicki was stood with her back to me in her yard, puffing on a cig. My heart fucking jumped a good'un, thinking it was that Lozza Price from down the garages, with that same bloody hair again. It weren't, though, it was Vick, hair hacked into a messy blonde bob. It was more yellow than blonde in the sunlight, a bit like a canary. Didn't like it much. Smiled anyway.

"Look different."

She spun around at the sound of my voice, smiling bright. "Like it? Fancied a change. Where the hell you been, Cal? Slay's been missing ya."

"Around," I said. "Busy, like."

"Deliveries?"

I flushed with guilt. I'd been slack on deliveries, too busy painting. Needed to go and see Jack Willis before he forgot my rounds, but I didn't want to freak Vicki out. "Yeah, working."

"I heard they beat you up," she said. "Got you good, didn't they? That's why you been staying away. I know you, Callum Jackson. I ain't a fool, know you didn't want me to see."

"Been around, Vick, just been busy."

"Rumours been flying all around the estate, Cal. Heard you were kissing that estate manager down by Al's. That true?"

"You sure know a lot, don't ya? Dunno where you get it all from."

She held up her mobile. "Facebook."

I fucking hated that shit and she knew it. "Me getting beat up's all over the internet is it? Un-fucking-likely, Vick. Ain't nobody knew about that." Her colour drained, and that's when I knew. "He's been round, ain't he? Jones? You'd better have called the fucking pigs."

"Ain't calling the pigs, Cal. He didn't stay long."

My hands clenched into fists in my pockets. "What'd he fucking want?"

"Said he could look after me, like. Me and Slay. Said he could tell the Stoneys to back off, leave me alone."

"Stoneys ain't coming after you and Slay, Vick. Debt's mine now."

She offered me a cigarette and I took it gladly. "He says Stoneys won't give a shit if you've taken the debt, still me they'll come for." She leaned into me, eyes wide and scared. "He said they're hardcore, Cal, the real deal. Showed me a vid on his phone, of them poisoning someone with some shit, lad convulsing all over the place, real sick. Couldn't even watch it. Ty thought it was funny, sick cunt. He said they cut off people's fingers too, burn them as well if they need to."

"He's full of shit, Vicki. Call the fucking pigs next time."

But he weren't full of shit and I knew it.

"He said you're dead meat. Said some tough guy from Croydon's after you, too. Don't reckon you'll be round much longer."

"That's complicated," I said. "Just mind your own, will you? I'll sort it."

"Where you been, Cal, really? You been hiding?"

"Summat like that."

"You wiv her? That Harding woman?"

I shrugged. "Got no answers, Vick. Just hanging out."

"What about me, Cal, when *we* gonna be hanging out?"

I felt fucking shitty, trying to protect her but making her so fucking sad. "Dunno, Vick, whenever you want. I'm here, yeah? Always will be."

"Tonight?" she asked. My heart dropped. I thought of Soph at hers, her sweet, warm arms. Her sweet, hot cunt all hungry for me. Vicki sighed. "Please, Cal. Hardly seen you."

I looked into Vicki's eyes and I knew I couldn't say no. Mates look out for each other, and Vick needed me. I could see it in her. "Alright, yeah. I'll come back later."

She looked so pissing happy it made me sick to my stomach.

Chapter Twelve

Callum

I always knew when Sophie was coming, but I never said so. She'd run up behind me, squeeze me tight and whisper *surprise* in my ear. Felt nice, that's why I didn't say nothing, but Case always made it obvious, ears pricked up and tail going for six whenever Soph came nearby. Her furry arse would go charging off, and I'd hear Sophie shushing her, rustling in her bag for treats. Cheap bribes, but they worked every time.

Casey loved Sophie Harding, just as much as I did.

"I'm done for the day," she whispered, planting sweet hot kisses on my neck. I reached back for her, hands on her hips as she studied my canvas.

"Look alright?"

"Better than alright. It's bloody beautiful. I guess Explicit made an impression last weekend."

I smiled. It was abstract, but not abstract enough for Soph from the looks. The slashes of colour across the canvas were chains, the play of white on black was the spotlight. Then the shadows... the curves of the woman in the foreground. A woman suspended entirely in chains, wrapped up tight for her punishment.

"Diva, right?"

"Aye."

Hadn't seen Masque and Cat play again, not yet. Kinda wanted to, though. Still felt weird about all that stuff, but not weird enough to wanna stop. Floggers and paddles and handcuffs and shit were becoming second nature now, but they weren't what got me off. Owning Sophie's sweet little cunt was what got me off. Her soft moans, the way she begged. Sometimes she'd look at me like I was an animal. I liked that, but it was the other times, when she looked at me like I was a man, a somebody, they were the times I loved.

She held up a bag. "I picked up steak for dinner, some for Casey, too."

My heart sank all over again. "Can't come over tonight, Soph. Need to go to Vick's."

If she was upset it didn't show. "I'll make a date with the microwave instead, then. Steak can wait."

"You could go out," I said. "See Raven. Or your family. Don't think I ain't noticed you're avoiding them."

She smiled. "I could... alternatively, I could wait until this Southbank shit's out the way and resurface when it's back to business as usual."

I pulled her into me, breathing in her hair. "Walk your own road. Don't skulk away in the shadows, not you, Soph. That ain't your place. Nothing to be scared of."

She sighed. "I'm not scared, it's just easier. If you knew my dad you'd know what I mean."

I wanted to say something. Something stupid like maybe one day I would know him. I didn't, though. My cheeks burned at the thought. Like we could ever be *something*. It felt like it, though, sometimes, it felt like we were. That's the thing I loved most of all.

"I'd better get going," she said. "Let you get to Vicki's."

"See ya tomorrow, then."

She pulled a face. "Where's Casey staying?"

"Shed," I shrugged. "With me."

Sophie folded her arms, her mouth all stern and pursed. "You're not staying in a shed, Callum, and neither is Casey. She's an indoors pooch now, I'm taking her home."

I looked at Case staring up at Soph like she was the bee's fucking knees, tongue lolling out all happy, like.

"I dunno, Soph. She might trash everything."

She rolled her eyes. "She's already done her worst. Another bin spillage isn't going to break me."

Sophie turned on her heels and took off, calling Casey along with her. Big brown eyes stared up at me, waiting for permission. Would be weird, being without her. Would be weird being without both of them.

I shrugged. "Go on, then, Case, go after her. Go find Sophie."

***

I played with Slay before Vicki put him down for the night. Pencil crayons in front of the TV. I drew him some pictures, of Case, and his mam, and of choo-choo trains, and he scribbled all over them, eyes fixed in concentration like he was a proper little artist.

"That's great, that is," I said, holding it up. "Really good, Slay. Clever, you are, sharp little man."

His smile lit me up.

Vick was quiet when she came back down. She'd changed into her nightie, one of her posh satin things. She sat by me on the sofa, pulling her legs under her.

"He loves you," she said again. "Thinks you're the dog's bloody bollocks, that lad."

"Love him, Vick, he's a smashing kid."

"Better than his real dad. Piece of shit."

"He'll get a proper dad one day, someone nice, who can take care of him. Take care of both of you."

"*You* take care of us, Cal." She reached out for my hand, squeezing my fingers.

"Gonna get this Stoney shit sorted, Vicki. Don't worry about it."

"Ain't your problem," she said. "It should be me sorting it. I'm so sorry, Cal. I know they beat you bad, and it's my fault, innit? I fucked up."

I pulled her over, wrapped an arm round her shoulder. "Don't be daft. Wouldn't change it. Only a few scratches, anyway."

"How we gonna get twelve hundred quid together? Ty said next week or they're gonna skin your arse."

"I'll do some deliveries," I said. "Some bigger ones. The biggest fucking ones."

"They'll send you down again and where'll we be then, eh? Don't wanna be without you, Cal. Hated it when you were inside."

My nerves were on edge, sensing danger, but I smiled it all off. "Might not need to do deliveries, anyway. Not now I got the studio."

"Studio?! What studio?"

I told Vicki all about it. About Sophie setting it up for me, about her mate Raven, and Raven's art dealer contacts, and all the new paintings I'd done and everything. Vicki listened to the whole lot, wide-eyed like a doll. She didn't interrupt and didn't ask questions, just took it all in until I finished.

"Jeez, Callum, that's some crazy shit."

"Mental, innit? Me with me own bloody art studio. Maybe I'll strike lucky, eh? Sell a painting to some posh toff in his manor."

"Can I come see it? Maybe we could hang out? I could bring some sarnies down at lunchtime, bring Slay too. He'd like that."

"Over in Haygrove," I said. "Too far for you and Slay. I'll come up here, though, keep popping in."

"It ain't that far, Cal. I don't mind."

"We'll see then, yeah?"

She dropped her eyes. "It's that Sophie, innit? You're with her all the time."

"I'm with her a bit, Vick, yeah." I felt like a fucking arsehole all over again.

"Is it serious?"

"Dunno what it is." I was telling the truth. "I like her. A lot."

"And she likes you?"

"Hope so," I sighed. "Dunno."

She pulled away a bit, shrugging it off. "Bit of fun, then, I guess, ain't it? Not like you got much in common." Her words twisted in my gut harder than they should have. I felt myself clamming up, shutters coming down. "She's a posh bird, ain't she? Probably likes a bit of rough." She elbowed me in the ribs, harder than a bloody joke, but I didn't say anything. "You'll be round here again quick smart when she's had her fill."

"I'm tired now, Vick. Let's call it a night, yeah?" I pulled my hoodie up.

She looked at the clock. "Ain't even ten o'clock. Ain't getting all tetchy about lover girl, are you? I was only joking."

"Raven's coming round for them pictures in a couple of days. Got a lot to do."

She hovered in the doorway so long I couldn't bear to look. "You can come up if you want, share the bed, like. More comfy."

"I'm alright here, Vick." I smiled at her and she smiled back, but it was an empty smile.

It took her fucking ages to go upstairs, and it took me even longer to bed down for the night.

***

Sophie

"It's a bloody work night," Bex laughed. "I'll be spelling people's fucking tats wrong tomorrow if you don't stop. I'll send them round to you for compensation."

She held out her glass regardless, ready for a refill. "Just need to get you drunk enough that you don't care."

Raven looked strange in this place, infinitely more flamboyant than the neutral colour scheme. She did a funny whistle again as she eyed the place, high-pitched enough that Casey jumped up on her lap. The dog took advantage when Bex didn't push her aside, curling up between us on the sofa.

"I still can't believe this is your pad," Bex said. "It's seriously swanky. Not even Masque's pad is this neat. I'll have to bring Cara next time, make a foursome of it."

"Harding's property empire sure buys the best."

"Mood lighting, voice activated entertainment system, view of the Thames… Christ on a bike. I'm surprised Cal's comfortable breathing in this place."

"Not so sure he is," I smiled. "He still perches on the edge of the sofa, scared to dirty it."

"Seems madam here isn't so self-restrained." Raven scruffed up Casey's ears until she rolled on her back, no longer even playing at being covert in her sofa-furring mission.

"Madam is taking over the place, one soft furnishing at a time."

"I'm impressed, didn't take you for much of a dog lover."

"What's not to love?" I grinned. "Well, besides the bin raiding and nose in all the cupboards and the fur on the pillows."

"You love it all," she laughed. "And her daddy too."

"I need to ask you something." I poured the rest of the bottle in my glass.

"Sounds ominous."

"About me," I explained. "Do I seem right to you?"

"Right?"

"Sane, I mean, healthy. Regular. Normal."

She smiled. "No, you don't seem right, thank fuck."

"I'm serious. I feel like I'm off the rails."

Her eyes fixed on mine. "Isn't that what the *Mr Dangerous* quest was all about? You're breaking out, baby, that's a good thing."

"I'm being reckless, impulsive... crazy. The stunt on the balcony, I mean seriously, Bex, what the fuck was that all about?"

"You'd have been fucking dead if he'd have lost his grip," she said. "Just be grateful you got your period and let it go, it's the least of your worries now. You two are all in. It's a collision of needs, baby, two people wanting more, and veering across the road and back before they find what works."

"Sounds poetic. I think he makes me crazy."

"Maybe he does. Is that bad?" Her eyes twinkled, and I just knew there was so much more she could be saying.

"Part of me thinks it's bad. Part of me can't live without it."

She shuffled up, leaning in conspiratorially even though we were the only ones there. "Talk about him, I want to hear all the loved-up crap."

I took a breath, then glugged back some wine. "I've never met anyone like him. He doesn't have the same filters that I have, doesn't have the same massive list of shit he feels he can and can't do. He doesn't second guess himself, and sure as hell isn't worried what everyone thinks of him, or how he looks, or how he appears on social media. He's refreshingly unrestrained."

"And..." she prompted.

"And he's wild, and raw, and aggressive... he'll take what he wants, when he wants it. He doesn't live in fear of convention. He doesn't hold back."

She smiled. "And..."

I sighed. "More?"

"Keep rolling, baby."

"And he's deep. He's a beautiful tragedy. A beautiful savage. The way he looks at the world, the way he paints... the way he loves."

"Now who's poetic?"

I whacked her with a cushion. "Told you I was fucking crazy."

"You're not crazy, baby. You're in love."

"That *is* fucking crazy, Bex. How can it ever work?"

She sighed, putting her glass down. "Please don't take this where I think it's headed."

"My job... my family..."

"Can all get stuffed," she cut in. "You either love him, or you don't, but make that decision for yourself, not for anyone else. The kid's got some issues, but he's a good kid, Sophie. Don't kick him to the kerb for the sake of lousy bloody convention, you're fucking better than that."

I really hoped so.

***

I sat bolt upright in bed, heart thumping. My ears strained, battling through the clouds in my muggy, alcohol-impaired brain. Casey was growling in the darkness, staring out into the space beyond the door.

I sighed in relief when I heard the knocking. Casey's tail brushed my arm, wagging like crazy, and her growls changed to whines as I padded to the doorway.

"Callum?"

"Yeah."

I opened the door, glancing at the oven clock. "Jeez, it's gone four a.m."

He brushed past, brooding, his hands stuffed in his pockets. Aside from saying hello to Casey he didn't utter a word, just pressed up against the doorway, staring. I could feel his eyes on me, gorgeous and feral. An old cotton nightshirt really hadn't been the most flattering choice of sleeping attire, but I hadn't been expecting him. I wrapped my arms around myself.

"What happened?"

He shook his head. Shrugged.

"You walked over from East Veil?"

"Yeah."

"Christ." I flicked the kitchen light on. "Want a coffee?"

No response.

"Wasn't expecting this," I said, filling the kettle. "I thought you were staying at Vicki's. I expected..."

I squealed as he slammed up behind, forcing me forward until I bashed into the running tap, cold water spraying over my shirt. The cotton clung like a second skin, cold and slick to my breasts as Callum's hot breath stroked my ear. The shock broke through my wine coma, and I was wide awake, heart quickening.

"Need you." His words were just a grunted whisper. "Now."

This was the animal Callum, the savage who gave me shivers, the man who made my pussy ache on sight. I dropped the kettle in the sink, using my hands as leverage to grind back against him. I could feel his hard on swelling through his jeans, pulsing against the crack of my ass.

His rough hands on my tits, twisting my nipples through the

fabric.

The cramps in my stomach reminded me of an unfortunate truth.

"Fuck, Callum," I groaned. "I can't."

He wasn't deterred, grabbing at my tits without restraint.

"Cal, stop. I'm on my period."

He grunted, but still he persisted, reaching down to claw at the hem of my nightdress. He yanked it over my head before I could object. I cringed at the reality of him seeing my period panties. I tried to move from his grip but he was having none of it.

"Need you," he growled. "Don't fucking care."

I cared. I cared a lot. I shifted against him, fighting my own desperation for his cock. His fingers pressed into the padding between my legs, hunting for my clit.

"Shit, Callum..."

"Gonna take you," he said. "Don't fight me."

My throat let out a pitiful squeak of self-consciousness as his thumb hooked inside the waist of my panties. I trembled against him, hating myself for not fighting harder. I moaned out in defeat as his fingers slid between my thighs."

"Fuck," he said. "Feels so nice."

Yes it did, he wasn't fucking lying. He dropped to a crouch, low enough to slide the fabric down around my hips. My underwear dropped to the floor, and I was naked and exposed.

"Gonna fuck you," he hissed.

Two fingers inside me made me groan like a whore. "Yes..."

"I wanna see you."

I groaned, all out of words.

"Wanna see your cunt bleed. Need to smell you."

Oh my fucking God. The squelching between my legs reeled my senses, but he felt too fucking good. I let him turn me, let him guide me, let him shunt me across the kitchen with his filthy wet hand between my thighs until we reached the bathroom doorway. I gasped at our reflection in the full-length mirror. My thighs were already dripping scarlet, bloody trails snaking their way to my ankles. His fingers squelched as he withdrew, an earthy metallic taint in the air as he clamped his bloodied hand across my tit.

I didn't want to watch, but I couldn't take my eyes off my own body, squirming for just a moment as he clasped the same bloodied hand around my throat. Crimson smears across pale skin.

"So pretty," he said. "I fucking like it."

"Fuck me..." I breathed. "Do it."

He pulled off his clothes in a flash, dumping his jeans to the floor as I watched his reflection. He was so gorgeous, absolutely fucking beautiful. I let out a grunt as he slipped his way inside. I parted so easy for his cock, so fucking wet. My pussy made such dirty noises, but none so dirty as him.

He pulled at my hair, hissing filth in my ear as he thrust inside. His fingers frigged my clit, dancing just where I needed them, and I was gone, groaning like a dirty fucking whore as the sensations took over. He came hard, faster than usual. His eyes were fierce all the way, holding my gaze right the way through until he was spent. He dropped me like a stone, catching his breath. The dark nest of his pubes was glistening red, his cock still twitching amidst the scarlet lake spreading down between his thighs. His hands were bloody, his chest too, and he looked fucking magnificent for it. Like a warrior back from battle, decorated with the blood of his conquests.

That's when I got him. Really got him. Callum Jackson was no Masque in the making. Masque was filthy to the extreme, but he was considered, controlled, polished to a mirror shine. Callum Jackson was a wild animal, governed by raw instinct, the feral urge for sex, and sweat, and blood, and heaving, writhing, primal fucking flesh. His eyes were savage, his hair unkempt, his muscles taut as strung wire. *He* was savage.

"You came back for that, didn't you?" I whispered. "You came back to claim what's yours."

"Is it?" he barked. "Is this mine?"

I looked down at the mess on my skin. "What do you think?"

"Dunno, Soph, don't fucking know." I made for the shower but he grabbed my wrist, pulling me so hard I slammed into his chest. "Never needed nothing, not from anyone. Not like this. I need this, Soph. Can't fucking lose it."

"This is fucking crazy, we're both fucking mad."

"Can live with crazy," he said. "Just can't live alone."

I touched his face, brushing a thumb over dark brows. "You aren't alone, Cal, not anymore."

"Say it, then," he snapped. "If you mean it, say it. Don't fucking lie, though, Sophie, if this ain't real for you then don't fucking pretend."

The words came easy, too fucking easy. "I love you, Cal. That real enough for you? That what you needed to hear?"

He buried his face in my hair, arms tighter around me than I'd ever felt.

I was happy enough to ignore the dread in my stomach, happy enough to kick the practicalities out of sight.

Happier still when we heard the bin crash over in the kitchen, and the night returned to normal.

***

Chapter Thirteen

Callum

"It's time, kid." Raven was smiling, but I struggled to smile back.

I'd been working all pissing day, trying to get these paintings ready for the dealer. Nothing I did looked right. They were all shit.

"Not ready."

"They're ready," she said. "Trust me, baby."

"He won't fucking like them," I snapped. "They're total fucking shit."

She slapped my hands away from the paints like I was a little kid at nursery. I didn't mind with her, though, didn't mind anything she bloody did.

"It's ok to be nervous. The best artists always are."

She started arranging my canvases, lining them up for transport. I gave in, letting her take what she wanted, too pissing late for nerves now.

"No Sophie?"

"In meetings all day."

"No rest for the wicked, hey?" I flinched as she uncovered the final canvas, heart pounding like a fucking freight train. "Oh, baby."

Her eyes were wide and sparkly, just like on the painting. "Did it for you. For your girlfriend, like," I grunted.

It was my favourite of them all, the one of Raven. She looked just like when I'd met her, eyes so twinkly and skin so alive. I'd painted her with a black cigarette, the hint of a smile as she breathed out smoke into a night sky. I wasn't expecting the crush of her arms around my neck, the warmth of her lips on my cheek. She felt good against me, with her strange hair and her strange clothes and her strange smell. Not clingy like when Vick did it, just nice.

"I love it," she breathed. "I really fucking love it, kid. Thank you."

I shrugged as she let go of me. "Weren't nothing much."

"Whatever you say, baby." A taxi pulled up outside, stopping right in front of the garage. "That's my ride, straight to dealer HQ. Sure you don't want to come?"

I shook my head. "Nah, you're alright."

"Don't you go slacking off on me now. We'll be needing more pieces for the exhibition."

My heart notched up another gear. "What exhibition?"

She smiled so fucking bright. "Only the biggest fucking London exhibition this side of Christmas, baby. Gallery's got a display, right up with the big boys, finest on the market. Current stuff too, a lot of urban, some modern. You'll be there, Cal, you mark my words. Jack's gonna shit a brick when he sees this stuff."

"Don't joke," I said. "Ain't fucking funny."

Her red mouth narrowed into a vicious flash. "I never fucking joke about art, kid, and I'd never fucking joke with you."

"Sorry." I put my hands in my hair, pacing about the place. "Just dunno what to think."

"It's a lot to take in."

"Aye. Lot on my mind."

I'd been waiting for it for weeks, but it still landed hard when it arrived. "You did tell Sophie, didn't you? About the Stoneys?" I didn't answer, just stared at my feet so I wouldn't see her face.

"Pissing hell, kid. I told you I'd keep my mouth shut, but you have to fucking tell her. She can help, it's no money to her, Cal, not with parents like hers."

"I don't want her money."

"Yeah, well, we don't want you fucking dead. She'll flip her fucking lid when she finds out you didn't tell her, and I'll be next in the firing line."

"I'll sort it."

"You'd better, baby, or I'll fucking tell her for you."

I guessed she weren't joking about that, neither.

***

Sophie

I'd been in crappy meetings all morning, itching to get away and make sure the great art collection had gone down without incident. Cal had been brooding to shit over the past few days, nerves kicking in. He wouldn't say that, of course, just shrugged it off as nothing.

My phone beeped as I stepped off the tube, and I fumbled in my bag for the handset, expecting a berating text from Bex. The reality was worse. So much fucking worse.

I have my sister stored in my phone under her full name. *Alexandra Juliette Allison Harding*. What the fuck did she want?

The text made it crystal clear.

Four missed Sundays and a complaint letter with your name on it. Tut, tut. Dad going ballistic. Be home at seven, I'm coming over.

I text back instantly.

Complaint letter?? Not convenient tonight. Busy, sorry.

We were having steak, Callum's favourite. Steak and sex, and probably more sex on the side. My phone pinged again before I could even switch the thing off.

Non negotiable. Call it an official landlord visit. Rather me than Dad, trust me.

My blood froze in my face. Reality knocking so hard I pulled up where I stood, brain spinning. I pictured the apartment; the dog-clawed sofa, the shredded cushions, the lacerated door panels. The dog bowls, the fur everywhere, Callum's measly belongings on the dresser. Fuck. Serious fucking fuck.

Make it eight, yeah?

I crossed my fucking fingers.

Seven thirty. I won't be late.

That was the best I was going to pissing get.

***

Only one canvas remained in the garage. Callum's work in progress was a six foot cityscape. Along the bottom of the image lay a dying man, and a crowd were huddled around him, taking selfies, smiling pretty for the camera.

"Feels like that," he said. "Round East Veil, anyway."

He was pensive, sitting on his stool, eyes downcast.

"It's going to be great," I smiled. "Better than great. Bex says the dealer really rates your work. He's going to love this one."

"Maybe."

"There's no maybe about it, Callum Jackson." I squeezed his muscled shoulders from behind. "You're a star."

"Don't feel much like one." He reached up for my hands, pulling me forward until I was flat to his back. I folded my arms around his chest, breathing him in. "Just wanna go home." *Home. He called it home.* "Need to talk and need to fuck. Need to be where you are."

"Talk? What about?" The hair on the back of my neck prickled at his tone.

"Just some shit going down. We'll talk about it later, yeah?"

I let out a sigh, but it didn't ease the nerves in my gut any. Here goes nothing. "About later," I said, "something's come up."

He spun around on his stool, guiding my hand to the heat of his crotch. "Something's coming up, alright. Can't wait to fuck you."

"I'm serious," I groaned. "I'm going to have to give this evening a miss. Sorry."

He looked taken aback. "You got plans?"

"No... Yes... it's complicated. Got some family crap kicking off, I'll call you when I'm done, though."

"I could help?" The look in his eyes was so genuine, it broke my heart to shoot him down.

"There's nothing for you to help with. I'll call when I'm done, first chance I get."

He shrugged. "Alright. I'll go to Vick's. Crash on her sofa 'till I can come over. We'll talk, though, yeah? Later?"

I swallowed the panic in my throat, head swimming with cleaning chores, and DIY and explanations. "Of course."

He started clearing his paints, putting them ever so neatly back on their racks. "Case can go with you, she don't like Vick's shed no more."

"Casey's probably better off with you," I said. "I'll be busy, and it's difficult... you know... taking care of her."

His eyes narrowed. "You don't wanna take Case?"

"It's not that I don't *want* to," I sighed. "Can't I just see you both later? Please?"

"Guess that'll have to do."

I kissed his beautiful mouth, lips tight against his like I never wanted to leave. I wished I was brave enough to tell my sister to get stuffed, hand in my notice on the property and set up a new life on my own. I could do. I could stand tall, hold my ground, tell them that I loved my job, and I loved that dog, and I loved Callum Jackson, too.

The flare of panic along my spine didn't agree.

Casey whined her furry head off as I left, big brown eyes following me along the path. I looked back over my shoulder at the low swing of her tail, the tilt of her head as she waited for the whistle.

And then I kept walking.

***

Callum

"Thank fuck you're here." Vicki was in her usual spot, puffing like crazy on a roll-up. "Had Ty over here again. He said we've got three days, Cal. Three bastard days!" Her hands were shaking life a leaf, tiny and white. "Where we gonna get fifteen hundred from in three days?"

"Fifteen hundred?!" I snapped. "It's twelve we owe."

"Interest," she said. "They want fifteen or there'll be trouble. He weren't messing around, Cal. I know him, he looked wired, but he weren't bluffing. They're coming for us. Oh God, Cal, what about Slay?"

"Chill the fuck out, Vick. Ain't nobody coming for you, I'll sort it."

"How?" Her eyes were desperate, scared like Casey's were when I found her on the street, wet and cold and hungry and so fucking sad. "I should pack, go to Mam's. You could come too, Cal, hide out til we get it together. Maybe your mate Sophie could get us one of them mutual exchanges? We could move. We could put you on the tenancy too, if you wanted."

I reached out for her tobacco, itching for a roll-up. "Gotta talk to you, Vicki. Been needing to say it for a while. Sophie ain't just a mate, Vick. Not anymore. We won't be getting no exchange, neither. You're staying here."

She stopped breathing, I swear. Just hovered without any words, staring at me like I'd taken a crap on her doorstep. "You *with* her? Like Facebook-official?"

"Not like on pissing Facebook," I groaned. "But, yeah, official. Said she loves me."

The memory felt warm in my chest, a good feeling.

Vicki made this horrible scoffing sound, just like my mam used to make when I said I was gonna be an artist one day. It went right through me, pulsed straight to my fists. Then she laughed, a cackley laugh. Didn't suit her like it suits Raven. "Loves you, does she?! Pissing hell, Callum, I've heard it all now."

"She does," I snapped. "Ain't nobody ever said that to me before, Vicki, nobody. I love her, too. Gonna get her to help us out, just until this art stuff comes through."

Her mouth shrivelled up like she'd been chomping on something sour. "Have you even listened to yourself lately? *Sophie loves me, says I'm her boyfriend.* Whatever, Callum. Like someone like her's ever gonna be with one of us. She don't even bloody know you, Cal."

"I am her boyfriend, Vick. I swear down."

She jabbed her hands in the air like some kind of crazy. "Where is she, then, this girlfriend of yours? Why ain't she come over with you, sat down and met your friends? Where's *her* friends? Have you met them? Met the family? Where's her Facebook status, eh? Last time I checked it said 'single', Cal, I've been checking her out. Bet she ain't gonna be changing it, neither. Posh bitch like her ain't gonna admit to being with someone like you, Callum Jackson, she's playing you for a fucking fool, man."

"Dunno about her status, Vick, you know I ain't on that shit. I've met her friends, though. They're cool."

"What about her fucking family, then? She's from that Harding lot, saw her old man in the paper last week selling that mansion down Billionaire's Row to some foreign king or some shit. Think he's gonna have you round for family dinner, do ya? *Oh, Callum, pass me a cucumber sandwich, will you? There's a good fellow.*"

"Don't be like this, Vick," I hissed.

"Someone's gotta be!" she snapped. "Someone's gotta give a shit enough to talk sense into that thick skull of yours. She's messing with you! Likes a bit of rough, no doubt, wants to feel like a bad girl. She's a stupid, selfish, stuck-up bitch."

"She ain't," I barked. "She fucking ain't, Vicki." My temper was flaring, getting close to the edge. "Don't be jealous, alright? You're my best mate, always will be. Ain't nothing gonna change just 'cause I got a girlfriend."

Her eyes were so angry. "Jealous?! Of her?! I ain't fucking jealous, Cal, I'm fucking looking out for ya."

"If you say so."

"I do fucking say so. You ain't all that much, Callum, and it's no good thinking you are. Just 'cause you got yourself a posh fuck buddy and some crappy garage down Haygrove. It don't make you Brad bloody Pitt. You're Callum bloody Jackson from East Veil, always bloody will be."

I stayed quiet, fighting back the urge to punch her spiteful little mouth. I felt that twinge in me, right down deep, the one that says I'm no fucking good and never will be. Vicki just kept on going.

"What the fuck you doing here, then, eh? If you're so bloody in love?"

"Came to see you."

"Why's Casey here? She weren't last time. Shed wasn't good enough for her the other day. Not today, though, eh?"

"Sophie's just busy, got some shit to do. She's calling later."

"Ah, so she's your girlfriend, but she's got some shit to do, so you can't go *home*..."

"Ain't like that. Thought you'd be pleased to fucking see me."

She laughed so fucking mean again. "She's probably off with her real boyfriend. Some posh guy who talks nice but don't fuck so good. That's why she's with you, Cal, make no mistake about it. She just wants your big fucking cock."

"Shut up, Vick."

"What's she busy with?"

"Dunno. Don't matter."

She shrugged. "Fucking soft, you are. Playing you for a right fucking fool, she is."

"I could go *home* now if I wanted, wouldn't matter." My mind flashed back to Roger in his stupid posh suit, fucking her in the room next door and laughing about me. "She's for real, Vick. I'm gonna bring her round here soon, so you can meet her properly."

"Why wait? Ring her now. Get her over here. I can say thanks for the money."

"Told ya, she's busy."

"Busy with another man's dick. Probably laughing about us poor people as she sucks on his gold-encrusted bollocks."

She'd pushed it too far. Way too fucking far. I slammed my fist into the wall by her head, shredding my knuckles on the brickwork. "Lucky I'm your fucking mate, Vicki Pollock, but I'd shut your nasty fucking mouth before I forget."

She shoved me, shunting me down the yard. "Go on, then, fuck off to her, if that's what you want. You'll be back, crying in my fucking arms when she shits all over you. We'll see who your friends are then."

"Yeah, we fucking will." I turned away before I throat-punched her, pulling my hood up and disappearing while she was still raving in the street. I didn't need to whistle Casey, she was as pleased as I was to be out of the fucking place.

I heard Vicki calling, squealing at me to go back, but there was only one place I was headed.

"Let's go where we belong, Case," I said. "Let's go find Sophie."

Her waggy tail sure agreed with that idea.

***

Took me a fair while to get there, but it didn't matter. I took the time to plan it out, rehearsing how I'd sit down with Sophie and tell her everything, all about the Stoneys and Vicki and the trouble I was in. I'd ask her for help and I'd pay her back. I wished I had some cash to buy her something nice, something to say thanks. Passed by some hotels with them posh plants outside and took the opportunity, pulling off some pretty flowers and bunching them inside my hoodie. I'd never got flowers for anyone before, never felt like I'd wanted to, but Sophie deserved all the flowers in the world, even if they were nicked.

I tried to push the fear away. She'd be cleaning, or summat. Having a girl's night in with Raven where they could talk and laugh and share stories about all their BDSM stuff. Maybe she had something special planned, some special outfit or something like that. An image of that twat Roger came to mind. What if she was … no, Roger wouldn't be there. No fucking way.

It would fucking destroy me if he was.

Was gone seven by the time we reached Canary Wharf. Casey picked up pace, bounding along ahead until she'd squat on the pavement with her tail going, itching for me to chase her. I shot after her several times and she'd bark her head off, jumping up on her back legs with her paws against my chest, tongue lolling like a goof while I fussed her.

"Good girl," I'd say. "Know where home is now, don't ya? Know where we belong."

I felt a prick over Vicki, but she'd asked for it. I'd make it up to her, and I'd show her, too. Show her what a nice person Sophie Harding was, and all the great things I saw in her. Maybe they could be friends one day.

Casey bolted straight through the foyer and into the lift, she even pawed at the right button, knowing the drill by now. "Hold your horses," I laughed. "She's only upstairs. We'll be there in a minute."

I got the flowers ready, purple and white things with a couple of roses. They were a bit battered but I straightened them out best I could. I pictured her face, smiling at me like I'd brought her the crown jewels. She'd like them, for sure.

My heart stuttered for a minute outside the door, ears straining for a hint of Roger. Of course he wouldn't be there. Not a chance.

Sophie opened the door straight away, but rather than smiling she jolted backwards, eyes fucking wild. She was dressed up smart, in a posh little suit like she wore to work, her make-up all perfect and hair curled under her chin.

"Surprise," I said, shoving the flowers at her. She took them, but didn't smell them, didn't say anything. My heart dropped through the floor, but I smiled anyway, pushing past her to get inside.

"We said I'd call," she snapped. "I'm not ready yet."

"*You* said you'd call," I said. "I just went along with it, thought it'd be a surprise and I could help." I looked around the place. It was clean right through, with no sign of Casey's bowls or the cushions she'd trashed. The sofa was turned the other way around, to hide where she'd been scratching it. I choked back the dread, stomping on through to the bedroom where the few bits of shit I had were missing. "What's going on?"

"Nothing," she hissed. "I've just got some things to do." She looked at the clock, nervous. "You need to go, Callum, just for a few hours."

"Why?" I folded my arms, throat all tight.

"I've got someone coming. Trust me, you won't want to meet them."

I fucking knew it. Deep down I knew. "It's Roger, ain't it? You're seeing fucking Roger."

Her pretty face turned dark. "Of course it's not fucking Roger! What the fuck, Cal? Are you fucking serious?"

"Who then?"

"My sister," she spat. "She's coming over."

The relief flooded over me like the fountain of fucking life. I smiled. "Shit, Soph, you had me worried pissing sick there. That's cool about your sister, should have said." I went through to the kitchen, flicked the kettle on. "I could've helped tidy up." I took a sniff under my armpits, they held up alright. "Could've had a shower, too. Wanna make a good impression, like."

Her expression pissed all over my parade. I didn't have time to react before the doorbell went again. Casey barked and Sophie flinched, waving her arms around in a panic. "Oh fuck," she said. "Jesus Christ, Callum, Jesus Christ. Please just play along, will you? For God's sake just play along."

I didn't know what she meant until she opened the door. Sophie's sister was taller than she was. A skinny thing with longer hair. Her nose was bigger, but she was pretty too. She sure didn't look pleased to be there, clomping her way in with heels and a clipboard under her arm.

Sophie's sister eyed me like a piece of crap on her shoe, and all thoughts I had of a great family introduction were smashed into pieces. "I didn't realise you had *guests*," she said.

I met Sophie's eyes and they were desperate, frantic. They were cold. "They were just leaving," she said. She ushered me into the hallway before I could react, Casey, too. "Thanks for dropping by," she hissed. "I'll check with the allocations team on Monday, Mr Jackson, see if we can get your application moving along. If you could call into the office I'll sort out the additional paperwork."

I stared in shock, from Sophie, to her snotty sister and back again. I raised my eyebrows, begging her to say something, anything. To backtrack and introduce me properly, tell her sister how happy she is with me, how much I mean to her.

She didn't say fucking anything, just opened the door and shooed me out like a fucking rodent.

She mouthed sorry before she closed the door in my face.

And I skulked back to the fucking sewer where I belonged.

***

Chapter Fourteen

Sophie

"That's a turn up for the books," Alexandra spat. "I thought *this* was a pile of horseshit, but clearly not." She waved the piece of paper in my face, but I couldn't make out any of it. "A complaint letter," she expanded. "Claiming you have a dog in the property and *undesirables* living here. This is Canary Wharf, Sophie, not one of your poxy council estates. We can't have people like *that* here. How on earth does it look?!"

My chest was still paining, torn into pieces by the hurt in Callum's eyes. In that one last moment, as I'd closed the door in his face, I hadn't seen the savage standing there, I'd seen the boy who'd thrown his pens from his shitty mother's balcony. A hurt, defeated, broken little boy.

Yet still I fucking lied. Still I held onto appearances like they fucking mattered.

"He's a tenant," I said.

"Sure he is," she snapped. "Don't insult my intelligence, Sophie. The guy looked at you like you were candy on a stick. He seemed pretty comfortable here, too, for a tenant."

"He's been around a few times. I'm helping him."

"Is that what they call it these days? Really, Sophie, you need to recalibrate your tastes and select something more becoming of you."

"Why are you here?" I stomped in her direction, folding my arms across my chest. "You've seen the place, now go. Write it up on your little form and get out of my business."

"This place *is* my business, and *you* are a lousy tenant." She kicked at the sofa, and my attempt to hide the damage looked pitiful. "That's *his* dog, then, is it?"

"Yes."

"So, who's dog has trashed *our* property?"

"It's not trashed," I seethed. "It just needs a bit of patching up."

I flinched as she shoved the door shut, rubbing down the tatty paint on the other side. "Patching up? You are joking? The place is a travesty."

"It's hardly a travesty!" I hissed. "It's got a bit of wear and tear."

"Maybe this is wear and tear by *your* poor people housing association standards, but believe me, we set the bar a little higher at Hardings."

"Sue me, then."

"Not planning on suing you, Sophie, just evicting you."

"You can't be serious. Over some scratches on the back of the door?!"

"Over destruction of property and breach of tenancy conditions. Our terms clearly state no pets, and reading between the lines would have made it damned clear that people like *him* aren't welcome here."

The gall of the woman took me aback. I stared into her spiteful eyes, reaching for the gangly teenager underneath the veneer. "People like *him*? You've got a short memory, Alex. People in glass houses…"

She shifted, uncomfortable. "That was years ago."

"Yes, it was. I'm sure Daddy would see it that way, too."

"You wouldn't!" she scoffed. "That's ridiculous."

"So's this," I said. "This is totally ridiculous, and you know it. Dad's trying to prove a point, about me choosing another career path rather than toeing the line like a good little Harding. But *you*. Why are *you* here, Alex?"

"It's my job."

"Cut the crap," I seethed. "Miss Self-righteous needs to take a long hard look in the mirror."

"I was a teenager," she snarled. "And I was grateful for your help."

"Grateful for my discretion."

"That too," she huffed. "Fucking hell, Sophie, does the guy really mean this much to you? Dad will never go along with it, and you know it."

My heart pounded. "I want the dog here. You'll have to swing it."

"The dog? Are you serious?"

"Deadly," I snapped. "I'll repair the damage, just keep quiet, will you? Like I did."

"I had an abortion not a tenancy breach. There weren't that many people around to make official complaints about *my* screw-up."

"Be creative, then," I insisted. "Hide it from Dad."

She blustered around the place, but I kept it calm. "Alright!" she said, finally. "I'll head off the dog complaints, but you're on your own with the relationship shit. If Dad finds out it will be your eviction, and most likely your funeral too."

"I'm aware of that," I said.

She ticked a load of boxes on her little form and made to leave. Finally. She hovered in the doorway, eyes softer than I'd known them. "About the abortion, and Jason, and the coke and all that. Thanks. I never said it properly at the time."

"You're welcome."

She smiled, a conspiratorial smile, leaning in close to make her confession. "I've got a dog too. Maybe we could go walk them someday."

She could have knocked me over with a feather. "You don't seem like the dog type."

"Neither do you," she said. "Mine's a pedigree, of course. Yorkshire terrier. Dad doesn't know about it."

"Seems we've all got our secrets, doesn't it?"

"Don't all families?" she smiled. "Seriously, though, if you want to keep a smooth ride please do just come along to the Southbank opening. It will get us all off your case, especially Dad."

I nodded. "I'll think about it."

She turned back in the doorway for a passing comment. "I'd go after him, if I were you. The guy looked like you'd ripped his bloody heart out. Looks like he'd eat glass for breakfast, but you, you've floored him. Well and truly."

It was the most sensible suggestion I'd heard from her in years.

***

I called and I called, pacing around the apartment and biting my nails until they hurt. I left messages he'd probably never hear, just so desperate to hear him pick up.

"Callum, I'm sorry. I fucked up, ok? It's my stupid family, not you. I love you. Please come home."

Nothing.

I took his things from the wardrobe, lay them back where they'd been. He had nothing much, just a couple of t-shirts and a spare pair of jeans. A few odd socks and a can of deodorant. I'd even hidden his toothbrush for Alex's visit. I took it out of the medicine cupboard and put it back on the rack. Shit, what a bitch I was.

I'd thrown his flowers down by the bin out of sight. They were wilting already, battered and pathetic looking. I put them in water, willed them to survive.

They had to survive. *We* had to survive.

When I hadn't heard from him by eleven I called a taxi. I sat silent in the backseat, staring out of the window and hating myself for the stupid choices I'd made, but hating myself more for being such a coward.

The garage was locked up and dark, no sign of life. I rode on, jumping out at the retail units and taking the rest on foot. I had no idea where I was looking, but the moment the taxi pulled away I felt totally out of my depth. This place was red-flagged in the daylight, coming here after dark was insanity.

A collection of girls from tower one were drinking on the benches. I approached with caution, and they laughed as they caught sight of me.

"Have any of you seen Callum Jackson?"

One girl spat out her vodka, giggling her stupid slutty face off. "I seen him. Enough of him to want to see him again…"

"Tonight," I said. "Have you seen him tonight?"

"Had a lover's tiff, 'ave ya?"

"Just tell me, will you?"

The girl stood up, breathing alcohol fumes too close for comfort. "You can't tell me what to do here, Miss Snotty. You ain't on office time."

"Please," I tried. "I need to find him."

"Saw him earlier," her blonde friend said. "Over by tower two. You know the alley, down by the old newsagents?"

I did know it. Knew it well enough to remember landing my ass on the tarmac. "Yes, thank you."

I ignored the catty comments all the way down the street, relieved to cross out of earshot. The relief didn't last long, not when I registered movement in the shadows. Two figures, big and dressed in black. I tried to ignore them, holding my head high as though my confidence was a shield. Maybe it would be.

I changed my mind on that as they closed in by the old alleyway, heading me off at the pass.

"Alright, Miss Perky Tits," one of them sneered. "We got something for ya. Wanna see?"

"No," I snapped. "I really fucking don't."

"Think you do," his mate said. "Think you'll fucking enjoy it."

"Please excuse me," I said. "I don't have time for any crap."

The two bodies came closer, backing me into the wall. "Should make time for this," one of them said. "I'm telling ya, you'll enjoy it."

"Get off me," I hissed, realising way too fucking late that those bitches had set me up. I shrieked as a hand landed on my breast, squeezing hard through my blouse.

"Nice rack. Hope your cunt's as juicy as your tits."

"Please," I hissed. "Just let me go. I'm the estate manager here, you must know me."

"You ain't no estate manager at this time of night," they laughed. "Just fucking take what you're offered, bitch. We'll take turns. Or you can take us both at once, one in the pink and one in the brown." Foul breath in my face, lips too close to me.

A rough hand crawled under my skirt, fingers jamming between my clenched thighs. I closed my eyes, breath hitching in my throat. "Spread 'em," he breathed. "Show us what you got. Gonna fuck you real good."

I screamed blue murder as his skull bounced off the wall. It made a cracking thwack sound, loud in my ear as his body thumped to the floor. His friend broke for cover, lurching away on skittish legs. He didn't get far, taken down to his knees by a well angled kick to the small of his back. I watched in horror as the savage pulled him back upright, pounding his face until there was only a bloodied mess. Callum was a demon in the darkness, a flailing hulk of grunting muscle. I listened to his ragged breath, the hiss of his anger through his teeth.

The body at my feet was barely moving. I sighed in relief as he groaned in pain, thanking fucking God he wasn't dead. I considered calling an ambulance, but Callum was already at me, dragging me away before I could get my thoughts together. I felt Casey's fur against my legs as he pulled me down the dark pathway, the swish of her tail across my arse. Thank fuck for that.

Once we turned the corner Callum slammed me almost as hard as he'd slammed my attacker. I squealed fresh as my head grazed the wall.

"What the fuck were you thinking?!" he seethed. "Could'a got yourself fucking raped, or worse. Are you fucking crazy?!"

He stalked away into the shadows where I couldn't see. I could hear him, though. His breathing hard as he paced.

"Shit, Callum, I was looking for you. I'm so fucking sorry about Alex. I should have told you she was coming."

"Don't matter now," he barked. "Know where I stand."

"You don't!" I said. "It's not how it looked."

"It's exactly how it fucking looked!" he yelled. "I'm fucking nothing to you, am I?! Just a piece of fucking meat. Liked it, didn't ya, fucking the fucking savage?! Liked my filthy cock in your ass, in your cunt, in your fucking face."

"That isn't what this is!" I hissed. "I promise."

He lunged from the shadows, pinning me like he'd done on the very first day we'd met. His body was a wall of hot iron against mine, chest heaving with every raspy breath. I stared up into hollow eyes, faint orange streetlight the only illumination in the night. Callum was magnificent in his anger, arms rigid as they caged me, jaw clenched tight with rage. "Wanted it rough, didn't ya? So fucking rough. Posh guys don't fuck like me, do they? Too much to lose, too much to give a fuck about to really scare you."

"That isn't right," I said. "It isn't like that."

His teeth pressed to my cheek. "You used me."

"No, I didn't."

"You don't fucking want me, just my cock."

"No!"

"She looked at me like I was a piece of shit, and you didn't say a fucking word. Not a fucking word. You threw me back onto the street like a used rubber."

"I wasn't throwing you out!" I screeched. "I just needed some time."

"YOU THREW ME OUT! Just like me fucking mam did. Ain't nobody wants a monster like me, do they? I ain't worth fucking shit!"

I flinched as he kicked out at the wall, landing his foot right between my legs and only just missing my knee. "I didn't throw you out, Callum, I swear."

"Didn't want me no more, did ya? Not when she was there. Judged me like her, didn't ya? Ashamed."

"I'm not ashamed."

"YOU WERE!" He took my wrists in one hand to hold them high, clamping his fingers tight around my throat. "Don't follow me," he growled. "Stay the fuck away."

I rubbed my neck while he retreated, my hand on Casey's back until she followed.

I hobbled my way along after him. My progress was slow and awkward, breath loud in my ears as I tried to follow in his footsteps.

A doggy whine alerted me to their location. It rang out just once, from my left, down by the bin storage.

"Callum?" I croaked. "Are you there?"

A security light glowed dull as I stepped into the trash yard. It was a stinky shithole, black bins pilled high along the walls. A couple of wheeled bins had been tipped on their side, spilling recycling waste across the tarmac.

"Callum?"

"You must have a fucking death wish." The light here suited him, caressed the hard lines of his face.

"I won't give up," I said. "I love you too much."

"Love my fucking cock, you mean."

"I love more than your cock, Callum."

He circled me like a lone wolf would hunt deer, eyes heavy and considered. "I'm a savage," he said. "That's what you want from me."

"No."

"You don't know where I've been, what I've seen. Don't know what I've done, Sophie. What I had to do to survive."

"Stop it," I snapped. "Please, Callum. Please let's just go home." I held out a hand but he didn't take it.

"You wet for me? I bet you are. You like it fucking dangerous."

"I like it at home," I said. "Let's go."

"Wanna play hard, is that it?"

"I want to you to come home!"

"Home? Here's my home, amongst the shit and the piss and the trash. Here's where *I* belong, Sophie. Wanna see who I am?"

"I know who you are!" I hissed. "And I know I hurt you, I know that. I didn't mean to!"

He pulled his hoodie off over his head. His chest was so fucking beautiful in that light. The darkness played with his tattoos, casting orange shadows over the plains of his chest. I sucked in my breath. He was so fucking beautiful. His abs rippled as he moved, the V of his hips trailing away under the low hang of his jeans.

"Run," he growled.

"No."

"You'd better."

"Never."

"I'll hurt you. Tear you apart. Take what I want."

I dropped my bag, shrugged off my jacket to leave me in just a flimsy blouse and a short skirt. "I'm yours."

"You ain't mine. Never have been."

"I'll prove it," I rasped. "Do whatever you want, you'll never get me to leave."

"That a fucking promise, is it?" he seethed. "Wanna make it up to me now? Too fucking late."

"Do it, Callum. Make me yours."

"SHUT UP!" he boomed.

Casey whined again from the shadows and he hissed her to be quiet. My clammy fingers fumbled with the buttons on my blouse, "You want this?"

He stopped pacing for a moment, dark eyes roving my skin. "Don't."

I slipped out of the blouse, let it drop to the floor. "What do I have to do, Callum? Tell me?"

"Fuck off," he said. "For your own good."

"No." I stood proud, with my shoulders back and head high. "Show me your worst."

I backed away as he lunged, but only for a moment. His grip was savage at the nape of my neck, twisting my head and driving me down onto all fours. He dragged me along by my hair as my knees grazed along the floor.

"*This* is who I am," he spat. "*This* is where I come from."

He pushed my face into the stack of rubbish bins, burying my nose amongst the stink until I retched. Only then did he let go, turning attention to the mounds of trash instead. He tore up the bags like a lunatic, spilling armfuls of filth and crap onto the tarmac. I heard the smashing of glass, the rattle of tin cans, and all around me the slop of residue filled my nostrils like an acrid soup.

Callum dropped to his knees at my side. His hands were rough as they hitched up my skirt, and rougher still as he tore into the flimsy lace of my panties. He bunched them up in his hand, then stuffed them into my mouth, shoving them in all the way to the back. I gagged on the fabric, my own taste ripe on my tongue.

"Keep fucking quiet."

The slime on the floor was cold around my knees. I groaned into my gag as the rancid sea reached my hands.

"Smell that. The scent of fucking survival." He sniffed it all in, revelling in the stench. "Never had to look through other people's leftovers for your dinner, have ya? Wouldn't have the first fucking clue. Don't pay to be picky when you got a belly screaming for food." He slapped his hand in the mess, then stroked my face, running liquid filth down my cheek. "You can be Queen of my world, if you like. Queen of the fucking streets. Better to be my dirty Queen than Daddy's little princess, don't ya think?"

I closed my eyes, desperate to block out the stench. "Let's paint you pretty, my new piece of art. *Living* art." He wrenched up my bra up until my tits hung freely, then daubed them in filth, rubbing it all around my nipples. "Fuck yeah, dirty bitch. Hurts to be degraded, don't it? Hurts to be fucking nothing."

He rooted around some cartons at his side, emptying the shit out until he found something to his liking. I daren't look. "You'll like this, Sophie, it'll really fucking suit you."

I screamed into the gag as he dumped a bottle of liquid on my head. Milk. It was milk. I forced back the vomit as milk dripped from my hair, sour and festering and fucking disgusting.

His laugh was bitter. "Run home to your nice world, leave us here where we belong, rich girl."

Tears welled over as my eyes met his, but still I didn't move. I didn't run from him.

"Not enough for ya yet?" he seethed. "Oh, I get it. You want more. You want me to decorate your pretty little cunt."

My stomach lurched.

"Let's see what we've fucking got here." He held up a scrappy box of cereal. "I'd have saved this for later as a kid, keeps longer, you see." He scooped up something that looked like baked beans, all clumpy on his fingers. "This, though, I'd have had to eat this straight away."

I shuffled away this time as he came for me, squealing as my knees crunched on something sharp. He pulled the panties from my mouth and I choked in relief but only for a second before his fingers were wrestling with my tongue, the putrid taste of stale food pounding my senses. I hacked up onto the tarmac, retching with everything I had. "Ain't no dessert if you don't eat your main," he sneered. "Ain't no place to be fucking picky."

I sobbed onto the floor, sobbed for me but mainly for him, the reality of life on the streets hitting harder than any of his filthy demonstrations. "I'm sorry," I wheezed. "I'm so sorry."

"Why be sorry?" he hissed. "Made me the man I am today, the man whose cock you want so much."

"I love you," I cried. "I made a mistake, that's all."

"You made a mistake coming here."

"No."

"Still want cock, do you? After all this?"

"I want *you*."

"Such a trooper for cock, you are." He slid his greasy fingers between my thighs, thumbing my clit as my tears fell. "This making you wet? Dirty bitch."

I shook my head, but his grip was good, circling my pussy in perfect motions.

"Gonna tear you down."

I nodded. "Do it."

"Want my big fat cock? Want me to fuck you?"

"Please," I cried. "Prove I'm yours."

"You like playing with the savage, don't ya? Like being fucking scared."

I didn't bother with words this time, just moaned in invitation.

"Let's see how scared you get before you fucking break."

He flipped me on my back in a heartbeat, amongst the dregs of sour milk and rotten food. I didn't fight, just took it. Breathing heavy as he loosened his jeans. I reached up for him, roving my hands over his chest, his stomach, all the way down until I found his cock waiting for me. It was thicker than my wrist, pumped stiff, veins bulging. The beautiful purple glans glistened in the darkness. He lowered himself onto me, slamming me with one savage thrust.

"I hurt you," I wheezed. "Hurt me back."

"Don't wanna hurt you," he groaned. "Wanna send you back where you fucking belong."

"I belong where you are."

"No you fucking don't," he growled. "Gonna break you."

My pussy felt so good with him inside me. I moaned as he fucked me, bucking to reach his thrusts. My hair was slick with grease and sour milk, my face sticky with fuck knows what, and still I bucked for him.

"Yes..." I moaned. "Fucking take me..."

"Fight me," he hissed. "Fight me and go home where you belong."

"Never."

"Fair enough," he snarled. I wasn't prepared for the hands around my throat. My eyes flew wild in shock as he cut off my breath, fingers scrabbling for his as he choked me. He leaned down, his mouth in my ear, his cock buried to the hilt and his weight all on one arm as he fucked me and stole my breath in unison. "Fight me. Fight off the savage and run away."

I took my hands away from his, reaching up gently to stroke his face. I felt him flinch. My eyes were filled with nothing but love as he took my breath, my pussy still wet for him, still hot for him, still desperate for him.

Casey whined, confused. Jumping around us and growling softly. I would have soothed her if I could.

There was panic as my body began to fight, a flailing against the pressure as I tried to gulp in air. I could hear Casey more frantic, barking and growling and whining in circles all around us. The world began to fade, but it felt fucking good. I felt Callum's lips on mine and managed a smile against his mouth.

My body took over as he freed me, coughing and spluttering and gasping for breath until my lungs recovered.

"Are you fucking mental?" he said.

"Something like that," I rasped.

My mouth was starving for his, hands in his hair desperate to force him down to me. He gave in to the urges, burying deep inside and fucking me the way we usually fuck.

So fucking dirty.

So fucking bad.

So fucking savage.

I thought I'd got him, pulled him back from the edge of pain, but as he approached climax his eyes turned dull again.

I felt him leaving me, disappearing back inside his hurt.

He got up without speaking, pulled his clothes on.

"Don't come here again," he said. "Ever."

"Callum..." I started, but his eyes stopped me dead in my tracks.

"Ever, Sophie. I never want to fucking see you again."

He called Casey, and she followed reluctantly, looking back at me with sad eyes. It jolted me into action and I jumped to my feet.

"Please, Callum, please don't do this."

"It's done. You don't love me."

"Yes, I do!" He didn't answer, just fastened his jeans. My hands were in my rancid hair, struggling for words. "What about Casey?" I hissed. "Please!"

"What about her?" he spat.

"She's not a stray anymore, Callum, she's an indoor dog now. She loves cuddles on the sofa, and a warm bed, and proper food every night."

"Don't we fucking all."

"Please," I begged. "Please let me take her."

He seemed to consider it, but again the shutters came down hard, eyes full of pain. "NO!" he boomed. "She's all I've fucking got!"

I covered my face with my hands as he stormed away, just to hide the tears.

His next words came with a crack of emotion, his voice wavering for just a moment.

"You've ripped my fucking heart out, Sophie! Ripped it fucking out!"

And mine.

I'd ripped mine out too.

✳✳✳

Callum

I was lost. Casey was edgy, lagging behind and whining all the time I circled the block. Just walking. Walking to nowhere.

I should've known, right from the beginning. Should've known a loser like me wasn't good enough for someone like her.

I don't know how I ended up at Vick's. I was at her door before I realised it, hammering so hard I nearly broke the fucker. She came to the door in her dressing gown, peering out through the crack.

"Jesus, it's you!" she screeched. "You scared me, thought it was the bloody Stoneys coming for me." She flung the door open wide.

"You were right, Vick. She weren't real, weren't serious."

"Shit, Cal." She pulled me into a hug and I didn't fight her. "Fucking hell, that's shit, babe. I'm sorry."

"Ain't your fault," I rasped. "You warned me."

"I was just being a jealous bitch."

"Nah, you were just saying it out loud. I ain't no good for someone like her."

"Wanna talk about it?" Her hands rubbed my back.

I shook my head against her. "Nah, just don't wanna be alone."

"You ain't alone, Cal. You'll never be alone, not with me and Slay around." Casey jumped up at the pair of us, nose snuffling.

I pulled away, and we stood in silence to smoke. The night was quiet, so fucking quiet. Too fucking quiet.

"Come inside," she said. "I'll get us a drink."

I shut Casey in the shed, and she grumbled a good while before she settled down, poor little sod. It would be hard on her, just like it would me. Vicki made us a cuppa and I perched on the sofa, brain fucking reeling. She sat down close to me, her hand on my knee.

"It'll be alright, Cal. *We'll* be alright."

"Aye." I didn't believe it, though, didn't believe a word of it. That fucking lump in my throat started up again.

"I'm here for you," Vicki said. "She ain't worth no upset, stuck-up cow. She ain't like us, Cal, we're different. We stick together, we get each other, from the same mould."

I nodded, not really sure what I was agreeing to. I hadn't got any fight left, just letting her yank my head to her chest. She nestled my face against her tits, arms wrapped round me, stroking my hair.

"I love you, Callum Jackson, even if she don't." I made to pull away but she held on tight. "Relax, Cal, let me hold you a minute. You need love, that's what you need. Real love this time, someone who really cares."

My nose pressed tight against her soft tits, and she kissed my head.

"Never really got chance to show you how much I love you, Cal. Can show you now, though, babe."

Guiding hands, teasing me backwards, my head on her thighs staring up at her smile. She loosened her dressing gown and pulled it open, her neat little tits on display. Her hands felt nice on my face, stroking me.

"That's it, Cal, just relax."

I was getting fucking hard again, horny over Sophie Harding on her knees in the rubbish. I forced the memory away. She was fucking gone now. Gone from me.

Vicki was stroking her tits. "Most relaxing thing in the world," she soothed, just ask Slay, sends him right off. Not you though, Cal, I'm gonna make you feel good."

A nipple flopped against my lips and I sucked it in. It tasted like baby lotion.

"Yes..." Vicki moaned. "You don't know how long I've wanted for this, Cal... so long..."

I tried to lose myself in her. Maybe she could love me, maybe she was the only one who ever would. I put it to the test, clamping my teeth fucking hard.

"Fuck, Callum, ow!" she hissed. "No wonder they say you're fucking rough!"

Her hand moved down my stomach, coming to rest at the bulge

in my jeans. She was gasping, little snatches of air, her greedy palm rubbing at my cock through the denim. I sucked her little tit right into my mouth and gave it all I got.

"Stop, Cal, stop!" she rasped. "Can't take no more of that. It really fucking hurts."

Hurts? She should be fucking moaning for more. Nah, she weren't the one for me. Not even close.

I hated her for it, but not as much as I hated myself for not loving her back. I slapped her hand away, sitting back up as she gawped at me, rubbing her teeth-marked tit.

"Sorry, Vick. This just ain't me."

She looked so hurt. She could join the fucking club.

"Sorry," she said, though she had nothing to be sorry about.

"Look, Vicki, I'm the one who's sorry, but you're a mate. Ain't no good trying to be something we're not."

"I love you, Cal. I just fucking love you."

I met her with tired eyes. "Please, Vick, not now, right?"

She shifted in her seat, coming closer. "Kiss me," she said. "Just once. If you don't feel anything then fine."

"Ain't no point," I said. "Ain't gonna make no difference. I know what mates feel like, Vick, and this is mates."

"Kiss me, Callum, please babe, just try it."

She pursed her lips and closed her eyes, like something from pissing primary school. I leaned in close enough to give her the briefest peck on the lips.

"Properly!" she snapped. "Kiss me proper, Cal."

"Fucking hell, Vick, it ain't gonna make no fucking difference."

I slammed my mouth on hers, shoving my tongue all the way in. It was fucking wet, and she was so keen, moaning in the back of her throat like it meant something. I pulled away. "Told ya," I said, "just mates."

"Not to me, babe," she whispered. She touched her lips with her fingers as though I'd given her the kiss of fucking life. "This isn't mates, Cal, this is so much more than mates."

I stood up. "I said not now, Vick, how many more times?"

"We'd be good together, you and me."

"I ain't good for anyone, and this ain't fucking right."

"Stay with me!" she begged. "Please!"

I walked away but she followed, grabbing my wrist by the door and coming in for another kiss. I shoved her away harder than I meant to. "What's fucking wrong with you?!"

"I'm in fucking love, Callum! That's what's fucking wrong with me!"

"You're fucking crazy, that's what you are."

"Love makes people do crazy things, Callum Jackson, real crazy things."

My stomach was tumbling. My brain was swimming too, swimming in pain, and hate, and rage, and love. Love for Sophie fucking Harding.

"Yes, it does." I hissed. "It really fucking does."

I slammed the door behind me, ignoring the whines from the shed.

"You're staying here, tonight," I said, holding a hand up to the little window. "You'll be better off here."

Casey cried as I left, then barked over and over. I could hear her from down the street, Vicki too. Both of them calling for me.

But I had a calling of my own.

***

Place gave me the creeps, no wonder they condemned the shithole. The tarmac was cracking all over, weeds poking through. I climbed the ramps slowly, taking care to stay in the middle, away from the crumbly edge. My paints were heavier than I thought, wrapped in a dirty tarpaulin tied up with rope. Got it from the garage, so it must have belonged to that dead guy. I raised the bottle of vodka in a toast.

"Cheers, dead guy. Nice one."

Stupid little bitches needed the drink less than I did. Just as well they didn't argue the point, neither. Weren't in the mood for it.

The roof of the multi-storey was higher than I remembered. Leaning out on the railing showed me the whole of fucking East Veil.

"You were right, Jimmy," I laughed. "They'll never reach to clean this one off."

I untied my makeshift hamper, wrapping the rope round my waist. I tied it tight, threading the other end through the railings and looping it into a knot. I checked it once before I set myself over the edge, spray can in one hand and my heart in the other. It creaked like a bitch before it held. I scuffed my heels against the concrete, sending chips flying to the floor below.

This would be my legacy.

The piece of art worth fucking dying for.

I leaned back, arms stretched wide, head dangling into nowhere while I thought of Sophie, and Jimmy, and Vicki, poor Casey too.

They were all gone from me now.

I let the darkness take over.

***

Sophie

No amount of make-up would fix my face. I'd cried myself to hysteria and back again, leaving a pair of panda eyes and blotchy, swollen cheeks in its wake. I hadn't moved all weekend, didn't want to. Instead I'd been sitting in the darkness breaking my fucking heart over Callum Jackson.

It hurt so fucking bad.

I dragged myself into the office, sloping to my station without eye contact. *Leave me the fuck alone, world. Just leave me the fuck alone.*

No such luck.

Christine wasn't alone when she approached my desk. She had Millie from HR on one side and one of the East Veil community support officers on the other.

"We need to speak with you," Millie said. "About Callum Jackson."

"What about Callum Jackson?!" My heart was racing so fast.

"There's been an incident, in East Veil."

My mouth was like paper. "An incident?"

"The multi-storey," Christine said. "You're aware of it, yes?"

I nodded.

"He was up there, on Friday evening. We found his paints below."

"Found his paints?! What about him?!" The tears were welling up, I could feel them coming. I breathed slowly in through my nose and out through my mouth. "Are you telling me what I think you're telling me? Is Callum ...?!"

Three faces stared at me, eyes wide at my reaction.

"No," Christine said. "Of course he's not."

She slammed down a glossy photo and my eyes shot as wide as theirs.

"Callum Jackson isn't dead," Christine seethed. "But you're fucking suspended."

***

Chapter Fifteen

Sophie

I couldn't answer Rebecca's calls, not until I'd signed out of the office. I was still reeling at the image.

There was no point denying it was me. It was too pissing obvious. He'd captured me perfectly, from the point at the end of my nose to the awkward bit of hair that would never stay flat on my head. I guessed it was his heart I'd been eating in the picture, and he'd captured that perfectly, too.

Suspended on full pay, at least they'd granted me that.

It wouldn't take them long to find the missing articles from the files, or locate Callum's garage.

My career was screwed.

"Don't ask how I am, Bex," I wheezed. "Just don't fucking ask."

"Shit, baby, that good, hey?"

"Everything's fucked," I cried, no longer giving a shit who could hear me. "I fucked things up with Callum, I fucked things up with work, I fucked things up with my parents."

"Back up," she hissed. "Just back the fuck up a second. You fucked things up with Callum, when?!"

"Friday," I said. "Would have let you known, but I was kinda tied up sobbing my heart out."

"Where is he now?" she said. "You did give him the money, didn't you? For the Stoney brothers? Please fucking tell me he's got the money!"

I froze.

"What fucking money?"

***

Callum

I watched Vicki's place from the wall across the way, just in case the Stoneys showed up early. She was going to her mam's for the afternoon.

I was fucking done for.

I'd been heading over with Case when I noticed them at the garages, them people from Sophie's work. They padlocked it up tight, writing on their stupid pads.

Another dream over.

My phone had been flashing all morning, but I didn't want to answer. Not until it was time.

It was time now.

"Yeah," I said. "Where's the meet?"

But it weren't Trent Stoney that answered me.

"Don't you fucking dare, kid, you hear me?! You go anywhere near them before I reach you and I'll skin you my fucking self."

I didn't know whether Raven was going to hug me or hit me as she charged across the street. As it turned out she hugged me first, then hit me. A hefty punch as well, right in the arm.

"You fucking dipshit," she snapped. "Why the fuck didn't you come to me? I'm not that pissing hard to find."

I shrugged, and she sighed so fucking loud, slamming an envelope in my hand. I raised my eyebrows.

"Twelve hundred," she said. "From the dealer. Call it an advance."

"What?"

"He loved your shit, kid, just like I said he would. Wants to put you on at the Southbank opening. Media viewing is tomorrow night so you'd better get your fucking act together."

I stared blankly at the envelope, too stunned to open it. "What's this for?"

"Standard advance," she said. "Well, almost. Persuaded him to throw in an extra two hundred to help sort your unfortunate predicament."

"Take more than that." I smiled sadly. "Might as well keep it, Raven. I owe them fifteen and they ain't gonna take any less." Her sparkly eyes filled with horror. "It's alright, like. I'm good with it."

"Don't be so pissing soft, you bloody idiot." She jammed a cigarette into my mouth and lit the end before lighting one up for herself. "Told you before, the pity party doesn't suit you, kid."

"Trent's gonna cut my fingers off," I smiled. "Great for a painter, eh? That's me fucking done for."

She rolled her eyes. "Yeah, fucking sure he is. Follow me and shut your bloody mouth."

I shoved the cash back at her, shaking my head.

"Don't even try and say no," she hissed. "Take it."

She'd dragged me to the cashpoint down by the subway, taken three hundred out of her own account. My cheeks burned with the shame.

"This ain't right, Raven."

"I'll take it out of your first sale. There'll be plenty of opportunities to pay me back, trust me. Your shit's the best in the whole fucking gallery. You're going to be a star tomorrow night, kid, I promise you."

I put the cash in the envelope with the rest, heart on fire. "Dunno what to say."

"Thanks is the standard answer," she smiled.

"Ain't much good with thanks," I said.

She hugged me tight, and I hugged her right fucking back.

I left Casey with Raven when I went to meet Trent Stoney. She waited across the way with her phone in her hand. Any longer than fifteen and she'd be calling the pigs, she said. I didn't doubt it.

Tyler was beaming like a fucking lunatic, face red and sweaty as he made his way into the garage block. The other arsehole didn't look bothered either way, and Trent looked like he usually does, keen to get his money and get the fuck out of there.

I handed it over, the biggest wedge I'd ever seen in my life. Broke my fucking heart, but the relief was so fucking worth it.

"Impressive," Trent said. "Didn't think you'd have a tin pot to fucking piss in." He threw the wedge to the arsehole at his shoulder. "Make sure it's all there."

We stood in silence until it was counted.

"Like to say it were nice doin' business with you, soft lad. But we both know it wasn't."

"We're done now then, yeah?" I said. "No more debt, no more interest?"

"Not unless your little slag wants to borrow again."

"She don't," I said. "We're done."

"Fair enough." He nodded his head for the others to follow and my breath loosened just a touch.

It was Tyler who started the trouble. His gobby mouth ran away with him, chattering around Trent like an old mother goose.

"Spit it out, you stupid cunt," Trent said. "What's the fucking problem?"

"Jackson," Tyler spat. "*He's* the fucking problem. We'd cut his fucking fingers off, you said."

"Not if he's brought the money, you fucking muppet."

Tyler's jaw slammed shut, eyes like tiny black marbles. "He fucking owes me," he growled. "Stole me girl, and me kid. His dog fucking bit me arm as well, yeah. Can hardly move the fucking thing."

"Heart bleeds," Trent scoffs. "We're fucking done here, Jones. Let's move it."

He didn't shift, not until Trent slapped him across the side of the head. "D'you fucking hear me, you thick cunt, we're fucking done here."

I couldn't hold back the smile, it swept across my face like a summer's fucking day.

"I'm coming for you, Jackson," Tyler spat. "That's a fucking promise."

"Not gonna be around much more," I laughed. "Not now I'm a fucking artist. Got my work in a gallery and everything. What a treat, ain't it?"

He brandished his bandaged arm, but I no longer gave a shit.

"I'll be coming soon, Jackson, don't you worry about that."

"Address is one two three kiss my fucking arse street," I said, flipping him the bird.

"I know where your address is," he barked. "And I'll be fucking coming."

I wouldn't lose any fucking sleep over it. I could take that cunt all day fucking long.

I'd enjoy it, too.

***

Raven left me with a kiss and a shitload of instructions. Where to be, what to say, what to do. She'd meet me in the afternoon next day, she said, all ready for my great gallery opening. I'd be so fucking scared I wouldn't know what to fucking do with myself. Loads of reporters would be there, celebrities and posh people too. Didn't know quite how I felt, but it was better than feeling fucking dead about Sophie.

I spotted Vicki and Slay in the distance as they made their way home. They'd left it until evening, enough time to count on the Stoneys being gone again. I ran up the street, shouting Vicki's name until she spun around gawping, hardly believing her pissing eyes. Casey nearly knocked her off her feet, stopping just shy of sending the pushchair flying.

"Fucking hell!" she screeched. "You're in one fucking piece!"

I lifted her up in my arms, spinning her around. "The art came through, Vick, fifteen hundred quid's worth. Stoneys cleaned me out, but it don't matter. Raven says there'll be more where that came from."

"That's fucking epic, Cal," she smiled. "Really fucking epic."

We walked towards her place, talking about the gallery, and the Stoneys and everything but the craziness on Friday night. It suited me just fine.

"Got some bread here," she said when we got to hers. "I'll make you a sarnie. Give me a hand with Slay, though, will ya?"

I made Case wait outside, her mouth slavering as Vicki started grating cheese. "You'll have one too," I said. "Chill your fucking beans."

I played drawing with Slay while Vicki made us toasties. She put the cheese on thick this time, too, thicker than I'd ever seen her make it.

"Well, it's a celebration, innit?" she said. "Callum Jackson the famous artist. It's so fucking awesome, Cal."

Yes it was. It really fucking was.

I whistled Case as I stepped outside. "Come on, girl," I said. "You're gonna fucking love this one. Got loads of fucking cheese on it."

She didn't come, didn't even move.

"Come on, Casey, don't be a sulker, it's cheese, look."

I stepped closer to notice she was panting. Panting really fucking hard.

"You alright, Case? What's up with ya?"

My foot kicked into something, something tough and slimy. I grabbed at it, and it felt rank in my hand. A sicked-up piece of meat.

"Jesus, Casey, where the hell'd you find this from, eh? Vicky ain't even got her bin out here."

And that's when I knew.

I stepped up to the gate just in time to see Jones disappear round the corner at the far end.

I was out like a bullet, already halfway up the street, steaming and raging and fucking gunning for him, but I didn't get chance before Vicki screamed.

"My God, Callum, you've gotta get back here right fucking now! Casey's having a fucking fit!"

**

Sophie

My phone flashed in my hand, exclaiming the ridiculous.
Callum.

No fucking way. My heart could hardly believe it.

"Cal?" I rasped. "Is that you?"

His breathing was ragged, crazy, like he was climbing a fucking mountain. "Help me. Please, Sophie, you have to fucking help me."

The line went dead, and my fingers skidded all over the keypad as I tried to call him back.

He picked up on the first ring.

"What's happened?!" I said. "Jesus, Cal, what is it? Are you hurt?"

A pained growl sounded from his throat. "Not me. It's Casey, that cunt Jones gave her something. She's shaking, and she's sick, and she's crying. She's really fucking bad, Soph, really bad."

My blood froze. "Where are you? Where is she?"

"Going down King's Road, to the vet at the bottom. Going quick as I can, but I'm carrying her, can't get there any quicker."

"Call a taxi!" I screeched.

"Got no cash. Got nothing, Soph. Please come. Please."

"Just get a taxi, Callum, please, for God's sake! I'll pay them when I get there!"

I'd never moved so fucking fast.

***

My taxi arrived just as Callum was getting Casey out of his. Her legs were rigid, twitching with strain, and her head was lolled back, eyes flickering. She was crying and panting at the same time, a terrible sound that punched me straight in the gut. It was so much worse than I'd imagined, and my eyes filled in a heartbeat, rushing to her side as he struggled to lift her out. He burst in through the doors, muscles tense enough to match hers, and I stared in horror at the vets' faces. The way they looked at Casey and then each other spoke volumes.

They ushered us into an examination room and Callum laid her flat on the table, stroking her head and talking to her all the time.

"What happened?" I cried. "What did he give her?"

He pulled out a rancid piece of meat from his pocket, and they rushed it off to the lab.

The vet shone a light in her eyes, opened her mouth too.

"Hyperextension, vomiting, rapid heart rate." He focused on Callum. "What symptoms were presenting when you found her?"

"Panting... crying... sick everywhere."

The vet stretched out his arms. "Was she stood like a sawhorse? Like this?"

Callum nodded. "Then she went all twitchy."

"We'll need to wash her stomach, attempt to remove the rest of the toxin. Please wait outside."

The fear in Callum's eyes broke my heart. His voice was so nervous, so unlike him. "Help her, please. Please make her ok again."

"We'll be doing our very best for her."

I took his arm, pulling gently. "Come on, Callum. Let them work. She's in the best hands."

He hovered just long enough to put his face to hers. "You've gotta get better now, alright? These nice people are gonna take care of you. Love you, Case, so much."

The savage's eyes were wet with tears when he rose, but he didn't linger any longer.

***

Callum collapsed in a heap in the corner once the vet was out of sight.

"I'm going to fucking kill him," he growled. "Just as soon as she's alright. Gonna cut his fucking heart out."

"No," I said. "He wants the fight. Don't play into his hands. You're better than that."

"Don't fucking feel like it."

"Casey wouldn't want it," I said. "She'd want you to think about your art, about staying out of prison, about how much I need you to come home with me. She needs us, both of us. We're her home now, Cal." I pressed my cheek into his back, soaking his hoodie with tears. "Please don't push me away."

"Ain't getting back together for Case's sake," he said.

My heart dropped, pain piling on top of pain.

I was numb as he reached for my hand, barely registering he was holding me until he said the words.

"I'm doing it for me."

***

We sat there for what felt like hours. Waiting, hoping, praying. We'd flinch every time we heard footsteps, but they'd only be offering coffee. I'd think I'd have it together, only for the image of her big brown eyes to reach out and bludgeon me all over again. Callum was quiet in his grief, locked up inside himself with just the occasional outburst, but for me it bled wild.

"You should go," he said. "You've got work and shit."

"I haven't. They suspended me."

"Why?"

"Doesn't matter now."

He didn't push it and I didn't share.

"It's all fucked," he said. "All of it. Got a fucking exhibition tomorrow, all my paintings and shit. I dreamed about it when I was a little kid, and now it's all fucked. Can't do it now she's like this."

I smiled, but it wasn't a happy smile, not really. "You're at the new Southbank complex."

"Dunno. Yeah, maybe."

"No maybe about it. It's the biggest event of the year. I know, my parents built the fucking place."

"Don't matter now, does it? Won't be going."

I reached out to touch him, the slightest touch of my fingers on his knee. "Of course it matters. You have to go, it's your big break."

"Won't mean anything now."

I sighed, a long sad sigh that rattled in my chest. "No matter what happens here tonight, Callum, that art means something. Don't let it go."

I kept quiet, letting his demons battle it out for themselves. So quiet that it came as a shock when he spoke again.

"Me mam threw me out first time when I was fourteen. Didn't have nowhere to go. Jimmy was dead, and I didn't have no one else."

"She wouldn't let you back home?"

"Too proud to ask, even then." He sighed. "I remember her telling me to get out, told me she hated me. Felt fucking rough. Didn't show it, like. Played tough, but it fucking hurt. Ain't never spoke about it before." His eyes met mine, hard. "That stuff with your sister felt like it was happening all over again."

I flinched inside. "I was a stupid cow trying to keep up appearances. I've been doing that my whole life." I leaned my head on his shoulder. "Hurting you was the last thing I wanted."

"Don't matter now," he said. "Thought it would be me and her missing you, but now you're here and she's fighting to get back to us."

Fresh tears pricked my eyes. "Puts things in perspective, doesn't it?" I paused awhile until I could speak the words aloud. "I'm going to tell my parents about us, Cal. Push me away all you like, I'm going to tell them anyway."

He reached out for my hand, squeezed it tight. "You're upset over Case, that's all."

"It's got nothing to do with Casey."

"She brought us together, didn't she?" he smiled. "Best thing that ever happened to me."

"Yes, she did. And loving her has brought us back together, Cal. Don't let all this be for nothing. It can't be for nothing."

"What now, then?" he said. "I'm off the fucking rails here, Soph. Got no fucking idea."

"We work it out," I said. "Like families do."

My beautiful savage took my hand, and finally the vet arrived.

***

Casey's tail wagged ever so slightly, but it was enough. Her eyes were focused, smiling up at us as we stroked her face.

"She's a real fighter," the vet said. "Didn't give up."

"Of course she wouldn't," I smiled. "She's like her owner."

"We'll need to keep her in a few days," the vet concluded. "Run some tests on her kidneys and take some blood samples. She needs to rest and recover, so please leave her with us until she's well enough to go home."

"Hear that, Case?" Callum said. "You're gonna come home, just as soon as these nice people have done some tests on ya."

Her tail flicked again, happy, like she understood every word. Maybe she did.

I hugged her tight before we left, and waited for my beautiful savage outside. I couldn't wait to take him home.

***

I didn't flick the light on. Callum reached for the switch himself but I stopped him, intercepting his hand with my fingers in his.

"Don't think," I said. "Just feel. Feel me. I'm right here."

His arms were crushing, wrapped tight around my waist as he buried his face in my neck. I felt him shudder.

"I need to tell you something," he whispered. "About Vicki. She wanted me... and I... I couldn't..."

I smoothed his hair. "It doesn't matter now."

"I didn't fuck her," he said. "Couldn't. There was only you, Soph. You're the only one I ever wanted."

He was so compliant as I took his clothes from him, dropping them onto the floor like dead skin as I pulled him along the bedroom. The sun was beginning to break outside, bathing us in the softest hue of dawn. I traced the dark lines on his chest, kissing my lips against the heavy beat of his heart.

"It's you and me now," I said. "We stand tall, we stand together. I'm going to be there tomorrow, with you, at your side. That's where I belong."

"Your parents..." he groaned. "Will they...?"

"They'll be there," I said. "Prancing about the place like they own it."

"Figures."

I reached up, angling his face to mine. "They'll be there, and I'm glad. No more appearances, Callum, just what's real. We're real."

"That stuff with the bins... I'm sorry, Soph. I wanted to scare you."

I lay back on the bed, wriggling out of my own clothes as the savage watched me. I reached between my legs, splaying myself open without reservation. "I like it when you scare me..."

He knelt on the floor before me, clammy hands hot on my thighs. The slightest smile played on his lips. "Then you really are fucking mental."

I smiled at the ceiling, arching my back as his tongue found the spot.

"Something like that…"

✳✳✳

Chapter Sixteen

Callum

I scanned the crowd, hands wringing, knuckles fucking white. I'd been here all afternoon, Raven too, helping with the display. Now it was open doors, and Sophie was the only thing on my mind.

"She'll be here, baby." Raven squeezed my arm, guiding me back towards my exhibit and away from the gathering media. "Trust me, she'll be here."

"That's her old man over there, ain't it?" I tipped my head in his direction. The guy was just like I'd imagined, all posh suits and comb-over hair. He was smiling for photos, standing right in front of the Hardings Property logo.

"That's him, yeah."

"He's gonna fucking hate me."

"It doesn't matter if he does, kid. His loss."

Sure wished I felt like that. I saw Adrian, the gallery guy, give me a nod as he showed off my artwork. People were looking, and they were smiling. Smiling at me. It felt so fucking weird.

Raven nudged me. "Incoming."

I turned around to catch Green Eyes on the approach, fingers gripped around the arm of the huge beast at her side. Couldn't fucking be, surely not. He looked so fucking different without the mask on, all suited and booted with a big fucking smile on his face.

"They're here for me?"

"Not just them," Raven smiled. Behind Masque and Cat were a load more from Explicit. Diva, and Trixie and Ash, and others I didn't know.

And then there was Sophie. *My* Sophie. She was hidden amongst the crowd, nervous eyes looking for me. They found me and she smiled. A smile of pride and love and everything else I ever wanted. She looked so fucking pretty, in a real posh frock, she was, sparkly and dark green. Really suited her.

She reached my side at the same time as the *Urban Life* journalist, a trendy woman in her forties, with thick-rimmed glasses and a microphone ready to shove in my face.

"You're new on the scene, Mr Jackson, please tell me what inspires your art."

"Life," I said. "Its love and its pain. Its heart, ya know?"

I thought of Casey's waggy tail, and all the love she brought me, turning to look at the picture of her high up on the wall. I'd painted it weeks ago, one of my favourites. The picture was choppy and careless, catching her in her best light, jumping up at my legs as I tried to paint, wanting to run and play and wrestle about on the floor.

"And your loves, Mr Jackson? Do you have a special someone in particular?"

I saw Sophie's dad in the crowd and bit my tongue. Sophie didn't bite hers, though. She stepped forward, bold and steadfast, snaking her hand through my arm and resting her head against my shoulder.

The journalist turned her attention to Sophie, shoving the microphone in her face instead.

"Are you the artist's muse?" she asked.

"One of them," Sophie smiled. "The human one. We have a dog, too, Casey. She's the model on the wall up there."

Sophie's parents came rushing forwards on sight of her, honing in on the conversation with horror on their faces. She didn't flinch, not for a second, meeting her dad's glare with her head held high.

"Can we have a picture of you together? For the magazine?"

Sophie smiled and pressed herself right against me for the whole world to see.

"I'm Sophie Harding, of Harding's Property," she said. "Callum Jackson's very proud girlfriend."

The look on Mr Harding's face told me he wasn't sharing the fucking sentiment, but Sophie didn't seem to care. Not one fucking bit.

***

Epilogue

Sophie

"Honey, I'm home." I grinned as I closed the door behind me, then waited for it. I was ready for Casey's assault, crouching down so she could cover me in doggy kisses while I threw aside my ID badge and all the other work shit.

Callum smiled at me from across the living room, and in his eyes there was still a hint of savage, not that most people would see it these days. His new jeans fitted him like a glove, hugging his toned arse like they'd been painted on him. Judging by the splotches of paint on his t-shirt there was probably some truth in that.

He stepped back to give me a better view of his canvas. The Sophie he'd painted was glowing, beaming with happiness at the tiny baby in her arms.

"It's beautiful..." I whispered. "You're so bloody good, Callum. I hope you realise just how talented you are."

"Love painting in this place," he said. "I'm so happy here, Soph."

"Me too. Beats the crap out of Canary Wharf." I walked past him, staring out of the window at our new little yard. "We'll be good here, Callum. The Haygrove people are really nice."

"Should hope so, *estate manager*. Else you'll have to sort 'em out, won't ya? Good you're getting right back on the horse, Soph, they had nothin' much on you and they knew it."

I watched him paint awhile, loving the way he moved, the way he gritted his teeth in concentration.

"You're going to make an incredible father."

"I wanna have six, at least," he said. "Loads of the little buggers."

The image reignited the flame I'd been harbouring all day. It didn't take much for it to flare into a fire.

I pressed up against my savage's back. "In that case we'd better get started."

I plucked the paintbrush from his grip, dropping it with a plonk into the water jug, then pulled up his t-shirt to plant hot kisses down his spine. He turned and reached for me, but I sidestepped. I shook my head. "I want you naked. I want you ready. I want you in that fucking bedroom, right now, Callum Jackson."

He stared down at me, eyes glinting. "You're a bit bossy tonight, don't ya think? Might have to do something about that..."

"Don't try me. I learnt from the best." I pointed to the bedroom. "Shut your mouth and do what the hell you're told."

He took his time about it, sloping slowly down the hallway with his eyes still on mine. I followed him in, standing triumphant as he adhered to my instruction.

"Naked," I said. "Now."

"You're pushing your luck, *Missy*," he said, but his hands were already at his jeans, sliding them down over perfect hips. I admired the steel plains of his stomach, wetting my lips as he yanked his top over his head. The intertwined skulls on his chest glowed with a sheen of perspiration and the savage smelled gorgeous. His musky scent went straight to my head. I took a breath, restrained the urge to jump on the bed and beg for a hammering.

"On your back, *Savage* – hands above your head."

"For fucking real?"

"*My* way tonight. All mine."

Fuck, how my pussy throbbed as he submitted. He lowered himself slowly, arching his back on the descent and stretching muscle-ripped arms right the way to the headboard, his perfect tats snaking to the V at his waist. My Callum was indeed a perfect fucking specimen.

"Come on then, Missy," he growled. "Do your fucking worst."

Oh, how I intended to.

The savage watched me with hungry eyes as I stripped naked, grunting his appreciation. He licked his lips when I played with my nipples. And he groaned out my name when I squeezed my tits together. Fuck, how I wanted his hot, wet mouth on me. His slavering kisses on tender skin, vicious teeth to mark them deep. I kneed onto the bed, stalking him slowly, teasing my mouth up his thighs until he gasped.

His beautiful cock jutted up at the ceiling, straining for my hot, wet throat.

"I'm going to ride that dick so hard, Savage, so fucking hard…"

"Fuck yeah," he growled. "Show me what you've got."

My tongue flickered, teasing his veiny shaft while my fingers worked his balls. He groaned and squirmed, knuckles white against the headboard as I sucked him all the way in.

"Got so much for you, Sophie," he hissed. "So fucking much. You'd better be ready for it."

I climbed up to straddle him, rolling my hips against his cock. Jesus, it hit the fucking spot. My pussy was swollen and ripe for him, craving the swell of his dick to stretch me wide.

"I'm going to fuck your brains out, Savage."

I impaled myself so slowly that he hissed out all his breath, growling his frustration through gritted teeth. I leaned forward, angling a hard nipple at his lips as I pinned his wrists tight to the bed. He sucked me so greedily, grunting into the soft white flesh of my tit. I moaned loud as his teeth clamped, begging him for more.

"I want your baby, Savage! I'm going to milk you fucking dry!"

He bucked, urging me on, and his eyes were wild, feral… so fucking savage they stole my breath.

I lay down on his chest, enjoying the slick heat of his sweaty flesh against mine. Our faces so close as he pumped me fast, grunting and moaning and wheezing mouth to mouth, eyes like pools of liquid coal staring right into mine.

I fucked him all fucking night long. I fucked him like a woman possessed, like a woman in love… like a woman who'd never get enough of his beautiful cock. I fucked him like I wanted his baby, but mostly I fucked him like I wanted him.

I fucked my Callum dirty.

I fucked my Callum bad.

I fucked my Callum *savage*.

THE END

Jade West

Acknowledgements

As always, I'd like to thank my incredible and tireless editor, John Hudspith, who really pulled out all the stops this time around. Couldn't do this without you!

Thanks to Letitia Hasser for another incredible cover design, and to my awesome PAs, Tracy and Shweta, for all the work they put in on my behalf.

Michelle, Lesley and all my other Bad Girls – you rock, thanks so much for all your help, it's much appreciated!

Thanks to all the blogs who have supported me, both with Dirty Bad Wrong and now with Savage. There are so many of you now, and I'm continually overwhelmed by your commitment, your passion and your generosity! Thank you!!

All my author friends who chew the cud, you know who you are! Thanks for brightening my days and making this journey so companionable.

And last but not least, my family, for putting up with my absence for weeks on end, while I immerse myself in fictional worlds. It means a lot that you are so supportive of my dreams.

Love you all, so much. <3

About Jade

Jade West is a contemporary erotic author, real life submissive, and former sex chat-line operator, who is plenty used to getting people all steamed up with her dirty mouth.

She embraces stalking, so please head on over and find her at:

www.jadewestauthor.com
www.facebook.com/jadewestauthor
www.twitter.com/jadewestauthor

Dirty Bad Savage

Jade West

Printed in Great Britain
by Amazon